The Paper Trail

Written by William Platt

Copyright © William Platt, 2011

All rights reserved

Supplemental editing provided by Kristina Moran

This is a work of fiction. Names, characters, places, and incidents either are the products of the author's imagination or are used fictitiously. Any resemblance to real persons, living or dead, is purely coincidental.

Acknowledgements

[1]Special thanks to the website www.njhm.com and their story The Iron Grave as sourced from:

- Forgotten Towns of Southern New Jersey, by Henry Charlton Beck, Rutgers University Press, 1936,

- The Roads of Home, by Henry Charlton Beck, Rutgers University Press, 1956,

- South Jersey Towns, by William McMahon, Rutgers University Press, 1973

- Smithville – The Result of Enterprise, by William C. Bolger, Burlington County Cultural & Heritage Commission, 1980

- The Travel Lady Magazine – The Other Smithville, Exploring New Jersey's Industrial Past by Marilyn Loeser

All gave me inspiration for chapters 11 and 15 of this book, giving me a factual insight into the life of H. B. Smith, a man whose real life story is even more compelling than that fictionalized in this book.

[2]Additional thanks go out to the recording artist Gordon Lightfoot. Lyrics to the song "Shadows" by Gordon Lightfoot Moose Music 1981 used by permission in chapters 29 and 31.

ISBN 978-0-9848001-0-0

For Bobby and Danny

Sometimes the difference between life and death is just a matter of inches, a few precious seconds, or a moment of carelessness. Occasionally the difference between right and wrong is even smaller, and the region between black and white fades to an indistinguishable sliver of grey.

Chapter 1 - First Day

I can still remember the first day of my paper route. Of course it really wasn't mine quite yet. Jimmy Reeder took me on a trial run. It was his route, and he was quitting, and I was taking over.

Jimmy really wasn't much of a friend. He was a Catholic and didn't go to my school, and besides, I think he was in high school. I think he was about fifteen or sixteen. I was only twelve. I had just started junior high. Jimmy had the paper route that delivered *The Camden Courier-Post* to my street. He had been delivering the paper to our house each afternoon for as long as I could remember. But then I really hadn't paid much attention. Until recently, the only thing I knew about the paper was that my dad read it when he got home. It arrived on the porch wrapped with a red rubber band every afternoon. It wasn't there when I got home from school. Jimmy brought it and threw it up on the porch from his big bike with the large basket in front.

My dad liked to read the paper after dinner. He'd sit in his chair and go through it page by page. If I looked at it, it was usually just to read the comics. They were in the back section. I liked the one about Nancy and Sluggo. It's strange now when you look back, what you can and can't remember. I know Nancy had a weirdly drawn prickly haircut; Sluggo's head was a buzz cut – a bald head with dots. I think they were boyfriend and girlfriend. Somebody had a dog. I don't remember why I liked this particular comic strip. I guess it was funny, but I really don't remember why.

Recently, I had started to get interested in the sports section. I had taken an interest in baseball, and I liked the Phillies. We lived in New Jersey, not far from Philadelphia. The Phillies were our team. They really weren't very good, and they didn't have a lot of good players. I guess I started to like the Phillies because I liked the game. You were part of a team, but you still kind of worked alone.

It was the end of August and school was set to begin in another week. Summer was almost over. I had spent the majority of the summer with Zachariah Bradford Mausser. His name was a real mouthful. That's why everybody called him Zack for short. He was my best friend. We had spent most of the summer together doing nothing in particular. The kind of stuff you do when you're twelve. We would play baseball together. We both enjoyed the game, but like the Phillies, neither of us was very good. I say we played baseball, but it was never an organized game. Most of the time, it was just me and Zack. We would go to the field behind the junior high school and have a catch. The field had a backstop, a big dirt infield and a big grass outfield with no fence. Behind left field there was a hill that trailed down to the creek. Hit it too far and it went down the hill towards the weeds and the water. We each had a glove and about five balls between the two of us. I had a 32 oz. bat. All bats were wood in those days, and had a player's name stamped on the barrel. I think my bat was called the Willie McCovey big stick. Willie McCovey didn't play for the Phillies. I don't know why I had that model bat. Zack had a bigger bat, maybe a Derron Johnson model. Anyway, we liked to shag fly balls. Well at least I liked to do that. Zack would toss up the ball with one hand and hit to me in the outfield, and I would run and catch it. We would do this for hours, but I'd probably only get about four or five good pop ups to catch over the course of an hour. The rest were grounders to the outfield. I liked to catch pop ups, and thought I could be a good centerfielder.

Zack would hit until his hands got sore. I would catch the balls, and throw them in to him. If we were lucky we had a good streak where Zack would hit the ball to me, I would catch it, and throw it back to him on target. That's the way it was supposed to work. The more likely scenario was that I was in left field, Zack would mess up and hit a dribbler in the infield, or something in the air to center or right, and I would have to run after it and get it. At least I got to run a bit. Looking back it's no wonder we never got any better at baseball. On most occasions, by the time I got the ball it had already stopped rolling. Then I would pick it up and throw it in to Zack. If I was lucky, my throw would hit the backstop. Depending on the distance, sometime I'd miss. Of course, sometimes Zack or I would uncork one, Zack hitting it over my head, or me throwing it past the backstop, which resulted in a lengthy session of ball hunt. This could go on for a few hours until we both got tired. Sometimes we would switch and I would bat and Zack would field. That usually didn't last long. My batting power was poor and I'd miss the ball a lot, and Zack really didn't like to field anyway.

We seemed to do this baseball thing most of that summer. We told everybody we were playing baseball, but it was in spirit only – at least we had the baseball equipment. It was pretty rare that we had any extra kids around to actually try to play a game. There were never any adults around and we never had any instruction on the proper way to do things. We'd hit and field, and run and get tired. If we remembered, somebody brought a jug of water. Then we would sit in the grass, and rest, and talk. On really hot days we would sit under a tree, by the hill to the side of left field. We would talk of things that interested boys our age. Who had the best bike? What die cast cars were better, Hot Wheels or Matchbox? What was the proper way to slide? How to make duck noises by blowing a blade of grass in your cupped hands. Important stuff. It didn't seem boring, and I remember it as a great time. We didn't care about how we looked, what we wore, or about girls. Times were simpler, before cable TV, video games, computers, or cell phones. We had no cares, and no responsibilities, but we did have lots of time.

With school vacation drawing to a close, we decided to finish our summer of baseball with a flourish. It was a Thursday, which left Friday and the weekend, then Labor Day and school. The idea was that we would invite some friends to play and have a real game. I invited the Karaszkiewitz brothers – Jimmy and Jackie. They were both good at the game. They had played Little League. Jimmy was the older of the two and he could pitch. He was a lefty. When you played baseball with him he could throw the ball so hard that it actually made a whizzing noise. It'd scare the heck out of you. Jackie was a bit more like me, he liked outfield and didn't hit much. Zack had invited Bruce Hendry, who lived across the street from him. Bruce had also played Little League. He had a short army style haircut which made his forehead look big. Once I had eaten lunch at Bruce's house with Zack, and I remember Bruce showing off. He took a spoonful of Nestlés Quick chocolate milk powder and put it in his mouth, then puffed it out. Kids did that type of stuff. It was cool, but I don't know why. Bruce had a kid named Peter Gallagher visiting at his house, so he brought him along too. We knew Peter from school. He had long hair and a pointy nose, with the faint trace of a mustache. He sat at our lunch table. He always bought his lunch from the cafeteria, and he always got soup. Peter wasn't very good at baseball, and he didn't have his own glove.

Michael Flaherty lived next door to me. He was a year younger than me, but of the six Flaherty kids, we were the closest, even though we went to different schools. Michael borrowed a glove from one of his brothers; I don't think he had one of his own. Michael invited his friend Donald Gaines, who was a friend of his from school. Donald had played Little League and was good at baseball, spitting, and cussing.

So by word of mouth, the group of us, eight in all, agreed to meet behind the junior high for a game. We all lived on the other side of the Pike from the school. The Pike was the major road that cut through town. In all, the ball field was about a fifteen minute walk across town for us, or less than ten minutes by bike. We all rode our bikes to the field except Peter, who hitched a ride with Bruce on his handlebars. We didn't all come together, but all straggled to the field in disjointed groups over a half-hour period. The Karaszkiewitz brothers were the last to get there, at about 12:15, and they had met up with Mike Burns on the way. We knew Mike from school; we called him Burnsy. He had short hair and wore glasses, and had big red ears. Mike already had a paper route – he served the morning *Philadelphia Inquirer*.

With Burnsy we had nine players, enough for a team. Of course there was no other team so we would have to split up to have a game. Typical, even with our large group, that there was never enough for a real baseball game. We broke into teams, with me, Mike Flaherty, and the two Karaszkiewitz brothers in the field, and the other five up to bat. We argued for a while about how we would play the game. Since Jimmy was a pitcher, he insisted he pitch, but there was no catcher, and not enough players to man an infield, let alone an outfield. After about four or five pitches with no one hitting the ball, it was decided this wasn't going to work.

We decided to change the game with each batter allowed to throw up the ball with one hand, and then hit it himself. The opposing fielders were positioned where shortstop and third base would be, along with left and center field. Miss the ball and it was a strike. Hit it to the right side of the field (first base or right field) and it was a foul ball. If it got caught, you were out. There was no running of bases, hits were based on no one catching it, and a home run was if you hit it over an outfielder's head. If you were a lefty, it didn't matter. Turn your body to the required angle to hit it to the third base side of the field.

I don't recall which side won the game. Jimmy Karaszkiewitz was definitely the best, hitting the ball much further than even the best shot I had seen Zack hit all summer. We lost two balls, and the group began to lose interest. Nobody really kept score anyway. It really didn't matter, after a single at bat and jaunt in the field, it was pretty clear who the best players were, and who were the worst. At the bottom were Mike Flaherty and Peter Gallagher – really no surprise there. Heck, neither of them even owned a glove. I didn't like it that I was the one who had to lend Peter my glove when he was in the field and we batted. Whenever he gave me the glove back, it was filled with foreign sweat, and was no longer molded exactly to my hand. Zack said he must have filled it with soup.

Jimmy was the best followed by Donald. Next was Zack. Me, Jackie, Burnsy, and Bruce were somewhere in between, but maybe I was just over-estimating myself.

I checked my watch and it was almost 3:00. We all were thirsty and hungry. I told the guys I had to leave, and that I was going to meet Jimmy Reeder and get his paper route. They all seemed impressed. I picked up my stuff and hopped on my bike to ride home. I had told Jimmy I would meet him at the specified 204 East Collins Avenue address at 3:30. I knew where the street was, so I figured it would take about fifteen minutes to get home, drop off my stuff, and ride to meet Jimmy.

I got home and like usual, nobody was there. I dropped my bat and glove in the garage, and ran inside to grab a pen and a piece of paper. Jimmy said to bring stuff to write things down so I would remember what I was supposed to do. I didn't want to be late, so I didn't get a drink before I left the house. I hopped back on my bike and started off for Collins Avenue. I think Jimmy had said it was the McGuillan's house where we would meet. I didn't know what to expect. I really wasn't interested in making money or having a job. My mom was the one who found out from Jimmy that he was quitting, and she was the one who suggested I take on the route. She said it would be a good experience and help prepare me for life and help me grow to be a responsible adult. I didn't realize on the ride to meet Jimmy how right she would turn out to be.

Chapter 2 - The Station

Our town was laid out with streets in a straightforward checkerboard fashion. The streets were parallel, with regular perpendicular intersections, forming a series of fairly regular blocks. Each block was typically fifteen to twenty houses in length by two to four houses in width, depending on property size. Most of the houses were single family, with homes about fifty years old. Property size was large enough for a small front yard, the house, a driveway that ran past the house to a detached garage, and a small backyard. Nobody had a lot of property, and houses were fairly close together, certainly close enough to yell over to talk to neighbors on either side.

The town had an east side and a west side. Our house as well as the houses of most of my friends was on the east side. The town was unofficially divided by the White Horse Pike, a county road busy enough that it had traffic lights. Usually you had to have permission to cross the Pike from your parents until you were at least ten. The west side was much bigger than the east side, probably four to five times bigger. The town schools were on the west side. The town was surrounded on three sides by a U-shaped creek which had been dammed on the east side to form a small lake. On our side between the Pike and the creek there were three blocks running east, and from my house, four blocks running north. To the south side, which traveled away from the creek, the streets went on for miles, forming blocks of houses than ran from town to town. Past the creek to the north and the east there were bridges that ran to other towns. They were small bridges, maybe fifty to one-hundred feet long, since the creek wasn't really very wide.

I hopped on my bike and started towards Collins Avenue. It wasn't very far, just down a block, then over two blocks. I was to meet Jimmy at 204 Collins Avenue, which turned out to be the second house once I got onto Collins. The house was about the same size as mine. It was two stories in height, with a grayish color stucco first level and a brown wood-sided second level. The house was for the most part unremarkable. Unlike mine, the front porch was enclosed, with multiple tall windows with closed blinds on either side of the front door. The house was positioned on a relatively steep hill, about eight feet higher than the street, which meant there was a separate set of five or six steps to get up the hill to the sidewalk leading to a separate set of steps to the front door. The driveway going up the side of the yard was asphalt paved, which followed the hill at a similar but slightly less inclined slope. The grass making up the front sloping hill was unkempt, mostly crab grass of various lengths. Riding up to the house, I thought how my dad had me cut our grass at home, and I was glad I didn't have to cut grass like this because it would be a real pain navigating the hill.

Looking up the driveway, I saw activity and a number of bikes parked in front of the garage, so I figured that was where I was supposed to go. There was a fence on the right side of the driveway opposite the house, just after riding up the hill. It was a stockade style fence, about six feet high so you couldn't see into the yard of the house next door. The fence was wooden and didn't look like it had been painted in quite a long time. The side of the house going up the driveway had some shrubs alongside it that were spindly and shabby, both overgrown and broken. Past the house but before the garage on the left side of the backyard was a rusted chain link fence with a swinging gate which was open. Inside the fence was a sidewalk to a second set of steps that ran to the house kitchen. The area within the fence had one of the biggest oak trees I had ever seen. In fact, it seemed to occupy most of the backyard. The tree trunk must have been three and a half feet in diameter, and it towered over the house. Within the fenced-in area, under the tree, was a large dog of some mixed shepherd breed. The dog was tied to the oak tree with a heavy chain. The dog was lying on the ground, in a soft powder of dirt under the tree. Most of the yard under the tree was just dirt with little grass, probably the result of the tree and its dense canopy of shade in combination with the roaming of the dog and his heavy chain being pulled over the yard. The dog didn't really budge as I pulled up before the garage, just maybe a slight raise of his head to look over at me as I rode up, but not a bark or a whimper to acknowledge me.

The single car garage had two doors that pulled open from the side, and the remnants of a long broken basketball backboard hung above the entrance. The panes of glass that had once filled the windows at the top of the garage doors were missing; probably the result of stray basketball shots of long ago. Looking inside the garage, I was surprised to see it was clean and orderly, with about 25 bundles of newspapers of various heights, spaced and set up in four lines within the garage. There were two boys in the garage, each sitting on a pile of papers, who were pulling newspapers from the bundles in front of them and wrapping rubber bands around them and putting them into a large canvas newspaper bag.

An old woman sat in a lawn chair near the front of the garage, reading the paper. The chair was made of aluminum with alternating green and white plastic straps interweaved to form a seat and back. She was smoking a cigarette, and her face was tan and wrinkled, either the result of too many days in the sun or too many smokes across her lips. Her hair was short, not quite shoulder length, and at first I thought it was blonde, but upon further inspection, it was more of a grayish white. She held her wire rimmed glasses in her hand as she read, but put them on when she looked up at me.

"Can I help you?" she asked in a voice that crackled from years of smoke.

"Yes, ma'am," I replied. "My name is Bill, and I'm going to be taking over Jimmy Reeder's paper route."

"Oh yeah, Jimmy, I almost forgot. I'll miss him. He's been serving since I took over the station about four years ago."

She stood up from the chair and standing she seemed even thinner than when she was sitting. "I got some forms you'll need to fill out and have your parents sign. You live close around here?"

"Yes, ma'am, over on Haddon, near the church," I answered.

"You live near the Flahertys?"

"Yep, right next door. Michael and Joey are my friends."

"Yeah, I know them from church. Michael and Joey go to school with my two sons Kevin and Patrick. My name is Mrs. McGuillan. You know Kevin or Pat?"

"Not really," I answered. "I've seen Pat around, but I really don't know him well."

"Oh, well you'll get to know him better if you'll be coming here each day; he just took off to serve his route." She looked at her watch. "Jimmy's not here yet; his papers are inside near the back. It's still a little early. I like everybody to be out of here by 4:30, that's my rule." She started to walk towards the house. "I'll get you the forms. You can go get your papers."

She left and went inside the house. I started into the garage and looked at the paper stacks. Looking at them closer, I noticed that each stack had a name written on the top paper in the corner. Watson, Gilmore, Milano, Leahy, Parker, Elfreth, Johnson, Merrick, Morrison.

'Oh, there it is… Reeder,' I thought.

As I was standing there, one of the two boys who had been wrapping papers finished, and stood up. I noticed that it was Mike Gaines, the older brother of Donald who I had been playing baseball with earlier that morning. Mike was several years older than I. He was husky and about a foot taller than me, and he had long brown hair that reached his shoulders. He had on a white and red T-shirt with the team name CAGERS written on it. I had never talked to Mike before. I had heard that Mike was really good at basketball, and played for the team at his school.

"So you're taking over Reeder's route?" Mike started. "You know, that route goes right by my house."

I wasn't positive where the Gaines' family lived, but it didn't matter. I had no idea exactly where Jimmy's paper route went anyway.

"I didn't know that," I shrugged.

"It doesn't matter," Mike explained. "We all deliver to our own houses anyway."

"Reeder's route is pretty good," Mike went on, "except for those places by the dam. I had them once and they're a pain."

Mike picked up the bag full of papers and slung it over one shoulder. The bag looked heavy, and because it was full, it stuck way out in front of him, pulling his shirt in an awkward fashion. The words *Camden Courier-Post* showed on the front of the bag, although the word *Post* was nearly impossible to read because the bag had a hole in it right where the "*t*" was supposed to be. Mike climbed onto his bike with the bag still over his shoulders, resting the bag on the bike's center bar. Carefully he pulled the strap from his shoulder and wrapped it about the handlebars. This made the bike a bit unstable and awkward to steer, but it didn't bother Mike and he took off down the driveway.

As he departed, Jimmy Reeder rode up the driveway, nodding to Mike as he passed.

"Sorry I'm late," Jimmy yelled. "Just a couple of minutes, and we'll get rolling.

Chapter 3 - Jimmy Arrives

My bike was a Schwinn Stingray, a hand-me-down from my older brother. The bike was dark purple, which was a bit odd for a boy's bike, but my brother always said it was the coolest and rarest color for a Stingray. There was no mistaking it for a girl's bike, however. The handlebars were pushed way forward, giving it a sort of "chopper" look, and its chrome fenders, white letter tires, and banana seat with the letter "S" emblazoned between double racing stripes gave it the look of a racer.

Jimmy's bike looked nothing like mine, and if my bike was to be viewed as a race chopper, Jimmy's bike was more like a Mack truck. His was a large men's style bike, black in color with heavy black fenders, large black tires, and a huge galvanized basket on the front handlebars.

Jimmy hopped off the bike before it came to a complete stop, and propped it up next to the fence. He had a canvas paper bag in the basket, and in the bag he had a partial plastic bag of red rubber bands.

He went straight in the garage and remarked, "Looks like forty to a bundle, pretty good for a Thursday."

He gave me a handful of rubber bands and motioned me to start folding. "Not like that," he corrected. "They'll rip." And he showed me how to fold the paper with the top of the front page inside the paper, folded so that the open side of the paper was inserted into the fold.

"If you do it like this, it won't rip when you throw it."

He then put the rubber band around the paper and picked up another. In a few minutes he had wrapped thirty papers to my ten. He then picked them up and put them in the bag so they stood up like soldiers, folded side up. He counted as he filled the bag.

"That's thirty-nine, forty, forty-one, and forty-two. Yep, forty-two, that's how many we should have," he instructed. He picked up the bag and squeezed it into his bike basket.

"You brought a notepad right?" he asked, and I responded, "Yes."

"Let's go," he said, and we took off down the hill, turning right up Collins Avenue. We rode up past the intersection of Collins and Coldspring, and stopped in front of 302 Collins. "First is the Pawlings," he said, and he threw the paper onto their top step. "Throw it Frisbee style, so it lands flat."

There were three other houses on this block; two paper deliveries in all for each side of the street, and we took turns throwing the papers up on the house steps, stopping in front of each house before loading and firing.

"I normally don't have to stop, but it'll take you some time before you can serve on the fly," he said.

This block of Collins Avenue was the shortest, and the closest to the creek. "We're pretty lucky with this route," Jimmy said. "We don't have to pick up the papers from the McGuillan's and then ride five blocks to the route before we hit our houses. Our first houses are right at the end of Collins."

We rode on to the end of the street, which after the intersection with Coldspring Avenue was a dead end. Beyond the dead end was a ravine with the creek, although it was difficult at first to notice the drop down to the creek because of all the trees growing up from the land below. It was about a twenty foot drop. To go down the ravine at the dead end was a set of stone stairs, overgrown by trees and weeds on either side of the steps. The steps were built during the Depression in the 1930's. Apparently at the time, the federal government paid people in the area to build things like these massive steps to keep people working, while serving a second function to develop and beautify the area. They built other things in the ravine like huge stone planters around trees, and stone walls and docks out into the lake by the dam for fishing.

Looking down the steps you could see the creek, and towards the north you could see the lake. Opposite the lake, you could make out the dam, but most of the dam had been fenced off with a high metal fence, with points near the top to keep people down by the creek from climbing on the dam and falling into the cascading water below.

Jimmy stopped and pointed beyond the metal fence that separated the dam from us, and noted a second fence that separated us from a set of four old homes on the Smythville property. "Those four houses are a pain," Jimmy noted. "To get to them, you have to go over to Ormond Avenue, and follow it down to the creek." "I usually get them last, on my way home," Jimmy said. "But you live in the opposite direction, so you'll have to figure out an alternate order to keep you from having to backtrack."

We rode back up to Coldspring Avenue and turned right, serving four houses on the same side of the street, all right next to each other. I looked across the street and saw Donald Gaines shooting a basketball on a hoop on his garage.

'Guess that's where the Gaines family lives,' I thought.

We kept riding on Coldspring Avenue, past Clinton Avenue and Haddon Avenue, then served four more papers on Coldspring between Haddon and Bettlewood Avenues. We then turned around and went back a block, and turned right up Haddon Avenue, which was the street I lived on. I followed Jimmy as he swerved from one side of the street to the other, serving up papers on the front porches or front steps of all the houses. He might serve four or five papers on one side of the street, then cross to the other side and backtrack a bit picking up the necessary homes on the other side of the street.

As we weaved from side to side, I carefully recorded the required house numbers. We were now traveling up the street from the creek end towards my house, and I noted that the homes closer to the creek were not quite as nice as those closer to the center of town near the Pike. It wasn't that they were in poorer shape, but more that they were smaller or maybe a single story as opposed to two stories in height. We rode up to Johnson Avenue, turned on to it for two houses, then turned back again onto Haddon, and back towards my house. Jimmy's basket was now almost empty, and the newspaper soldiers in the basket were now falling over as they no longer had their comrades to keep them from tipping on their side.

We hit my block, now riding and serving on one side of the street, then crossing over past the church, to serve the other side of the street while moving in the opposite direction. Jimmy gave me the honor of throwing the paper up on my own front porch, which I did in perfect fashion.

We rode past my house and back toward Johnson, and I thought about how I would have to change things a bit to keep from back tracking. We again reached the intersection of Haddon and Johnson, and Jimmy said he was heading for his home and to do the four houses near the dam. He said I didn't have to follow but I did, knowing I'd have to get these in a few days when I was going it alone, so I better see where they were today.

We took a right at Johnson, riding back past Collins, and eventually to Ormond Avenue. We followed Ormond down towards the creek and the dam. As we got closer to the Smythville homes, the street got narrower and void of houses, with just trees and tall grass on either side of the street. Eventually the grade of the street began to change, as it sloped down towards the creek, and we started coasting downhill faster. We finally arrived on Landing Street. In all there were four houses, three at the close end of the street and the fourth down the street a bit further, looking directly over the creek and the dam. All four houses were really old, maybe over a hundred years, and they showed their age. At the last house, Jimmy got off his bike and meticulously placed the paper on the porch floor, just to the left of the door. "The lady who lives in this house is really old," Jimmy whispered. "I really feel bad for her. If you take care of her, she'll take care of you."

We turned back up the road and onto Ormond Avenue. Jimmy was talking but I wasn't paying much attention. The day had been long, and I was thinking about Jimmy having done this for four years. As we again reached Johnson Avenue, we stopped. Jimmy said we should meet tomorrow at the paper station much earlier, about 2:30. "We need to get an early start. Tomorrow's Friday, it's the end of the week, and we got to collect. We need to be done collecting and back to McGuillan's house by 6:00 to pay her. That's the latest she gives us," Jimmy said.

"Alright," I said, "2:30."

With that Jimmy turned left onto Johnson Avenue going towards his home. I jotted down *2:30 collecting Friday, must be done by 6:30 to pay McGuillan.* Then I shoved the paper and pen back into my pocket, and started off in the opposite direction towards home.

My mind started to wander, from the end of summer, to baseball with Zack, and back to the paper route. I thought of Jimmy and the old lady. "What did he mean take care of her and she'll take care of you?"

'Collecting,' I thought as I pedaled for home. 'Crap, did he say she needs to be paid by 6:00 or 6:30?'

Chapter 4 – Collecting

The next morning I was up and eating by 7:30 AM. It was early, and it already felt like it was eighty degrees, pretty hot and humid for the end of August. It had been really warm last night in bed, so I slept downstairs on the sun porch couch where the house temperature and breeze felt about ten degrees cooler. Mom and Dad had already left for work. I had just sat down at the kitchen table when I heard a jingling noise by the back screen door. Zack always carried around a large set of keys on a chain attached to his belt, and I could recognize the sound they made a mile away.

Before he had a chance to knock, I yelled, "Come in!" and he did. I was eating Cheerios and a banana, and he came over to the table and sat across from me. I asked if he wanted something to eat, but he said he had already eaten and wasn't hungry. Instead he took an Oreo from the cookie jar in the middle of the table and poured himself a glass of milk. He had come over early because his mom was taking him to W.T. Grants just after lunch to buy some new school clothes. I told him that my mom had already taken me last week to get new clothes, but we hadn't gone to Grants. "It's weird," I observed, "that you always wear some nice school clothes that your mom picks out the first day of school, then just wear your old stuff the rest of the year."

Zack said he was excited. He couldn't care less about the clothes, but he had heard reports from Bruce Cunningham that Grants had the elusive Hot Wheels Volkswagen Beetle. Just the thought of it even got me excited. Not only was it impossible to find, but it also had a sunroof that slid open. I told him I'd pay him double if he got me one too. Of course I didn't have any money, but I would very soon, what with the paper route and all. Zack asked about the paper route, but really didn't appear very interested, except for the part about the four old houses by the Smythville Dam.

We decided we didn't have time to go play baseball behind the junior high. Besides, Zack said, we were down to a single ball, and he asked me if I had the others. I told Zack that I didn't have them. "You guys were still playing when I left," I reminded him.

We decided since this was pretty much our last free morning, we would complete our Wiffle ball tournament. Zack was winning seven games to five, but I had pitched more strikeouts and had scored more total runs. Of course like everything else we played, this game used our own rules. We set up two folding lawn chairs in the back yard. The first was set on the ground normally. The second was placed upside down and backwards on the first – so that the arms of one chair lay on the arms of the second. This exposed the back of the upside down chair. We then threw a towel over the top chair's upside down bottom legs, so that the towel hung down over the top chair. We used a Wiffle ball and Wiffle bat from my garage. Throw a ball and hit the towel or the chair and it's a strike, miss the chair or towel and it's a ball. Past the pitcher in the air is a hit. Past the maple tree in the air is a double. Over the back fence is a home run. Three outs per inning.

I pitched first, caught one off the garage roof for the first out, and then struck out Zack with three straight curve balls. Then he slammed one over the fence for a home run. One to nothing. We both climbed over the back fence to get the ball, but we couldn't find it. It had gotten lost in the ferns in the yard behind ours.

"Talk about a short game," I lamented. "Let's look in the garage for another ball, or this game won't count!"

We looked for about twenty minutes but it was useless. The garage was a mess, and Zack was becoming more interested in the junk in the garage than looking for another ball.

"Where did your dad get all these jars of screws?" he asked. "And there must be a hundred hardened paintbrushes in here."

I looked at the various pots on the floor that contained paintbrushes. At one time the jars contained turpentine, and the brushes were soaking to get clean, but the turpentine had long since evaporated, leaving lots of hard dirty brushes. Just like the brushes, my dad collected a lot of junk, and he never threw anything out.

"Think your dad would miss the Turtle Wax?" Zack asked. "I could use it on the Nash Rambler."

"Better leave it for now," I replied.

A few moments later Zack found a basketball, and we officially gave up on the Wiffle ball game.

"Let's play HORSE," he said. Twenty minutes later, the game was over. Zack won HOR to HORSE, finishing with his famous off the backboard foul shot.

Zack looked at his watch and it was half past eleven so he figured he had better leave. I watched him ride off on his bike, a ten-speed Schwinn Continental he had bought the end of June with his own money.

"I guess Zack's bike *is* really neat," I thought. "Maybe I'll save up my newspaper money to get a ten-speed like his. It has been getting harder keeping up with him when we ride together anyway."

I went in the house to get some lunch. My brother had just woken-up and asked what all the noise in the garage was about.

"Just me and Zack looking for something," I said.

"Yeah, well you guys will be looking forever, if it's for your brains," my brother replied.

I grabbed a cheese sandwich and went back outside. I wandered back by the fence and saw the Wiffle ball through the corner of my eye. It hadn't gone over the fence after all. It was right in front, behind a clump of grass. I picked up the ball and put it and the bat back in the garage. I thought of Zack and how he'd never believe me. Then I thought of the Volkswagen Beetle Hot Wheel. Remembering the Nash Rambler, I picked up the can of Turtle Wax and put it next to the ball and bat for safekeeping. Then I went back inside the house.

At 2:15, I grabbed my pen and paper and rode my bike to the paper station. I got there about 2:25, and a *Camden Courier- Post* truck was backed into the driveway. I made my way around the truck and saw the driver unloading bundles of newspapers into the garage. The newspaper bundles had sheets of heavy brown kraft paper on the top and bottom, and were tied together with wire. The papers looked thicker than the day before, and I heard the driver tell Mrs. McGuillan they were thirty to a bundle. He also said there were inserts, and he pushed out several bundles of four page advertisements for Korvettes. Mrs. McGuillan checked the count, told the driver "ok", and he pulled shut the back door of the truck and drove off. Mrs. McGuillan grabbed her list off a table in the corner of the garage and quickly put 23 bundles of papers in rows, then cut the wire from each bundle, pulled it out from under each stack, and threw them out in a trash can in the corner. She then opened up several other bundles, and added papers to the bundles until the count was correct for each route. She finished off each stack by writing the carrier's name on the top paper of each stack.

The stacks of papers varied from a minimum of 22 for Milano, to 64 for Parker. On average most routes were about 35 papers. She looked at me, when she had counted out the 42 stack and said, "I got those forms for your parents to fill out." Then she handed me the forms. "Get 'em back to me filled out by the end of next week," she said.

When she got done all the piles, she counted out the circulars and placed these on the top paper of each stack. She wasn't nearly as careful counting the circulars, I guess, because there were lots of extras.

Jimmy pulled up a few minutes later, said hello, and then started to place a circular inside of each paper. He said we wouldn't fold and band the papers today because he had to collect.

I asked him why we hadn't gotten circulars the previous day. He explained that we typically got circulars before holidays and busy shopping days, and that we made an extra penny per paper for inserting the circular. "That's an extra forty-two cents," he said.

I shrugged my shoulders. Forty-two cents didn't seem like much. "Well how much do we make for each of the papers," I asked.

Jimmy began his reply, "Well we get three cents a paper per day, times forty-two papers times six days a week is...."

"That's $1.26 times six is $7.56 a week," I interrupted. I was good at math.

"Yeah well the *Courier* home delivery rate is 75 cents a week for the six papers, but they only charge us 57 cents", Jimmy responded. "The key is to do a good job, get the paper on time and dry, and you can make a lot more in tips. Most people will give you an extra dime, but really good tippers will pay you a dollar and let you keep the extra quarter. "

"I started to do the math in my head, "Wow, forty-two times twenty five cents is over ten dollars extra."

"Don't count on it," Jimmy said. "But on average if you do a good job, you should make about twelve dollars a week between the papers and the tips."

"At that rate, I'd have a ten-speed by November," I thought.

Jimmy had finished with the circulars, and had put the stack of papers in his bag and was putting the bag in his basket. He climbed on his bike and waved at me to follow. Just like the day before, we went down the hill and down Collins Avenue towards house one – occupied by the Pawlings.

At the corner of Coldspring and Collins, we parked our bikes. Jimmy carefully positioned the basket and handlebars to keep the bicycle from falling over. He pulled four papers from the basket and we headed out on foot. In one hand he held the papers; in the other he held a canvas sack with a drawstring. The sack had some money in it, about two dollars in change and a few dollar bills.

"It's good to have some change to start," Jimmy explained. "Or else you might have to come back later if they don't have the right amount. But don't offer up the change right away. If they're only a bit short, they're more likely to let you keep the difference."

We reached the Pawlings' doorstep and it was then I noticed that Jimmy had a book of tickets. He called it a book, but it really wasn't. The book was about the width and thickness of a paperback book, and maybe about one and a half times as long. It consisted of forty-two perforated sheets with a few extras in the back. The sheets all had two holes punched in the top corners, and two silver rings ran through the sheets to keep them together. On either side of the sheets, was a black imitation leather cover and back. Each customer had their own sheet, which had their name and address written on it. There was also a spot for a phone number, but most of the phone number spaces had been left blank by Jimmy. Each of the sheets was perforated so that it had about fifty to sixty perforated squares, each a little smaller than a postage stamp. Each perforated stamp, or ticket as they were called, had the word *Courier-Post* written on it, and the start and end date of the week. The idea was that when each customer paid, you would rip out the perforated ticket for the week and give it to them as a receipt. Sort of protection against you double charging the customer, but even more likely a simple method devised for paperboys to remember who had paid and who had not.

The ticket was even more important for keeping track of who had missed paying for the previous week or weeks. Some customers were notorious for never being home while collecting, and for missing several weeks' payment. "This was especially annoying," Jimmy explained, "because you had to pay Mrs. McGuillan for the papers no matter what, even if your customers had not paid you."

The bad part was that if you missed a bunch of people, you didn't make a cent. "You really don't get paid until you catch the last dozen or so people," Jimmy explained. "Tips or no tips!"

I looked at Jimmy's ticket book. The majority of the customers' pages all had the tickets removed to the same spot, giving them a uniform shaped appearance. Several other customers had an extra ticket still attached, which made them stand out. A couple had multiple extra tickets.

"Don't let the non-paying customers pile up," Jimmy cautioned. "First of all, you don't get your money, and secondly they get pissed off and think you are lying and double charging." If they pile up too long, they usually argue with you and end up quitting, and the more they owe, the less likely they are to tip."

Jimmy rang the doorbell, and out stepped Denise Pawling. She was in her mid-teens and clearly annoyed that the paperboy was at the door.

"Collecting," Jimmy sang out.

"MOM, THE PAPERBOY IS HERE!" she yelled.

Denise left the doorway, and about a minute later, her mother showed up. "Just one week?" she asked.

Jimmy said "yes" and told her that this was his last week and that I was taking over. "Well, we'll miss you," she said. She handed Jimmy a dollar and she told him to keep the change. Jimmy ripped off the ticket and handed it to her. "One down, forty-one to go."

We finished off the other three houses on Collins, and the six on Coldspring in similar fashion. Of the ten houses so far, only one had no one home. We moved on to Haddon Avenue, with the first stop at the Boyds'.

"Mrs. Boyd leaves the money on the porch," Jimmy said. He opened the screen door into the porch and sure enough, there was a small table with seventy-five cents on it. Two quarters, two dimes, and a nickel. Jimmy ripped out the ticket and left it on the table. "Wish they were all as easy as this," Jimmy said.

Right next door was the Irelands' house, which couldn't have been more different. We walked up the steps of the porch and rang the doorbell. The screen door was open and we could hear the TV on inside, but no one was answering. Two minutes and we rang the bell again.

"Paperboy!" Jimmy hollered in. Still nothing. "Paperboy!" he called a little louder. A bit of rumbling and a bearded teenage boy came to the door.

"I'll get my mom," he said. "Mom," he yelled, "Paperboy!"

A few minutes later, Mrs. Ireland came to the door with a baby in her hands. "I'm a little short on cash," she explained. "Can you come back next week?"

"Yeah," Jimmy explained, "but you already owe me for three weeks. So next week it'll be $3.00."

"Are you sure? It seems like you were just here." She seemed annoyed. "I don't read the paper anyway; you really should see my husband."

Jimmy showed her the ticket book and said he would try back later that night or on the weekend, when her husband was there. "By the way, this is my last week. Bill here will be taking over," Jimmy added.

He handed her the paper and we walked away. "Creep," Jimmy said. "And her husband's not much better."

I was beginning to think this collecting stuff was going to be the worst part of the job.

When we reached my block of Haddon Avenue things were a lot better. I knew most of the people on the block and they were all sad to see Jimmy leave, but were also glad to see me taking over.

"At least we know who to call if the paper is late," was the common reply.

With thirty eight houses down, Jimmy noted we had enough money to pay Mrs. McGuillan. "We'll stop and pay before the Smythville houses," he said.

We arrived at the station at 5:15, and pulled up the driveway. Mrs. McGuillan was sitting at the table in the garage with the radio on. Christine Milano was with her, paying her bill. We stood by the garage door and waited, Christine counting out her $12.54 to pay for her papers. She had the smallest route, two blocks south on Johnson, then the length of Oakland Avenue. Christine went to Catholic school, so I didn't really know much of her. She wore glasses, had shoulder length brown hair, and was pretty plain. The only reason she stood out was that she was the only girl with a paper route. She joked with Mrs. McGuillan about the summer coming to an end, and school starting next week. She asked about Mrs. McGuillan's daughter Marie, who was in her class. They were entering the ninth grade.

Christine had her money stacked on the table, mostly coins, and when she finished counting, Mrs. McGuillan took the coins and bills and put them into a cash box, segregated with sections for pennies, dimes, nickels, quarters, and bills. Christine walked past us, said goodbye to Jimmy, and motioned us into the garage. Jimmy dumped out the money from his cloth sack and started counting. He counted out the change first, and then the bills. He needed to pay $23.94, and had over $13.00 in coins. He added a five-dollar bill and six ones, and Mrs. McGuillan gave him back six cents. Mrs. McGuillan wished Jimmy luck, and said she had enjoyed working with him the past few years. She asked him if he had another job lined up, but he said he was hoping to take it easy this fall, and join the high school track team.

"Good luck," she said as we walked away. "Hope to read about your track wins in the paper," she joked.

We got on our bikes for the trip to the Smythville homes. It was now almost 5:45 and the old lady at the end of Landing Street would be concerned about her paper being late. Jimmy pumped his bike a bit faster, and I stood up, and pumped faster still to keep up with him. Down Ormond, past the trees, grass, and the sloping hill towards the creek. Onto the gravel bed that was Landing Street we pedaled, and then skidded to a stop.

Jimmy hopped off his bike with the last four papers in hand, and we started up to house 101. The house was owned by Mrs. Hussong. Jimmy rapped at the door, and we heard movement inside. Mrs. Hussong must have been eighty years old. Her hair was grey and pulled back into a bun on her head. She moved slowly, carefully holding the railing as she leaned her head out the door. She smiled when she saw Jimmy, and handed him an envelope with seventy five cents in it. Jimmy thanked her, and said that this would be his last week. "Bill's taking over the route," he repeated, for what seemed like the millionth time I heard it that day.

The next three houses were just as run down as the first. They were small homes, made of brick, with small wooden porches, not much more than two steps off the ground. The homes were backed up to the woods on one side, with the gravel Landing Street before them. The homes and Landing Street fronted a small hill of about six feet, which dropped down to a grassy area overlooking the creek and its large iron fence.

Mrs. Dildine and her husband lived in the next house. The two of them had lived in the house for over 45 years. Both of them were even older than Mrs. Hussong. Mrs. Dildine sat on a rocker on her porch. On a table next to her was a cup with the seventy-five cents. She paid Jimmy, asking for the ticket and carefully putting it into her pocket. She listened intently as Jimmy gave his farewell speech, her head nodding continuously through the oration, and continuing as we left the house and went off the porch.

House 103 was Mrs. Welsh, and further down the street in house 104 was Mrs. Mac Mullin. All were sad to see Jimmy leave, and all asked me to try to live up to his high standards. As we walked back towards our bikes, Jimmy remarked how these four houses always seemed so desolate and alone from the rest of the world.

"It's kind of creepy at night in the winter," Jimmy said. "There's really not much light except for the streetlight near the dam and the faint glow from the front windows. I really don't think any of 'em has a car. I'm not sure how they get around or get food to eat."

We got back to our bikes, Jimmy's paper bag now finally empty, and it now past 6:30. Jimmy put the canvas money sack in his pocket, it now containing at least eleven dollars to my guestimate. He then handed me his ticket book and paper bag.

"Today's my last day," he said. "You're serving alone tomorrow to finish off the week. No papers ever on Sunday, then you start fresh next week. If you look in the ticket book you'll see you're owed at least eight dollars. That should more than cover you for the last couple of days and what you're owed for tomorrow. Have fun with the route and take care. Stop by if you have any questions, but I think you're pretty much set."

The surprise that my crash course training session was over suddenly hit me, and I grabbed my pants pocket to make sure my house list was still there. Of course the ticket book had pretty much the same information. I took the paper bag from Jimmy and draped it across the Stingray handlebars, doubling it up twice on each grip to make sure it wouldn't fall off, then carefully placing the ticket book into the bag. When I looked up, Jimmy had already started up the road, and I hit my kickstand up and started to follow. Jimmy's bike was bigger than mine, and he pedaled ahead way faster than me. I headed up the hill and started past the woods and tall grass along Ormond Avenue. In the distance I saw Jimmy, then as suddenly as he took off, he started back towards me. I kept pedaling and he drew closer. Our bikes met and we both stopped.

"Hey, I almost forgot," he yelled.

Then he took the partially filled bag of red plastic rubber bands from his pocket and handed them to me. "You'll be needing these," he said. Then he turned around and pedaled towards home, as darkness started falling, and the summer of my twelfth year came to an end.

Chapter 5 - The People

Remembering back to those days, it's difficult to understand the forces that kept everything going. I'm not sure if the systems we followed were universal to any particular newspaper publishers, or geographical area, but I doubt it. In our little paper station there were 23 of us who carried out our tradition six days a week. When a carrier decided to quit, the route was not advertised as having an opening, but instead word of it was informally passed from brother to brother, friend to friend, or acquaintance to acquaintance, with the responsibility of the outgoing server to find his own replacement, similar to how Jimmy found and recruited me.

Likewise, the routes were not laid out perfectly. Most centered on one or two main streets of houses, but nearly all had a tail of several stragglers, much like the Smythville homes of my route that were strangely out of place and fell like a handful of outliers on the hypothetical bell-shaped distribution. This could have been due to past nepotism, like Mike Gaines serving to his own house while his route was centered blocks away, or it could have been due to the paper's practice of giving a monetary prize of a few dollars to each carrier who drummed up a new customer. By the end of my time with the paper, I had served the *The Camden Courier-Post* for over five years; traveling the same route day in and day out to get to the end block of Coldspring Avenue. Yet even though I knew every carrier in the area, it now seems ironic that I never knew who served the homes on the first two blocks of that street.

We carriers persisted in our efforts with a sort of tunnel vision. We were driven by a self-satisfying reward system, fueled by tips and the desire to avoid complaints by our customers. While we may have viewed the station manager Mrs. McGuillan as a sort of informal boss, she really hadn't a care what we did with the papers once we left her garage. If we accidently forgot a house, or a paper landed off a step and into a bush, she received no complaint or gave no reprimand. Of course there was one authority figure, the district manager Mrs. Galinskie, who collected our money from Mrs. McGuillan and countless other paper stations across southern New Jersey, and funneled the money mysteriously back to the paper's true business unit. We rarely saw Mrs. Galinskie, but she knew each of our names, probably as vaguely as we knew the names of each of the customers on our route. Complaints, if severe, could be channeled back to us through Mrs. Galinskie, but that was rare; perhaps just as rare as an invitation for us to add a new customer to our routes because someone had called the paper requesting to start home delivery.

While we all functioned independently, the paper station was our hub, a home base of operation, and we were lucky to have a good station manager. While I'm not sure who came up with the concept, I'm sure the original idea was that the station was a truck dump off spot, where the carriers would come to pick up their papers and immediately leave. Mrs. McGuillan didn't make much more money than we did, setting up the paper stacks six times a week and collecting money from 23 assorted personalities every Friday night. She could have been strict and told us to pick up our papers and beat it, but instead she let us sit awhile and joke with her and each other as we folded our papers prior to departing. Sure she had a son about our age who had a route, but most of us were not close with him, or for that matter any of her other children.

Of those carriers in the early days, I can recall Mike Gaines, Conrad Stipp, Kevin Leahy, Christine Milano, Joey Gilmore, and Danny Dobalo, all of whom were Catholic and attended the same school as Pat McGuillan, Mrs. McGuillan's son who also served as a carrier. The McGuillans had at least five children, two of whom were considerably older than me. Then there was Pat, Mike, and Patty who were all within a few years of my age. Betty was a redhead and quite attractive, and sometimes she would fill in for her mother. She had freckles in the summer and wore skimpy shorts which I'm sure inspired several of us to fold our papers just a bit slower in the garage during our adolescent years.

There were also a few older kids, like Donald Elfreth and Dave Parker, who were quiet, kept to themselves, and usually picked up their papers later in the day after most of the others had gone. Dave Parker had the largest route with over 60 papers. On days of thirty to a bundle, he could barely fit all his papers in his bag; if there were only twenty, he had to make two trips. Among his customers were tenants of the Heather House, an apartment complex in what we called the Heather Glen section of town. I never was personally in the Heather House, but it looked nice from the outside, and I heard that Dave could drop off over forty papers just inside the apartment.

A younger group of kids consisting of me, Jon Shelly, Dennis Watson, Jim Cilento, Leonard Algiere, Russell Johnson, and Alvin Morrison rounds out the names I can remember. We became friends and enjoyed good natured ribbing of each other. This particularly applied to Alvin, who it turned out had accidently set his house on fire when he was about eight years old, something he could never live down. The fireman had arrived in time to put out the fire, and fortunately nobody had been seriously hurt, but a large part of the house had burned up pretty bad. Alvin was subsequently labeled Louis the Torch, which became his nickname to everybody in the station. The funny thing is Alvin was one of the nicest, most mild mannered kids that we knew and really didn't deserve the abuse. He grew up to become quite an accomplished musician, and later a successful Episcopal minister.

I recall that I met Alvin for the first time that Saturday after Jimmy turned the route over to me. At the time I knew nothing of the fire story. I was folding my papers sitting alongside Alvin and Jon Shelly. The papers were unusually light, like sixty to a bundle, and the short stacks brought on the feeling of an easy day. The paper had a headline about a plane crash somewhere in Alaska, and it was reported that all of the hundred or so passengers on board had died instantly on impact.

The story said something about some kind of equipment malfunction that caused the plane to lose altitude and descend and finally crash into a mountain.

"I can't imagine how scary it would be on the plane during those final moments," I said, looking at Jon.

Alvin looked up from his folding and spoke to no one in particular. "When you know you're really close to the end, everything slows down. At first you panic, and then you realize you're not alone and a strange calm comes over you. Then a bright light comes to help you, and together you decide if it's time for you to stay or to move on to a better place."

I looked over at Alvin and he was staring off into the distance, like he was reliving some past experience. The expression in Alvin's eyes made me feel he knew what he was talking about.

Jon Shelly started to giggle. "Well, anyplace without a Morrison would be a better place," he snickered.

Alvin looked down, and the garage got quiet. I didn't know what to say, so I kept my mouth shut. Alvin looked over to Shelly and said, "It's a shame I didn't know you earlier, it would have made the decision a lot easier."

Shelly laughed and shot a rubber band at Alvin. The rubber band missed and flew right into Alvin's paper bag.

"That's one for me!" laughed Alvin.

I finished folding my papers, so I picked up the bag and started for my bicycle. Even though the papers were light that day, I struggled a bit putting the bag on my bike. Both Alvin and Jon knew I was a new and both got up to help, each offering tips on the best way to wrap the strap onto the handlebars to secure it. I thanked them and took off down to Coldspring. The previous day's heat and humidity had lifted, and the air seemed clearer and the sky bluer than I remembered before. I made my way through the route, remembering the ticket book and the houses that had not paid the day before. I had a good feeling inside, maybe it was because I was working on my own, maybe it was the weather, or maybe it had something to do with Alvin and Jon Shelly.

I stopped at the Irelands' house and saw a man in the driveway washing a car, who I assumed was Mr. Ireland. I knew Jimmy and the ticket book said they owed three weeks, but I decided not to push my luck. I introduced myself, and told the man they owed two weeks. Mr. Ireland pulled out two dollars and I gave him his fifty cents change.

"My first dollar earned," I thought as I put the money in my pocket and rode off.

I continued up the street and delivered the rest of the papers, catching four of the remaining five homes for the payment that had been missed the day before. I zoomed past my house, throwing the paper on the porch, and started back towards the Smythville four. The bike was much easier to steer now that the bag on the handlebars held only the four banded papers. I glanced at the time, and saw it had barely been 35 minutes since I left the station to get this far, and that was even after stopping at a few houses to collect. "If it weren't for the backtracking, this route would be a cinch," I thought.

I rode over to Ormond, coasted down past the woods to Landing, and to the four Smythville homes. When I got to the last house, Mrs. Mac Mullin was waiting on the porch. She asked me my name again, then she asked me if I could help her put up a holiday banner. She pointed to a box on the porch which contained one of those red, white, and blue buntings that are hung in places like ballparks to celebrate the Fourth of July and other patriotic holidays. I took the bunting out of the box and Mrs. Mac Mullin stood up and pointed to where she wanted it hung on the porch railing. There was some string left on the bunting from the last time it had been hung up, and I tied it to the railing, once at the top at both ends, and once at the bottom at its widest point. Mrs. Mac Mullin thanked me, and I asked if there was anything else she needed. She said no and I started off, turning back to admire the bunting on the railing. The bunting colors were faded from age, but it still looked good on the porch. I figured she wanted it up to celebrate Labor Day, and I wondered if anyone else would see it besides me. After all, nobody ever came down the street. I gazed down the hill and looked at the dam and the water flowing over it. Behind the dam were the remnants of the timeworn brick factory that had once gotten its power from the dam.

I rode over by the dam and along the fence that separated me from it and the creek, following it away from Landing Street along a dirt path. The water was dark in color, stained from the cedar trees that populated the woods along creek, including those that had toppled in over the years and now lay by the banks jutting into the flowing water. I continued for about thirty feet, until I was into the woods and halted by another fence that prevented me from going further. At that point, the fence parallel to the creek had a tall gate which was held closed by a chain that was joined by a silver colored lock. The area inside the gate was overgrown, and it appeared that whoever had locked the gate rarely if ever went inside. Although overgrown, the dirt path continued inside the fence along the creek, past the old factory and on for at least another hundred yards beyond that. There was a sign on the fence that read "Former site of Benjamin Shreve Dam circa 1830. Replaced by Smythville Dam Circa 1937".

The path, the creek, and the fence all continued in the direction towards Coldspring Avenue. I thought, 'It really would make a nice short cut if you could get through.'

I turned around and walked back along the path, stopping for a second before the dam to pick up a few stones to throw over the fence and into the water. One stone skipped along the water, and over the dam, falling onto a narrow concrete ledge just to the side of the cascading water and hitting an empty soda can that had come to rest on the ledge.

"There's one for me," I thought, raising my arms in victory, as the dislodged can fell off the ledge and into the water. I turned around suddenly, strangely feeling I was being watched, but saw nothing up the hill except Mrs. Mac Mullin's house with the red, white, and blue banner. I started back on the path again, stopping to pick up my bike and the empty paper bag along the way, then started back towards Landing Street and Ormond Avenue towards home.

Chapter 6 – Zack

Bettlewood Avenue was one block over from my house, in the opposite direction from the paper station. At one time, the street was probably the nicest in our town. The homes on the street were larger than most, each with an old Victorian style, with multi-gabled roofs, and multi-colored ornate moldings and large porches. The street was lined with large elm and oak trees, which provided an overhead canopy of shade during the summer. Like the other streets in town, it was just a single lane in each direction; but it was built a bit wider than most so that even with cars parked on both sides, you could travel up and down the street pretty fast, even when another car happened by in the opposite direction. I suppose the street was built wider and the homes more elegantly because Bettlewood Avenue had a bridge that crossed over the creek and led into Collingswood, the next town over.

Zack lived on Bettlewood Avenue, near the end of the second block from the Pike. The bridge to Collingswood was about two blocks further east. The bridge was not long, maybe 75 feet in length and made of cement, with heavy concrete side railings and sidewalks on either side where people would gather to fish or gaze out at the water on either side. On the south side of the bridge, the creek blossomed into a small lake due to the backflow created by the Smythville Dam. The dam was at least eight blocks off in the southern direction. Looking from the bridge, it was difficult to see the dam or the old Smythville factory, as it was blocked from sight by the curvature of the creek into the woods.

The Mausser house was much larger than mine, with both a front and a side porch. The front porch had at one time been open, but had been redesigned by Zack's father so that it was now enclosed, with several large front and side windows. In the summer, the windows were fitted with large screens, and there were two comfortable couches on both sides of the porch for sitting, reading, and taking in the breeze which blew in from off of the street. The side porch was open, with thick white wooden railings and a slate gray colored wood plank floor. It was on the side of the house opposite the driveway, with steps that led out to a side yard patio and then out to the backyard. The side porch was pretty much free of furniture, with two lone lawn chairs which sat angled with their backs up to the railing. This side porch was a favorite spot for Zack and me to play. It was seldom visited by anyone else in the Mausser household, so we could set up our toy cars and build homes and towns out of wooden blocks, and leave the set-up intact for days without anyone disturbing it.

It was Sunday, shortly after church and I had decided to pay Zack a visit. I hadn't seen him since his trip to W. T. Grants, and I wondered if he had gotten the Hot Wheels Volkswagen Beetle. We had phones of course, but I would never have dreamt of calling when I could ride my bike over to find out in person. My paper bag was getting quite handy, and I left it on my handlebars, and put my collector's case of cars in the bag, just in case Zack and I decided to play with them on the porch. I also brought my six dollars, in case Zack had gotten a Volkswagen for me. When I got to Zack's house, he was out back painting the garage.

Zack was my best friend and had been for as long as I could remember. We could be together for days and never tire of each other's company. We talked openly on all subjects, and were never ashamed or scared of embarrassing ourselves to each other in anything we did or said. I was in the smarter class at school than Zack. In fact he was actually a year older than me, having been left back a year in the first grade for being a bit slow. That was ancient history now, and though I may have been book smarter, Zack was clearly smarter than me when it came to practical items, like how to fix a bike, mix cement, or paint a garage.

Compared to me, Zack was a stocky kid, with large arms, broad shoulders and a head of thick black curly hair. He always dressed in jeans, and usually wore either a flannel shirt when it was cool, or a T-shirt when it was warm with some masculine theme like Ford Tough Trucks or John Deere Tractors. With the exception of when we played baseball, he usually wore work boots, and he always carried a key chain, which attached to his pants at a belt loop on his right hand side. At the other end of the chain was a metal key ring with about 25 keys to various things that Zack felt were important. Zack loved to do things with his hands. At school he played the drums in the band, and at home he loved to build with his father's tools. Even at thirteen, he knew what he wanted to be when he was older, and he often said that he would one day be a craftsman and a full percussionist.

"Hey, Zack," I said as I rode my bike up by him while he was painting. "What's up with the garage?"

"Well, my mom's always lookin' at the garage from the kitchen window and she gets depressed. Last week she said it's all so barren now, stripped of color." Zack said. "So I told her I would clean and paint the garage if she bought some paint. She laughed and said it's a lot more than just that, but it would be a great start toward straightening things back up."

I looked at the can of Grant's finest White Exterior Enamel, the jug of Clorox bleach, and the bucket of water with a large scrub brush sticking out of it. Zack was on a ladder, at the far end of the single car garage, with a paint brush in his hand. He had painted the side of the garage facing the house, which included a door on the side, and a side window. I could see from the fresh paint that he was nearly done painting the entire side.

"It looks great. Are you painting the whole garage?" I asked.

"No, just this side at least for now," Zack replied. "The other sides don't look as bad from the mildew because they're not in the shade all the time."

I knew what he meant, but I could still never imagine anybody repainting a garage, even if it was just a fresh coat of white paint, unless the plan was to paint the whole thing.

"How was Grants?" I asked.

"Not too good," he replied. "No Volkswagen, all they had was the blue Eldorado and the red Firebird."

"Nuts," I said in disappointment, knowing we both already had each of these, even in the same colors as the ones at Grants. "Are they getting anymore in soon?"

"The guy at Grants said they get stuff in each Thursday, but he said that even if they got in the Volkswagen they would all be gone in a day. Everybody's lookin' for it," Zack lamented.

He had just about finished painting the side, and was now at the end of the garage and off the ladder. After a few more dips and strokes, he said he was done.

"Looks pretty good, huh?" Zack asked. And I agreed, "Yeah, looks a lot brighter and cheerful."

Zack put the lid on the can and banged it down with his fist. He then dumped out the bucket of bleach in the gravel in the driveway, and washed it briefly with the hose. He then swung open the garage door and squeezed down the side to go to the back and get some turpentine and a jar to soak the brush. I could see the Nash Rambler in the garage. It was Zack's grandfather's car, an old blue 1955 model. We called his grandfather Pop-Pop. He was Zack's father's father. He was in his late 70's and he didn't drive anymore or really do much of anything. Zack said that Pop-Pop had given the car to him, and he was going to fix it up so it ran better, and polish it up so its dull dark blue color and chrome bumpers would shine like new. The car was kind of small and plain, but it really wasn't in very bad shape, and I thought Zack was lucky that his Pop-Pop had given it to him.

"I forgot to ask my dad about the Turtle Wax for the Nash Rambler," I said to Zack.

"That's ok, but try to remember," Zack returned, "With that can I could wax the whole car. It'd be sharp."

Zack started for the house. His house had no back door, but did have one on the side near the driveway. We walked in the door onto a landing that went either up into the first floor or down into the basement. Zack turned on the basement lights and we went down into the cellar. The cellar was full of Zack's father's power tools and saws. There was also a lot of wood. Zack put the can of paint on the workshop table and wrote the word *garage* on it. We then headed upstairs.

The steps led into an area between the kitchen and dining room. The kitchen was wide with an open design and clearly bore the look of being under construction. Actually, the work had been going on for some time. Zack's father was primarily a carpenter by trade, with a side business as a locksmith. He had started work on the kitchen years ago, tearing out the old cabinets and wood moldings and replacing them with new. But the work was never finished. At the time, the family couldn't agree on which of the new style cabinets they liked best. So Zack's dad put up a couple of each style for the family to choose, but no decision had ever been made.

Zack went straight into the kitchen to the sink and started to wash his hands, scrubbing any remnants of white paint from them. He looked out the kitchen window which was above the sink and commented on the pleasant view of the freshly painted garage. "I can't wait until my mom gets home to see the garage. She'll sure be happy when she stands here now. She always gets so upset when she stands in the kitchen and washes the dishes. Sometimes she just stares out the window and cries."

He finished washing his hands and went over to a light tan colored cabinet on the left side of the window and pulled out three glasses, "You want something to drink?" he asked. "We got some iced tea."

I said yes and walked over to the table. Zack came over with three glasses of iced tea and a bag of pretzels, which he grabbed from a walnut colored cabinet. The cabinet had a series of track lights focused on its side. They looked a bit awkward and out of adjustment. He motioned to me to pick up the bag of pretzels and my drink, and we started out to the side porch. Just beyond the side porch back steps, ran the pavement to the backyard, which stopped on a small flagstone patio under the shade of a large buttonwood tree. There was a piece of wooden yard furniture of a popular style of the time that sat on the patio. It consisted of two redwood chairs on either side of a center table, all of which were connected and were built on wooden wheels, so that the unit could be rolled around to different parts of the yard if someone so had the desire. This patio was a favorite sitting spot for Pop-Pop. He could sit there and smoke his pipe without bothering anybody, and he could feed the birds and squirrels in the backyard, which seemed to help him pass the time. Pop-Pop looked the same as always, with his white hair parted to one side, cane in hand, and wearing tan pants and a plaid colored shirt with a dark blue button-down sweater. I swear it didn't matter what the season, he always seemed to have on a button down sweater. Zack gave Pop-Pop one of the glasses of iced tea and a handful of pretzels.

"Whoa, a treat to wet the whistle of the old man," he crooned. "Thank you kindly. And if you don't mind, I'll take a couple of extra pretzels for my friends," he said as he motioned to some birds over on the grass. "What you been doin'?" he asked.

"Aw, nothing much," Zack replied. "I just thought you might like a drink."

We left Pop-Pop and started back for the side porch. We sat there for a few minutes and finished the drinks and the pretzels, and talked.

"You know that guy at Grants said he heard that soon they'll be coming out with a whole new set of Hot Wheels," Zack started. "I just can't understand how they can come out with new ones when you can't even find the old ones. Oh, then I looked at the Matchbox cars and they had an orange dump truck with Birmingham written on the sides. The back truck bed actually lifts and the tailgate opens. Mom let me get it. I got it upstairs in my room."

Zack got up from the porch and I followed. We went back in the house and dropped off the glasses and the empty pretzel bag. Then we passed through the living room, past the entrance to the front porch, and upstairs to Zack's bedroom. Zack's bed wasn't made and his church clothes were lying on top of the rolled up covers. His room was packed with stuff that was neat to look at. There was a clear model of a V-8 engine, and if you turned a crank, you could see the eight pistons cycle and valves open. There was a small brass steam engine, with a black boiler with a small fuel furnace that burned white blocks of some kind of fuel that looked like a lump of sugar. The steam engine really worked. I remember Zack's dad filling the boiler with water, and lighting the furnace years ago. We watched and listened as the steam in the boiler began to crackle, and watched as if by magic as the wheel on the engine began to spin from the steam pressure inside. I can remember Mr. Mausser with his white hair and huge hands opening the valve from the boiler to a small whistle on the engine, and listening to the shrill shriek of the steam. Mr. Mausser had lost half of his index finger in a carpentry accident when he was younger, and I remember him pointing at us with the stub, telling us to be careful with the engine, because it really was a machine, and not a toy, and we could hurt ourselves either from the heat or the mechanical action of its wheels and levers if we weren't careful.

Zack walked over to the far side of the bed to get the Matchbox dump truck. On the wall was a large wooden shelf, maybe four feet long by three feet high that Zack's dad had made for him. The shelf was perfectly made, with mitered joints about the outside, and rabbeted tongue and groove shelves to rest stuff on. There were about fifteen shelves in all, each perfectly sized to allow a Matchbox or Hot Wheels car to rest on. The wood was stained a light oak color that made the wood grain stand out and gave it the character of a fine store bought piece of furniture. The shelf was a little more than half filled with cars, starting on the top and running the length of the shelf. The cars were arranged by type, with Hot Wheels on the top shelf, and construction vehicles in the lowest of the middle shelves. The new orange Birmingham dump truck was on this shelf. Zack took it down and showed me how the bed could be lifted and the tailgate opened. He handed me the truck and I repeated Zack's manipulations of the lift and gate, marveling at its authenticity, although I had never really seen an orange dump truck before.

Zack had two older sisters and an older brother. His sisters were both going to college; one in Tennessee and the other in South Carolina, so for all practical purposes, neither of them lived at home anymore. Their bedroom was adjacent to Zack' bedroom. Far down the hall was Mrs. Mausser's bedroom, and in between was Pop-Pop's bedroom.

That weekend, Zack's mother had accompanied the younger of the two sisters back to South Carolina, so she was presently not at home. Zack's brother Randy was about five years older than him. Randy was friends with my brother and they had put together an elaborate HO train platform up in the attic of Zack's house. Randy had actually moved his bedroom up to the attic when Pop-Pop came to live with them. There were two rooms to the attic, Randy's bedroom and the train room. Unlike my house where you needed a ladder to get up into the attic, you could get into the attic in Zack's house from a set of steps in the second floor hallway.

Zack asked if I wanted to see the train platform and I said yes. We climbed up the attic steps, the temperature getting warmer with each step up. The steps opened up to an "A" framed room. In the center of the room was a large plywood table, resting on heavy hewn legs which raised it about three feet off the floor. Near the center of the platform was the platform control center with three transformers and a series of buttons for turning on lights and moving track switches. Zack's father had built the train platform for Randy. Some sections were painted to resemble water, and others were covered with a green fuzzy paint to make them look like grass. Still other elevated sections were covered with a tan or brown graveled paint that resembled mountainous sections. The platform was exceptional, and my brother and Randy spent a considerable amount of time, putting up new track sections and adding houses, trees, and factories to make it seem like a real town.

Zack started to talk about a new GG1 engine his brother had gotten when we heard a call from Pop-Pop from downstairs.

Zack started down the attic steps and I followed. We continued down the second flight of stairs to the living room where Pop-Pop was calling. When we got there he was standing at the bottom of the steps.

"Oh, there you guys are," he said. "I thought you might have left to play ball or something. I just noticed what a great job you did on the garage. What a saint, and you didn't even ask for any help. You're getting to be quite the image of your father. Bet he's looking down from heaven right now and is darn proud of what a fine son you've turned out to be. Sorry to disturb your fun; I just wanted to be sure to thank you."

Chapter 7 – The Lock Shop

Zack's father had died a little over two and a half years earlier. He was a workhorse who had really never been sick a day in his life. But one day he came home severely exhausted and faint. The doctors said he had developed a type of lymphoma. That was a few days before Halloween, and by Christmas he was dead.

To his credit, he had been a hard worker all of his life. He had started out working with his father in town as an apprentice in his locksmith shop; and eventually he took over the business. Over the years the job expanded, first requiring him to repair locks, then install new doors, and eventually the job extended to that of a full service carpenter. Mr. Mausser loved working with wood and became an expert at the trade. While he kept the locksmith shop, the service of locks gradually became more of a hobby than a career. As large mass hardware department stores like Channel, and Rickles became popular, with their selections of do-it yourself lock and key hardware, it became more difficult to eke out a living as a locksmith. This was something that was difficult for Pop-Pop to handle, but not Zack's dad. The store still served as a way to attract business, and many times the repair of a lock led to other carpentry services, referrals, and a considerable amount of work. Pop-Pop would man the store in his gentlemanly way, while Zack's dad set out on the big dollar jobs that paid the bills. While he could do nearly anything from fix a lock to build a house, his real love was working with wood, and he could build a cabinet from scratch that rivaled even the best furniture maker. His reputation in the town was golden, and business was very good, albeit very busy.

I learned of Mr. Mausser's illness from my parents, who had heard the news at the church in which we all were members. I remember it being a time of great sadness for the congregation, as among other things, he was a pillar to the council as well as the community. Even approaching death he kept up his good spirits, and I recall conversations of my parents concerning his impending funeral. It seems in his last weeks,

Mr. Mausser had decided he wanted to make his own coffin. After all, he had said, he knew no one better at woodworking, he loved the trade, and if he was going to spend the rest of his life in a box, he wanted it to be to his liking. So he made the coffin in his workshop in the basement of the house, designing the size and shape himself, and finishing it to a finely polished walnut finish which was his particular favorite. As a finishing touch, he installed a two-way lock on the cover so, he said, it could be opened from both sides – "just in case." He then made up six gold keys to operate the lock, one for himself, one for his wife, and one for each of his four children. The keys were placed in an envelope, and it was his last wish that upon his death, that he be buried with one of the keys, and that the remainder be given to each member of his family. "Just in case I can't get out," he joked. The gold key was one of the keys Zack kept on his key chain. He said he would keep it with him until the day he and his father would meet again in heaven.

Zack and I were at the bottom of the steps talking to Pop-Pop, the orange Birmingham dump truck still in my hand. Pop-Pop continued his oration on the garage, and as he spoke he became more animated.

"You know what would make the garage look even more personable? What if you brought up that sign from the lock shop and put it over the side door of the garage. Not the big sign from out front, the smaller one from inside over the entrance to the storage room. You know, the one with your father's name on it. It would look nice, and when we looked out in the yard we could think of him, bringing back pleasant memories for us and your mom."

Zack knew the sign and where it hung. "But the shop won't be the same without it," Zack commented.

Pop-Pop continued his discussion. "Well it's goin' on three years and that store still ain't been sold, and we're all kind of kidding ourselves.....and that means mostly me. You can't sell a man's business when the business was the man. We all know his knowledge, and service, and dedication were the only reason people would keep coming. I think it's time we said goodbye to the shop, and let it go to rest, just like your dad."

Zack seemed perplexed at first, and then became resolute. "The one over the door you say, you want me to get it?"

"Yeah, it'd make me and your mom happy," Pop-Pop replied. "I'd come with you, if I was any help. But my legs aren't what they used to be. It'd take me damn near two hours to walk there, and I can't drive anymore."

Zack agreed to go and asked me to go with him. "We'll have to walk," Zack said. "I don' know if we could carry the sign on a bike."

So we set out to the locksmith shop. It wasn't that far, just up to the Pike and over a block and a half. I was more than happy to go. I hadn't been there for years. The walk took us only five minutes. When we got there the store looked the same as I remembered, except for the CLOSED and FOR SALE signs in the front window.

The store really wasn't that big, and it blended in with most of the other stores on the Pike. It looked as though it had once been a house, except for the big window in front and the glass entrance door. On the window were stenciled the words "Mausser Locksmith Shop", with the words, "Full Lock Service and Sales", stenciled underneath. The lettering was gold and outlined in black. The shop front was narrow and connected to two other stores on either side. On one side was Ralph the Barbers, on the other side was Swartz's Photo Shop. Above each shop was a small apartment. Ralph lived in the apartment above his barber shop. Mr. Feeny, a friend of Pop-Pop's lived above the locksmith shop. I'm guessing Mr. Swartz lived over his photo shop.

Zack pulled out his keys and instantly selected the one to the shop. When we walked inside, the air was stale, like no one had been inside to air out the building in quite a while. The shop had a counter and a cash register on the back wall. To the left of the counter was an entranceway to a back room that held boxes of parts and miscellaneous locks. A sign hung above the door that read "Randolph Mausser - Registered Locksmith - Providing Security for Over 25 Years." Zack motioned that this was the sign we'd be taking down. On the right hand side was a second counter with a key cutting machine and a revolving carriage of keys of different types, sizes, and shapes. In the front of the store were displays of types of door locks and hardware, but the displays were sparse and looked pretty near cleaned out. Zack explained that most of the hardware had been sold off shortly after his father died. He explained that his mom had put the business up for sale, but there had been no takers. The store property itself was not owned by the Maussers but was leased from Ralph the barber. Ralph was in no hurry to evict the locksmith shop, partially because he and Pop-Pop had been friends nearly forever. The bigger reason was that there were similarly unoccupied shops on the block along the Pike, so why create another? At least the appearance of a shop next to the barber shop was better than a blank empty window and a barren interior.

We walked around inside and Zack asked if I wanted to see some things that were neat. I said yes, and we went into the backroom. Along the far left side in the backroom there were a series of benches, vises, and at least a dozen tool chests that were full of tools of the trade. The chests were organized and labeled with their contents. I read through some of the drawer names: files, key blanks, master keys, bolt stumps, slim jims, lock picks, tubular locks, tubular lock picks, Maison keys, car keys, double sided keys, four sided keys, paracentric keys, abloy keys, skeleton keys, Zeiss keys, and Do Not Duplicate keys.

I opened the drawer that said lock picks and found a series of boxes containing torsion wrenches, hook picks, half diamond picks, rakes, snake rakes, picks, and double round picks. There was a whole drawer full of bump keys of various shapes and sizes, along with four or five drawers of lock cylinders. On the side table were at least ten horizontal stacks of compartmentalized steel covered boxes on a series of pull out slides. These boxes contained lock bittings, shims, and pins of hundreds of shapes, lengths, widths, and styles.

There were several posters on the walls showing the internals of locks with a cross section of the cylinder, key pins, and driver pins, and how they would align properly along the key plug shear line if the proper key was in place. The posters referenced a series of letters and dimensions, with each poster presumably explaining the coding system for some manufacturer's pin nomenclature.

In the drawers under the benches were sets of hammers and screwdrivers of every conceivable size, with an emphasis on extremely small sizes. On the benches were a series of torsion meters, and manufacturer's books, and to the right were at least three feet of different manufacturer's reference catalogs.

A cabinet to the side was labeled drills and a second was labeled saws, still another labeled pick guns, with manual and electric guns positioned on either side. The rest of the back room was full of a series of shelves with an exhaustive inventory of locks of every conceivable size and type, including door locks, dead locks, combination locks, and standard keyed entry locks.

I asked Zack what a pick gun was, and he showed me how you could use one to open a lock without the proper key by simply applying some leverage and pulling the trigger to bump it open. He then showed me how he could do the same using a bump key and a hammer.

"My dad showed me a lot, some of the stuff seemed simple, but a lot was really amazing," Zack said. "But my dad could literally look at a key or a lock cylinder and pretty much tell you who made it and what its pin design was. Heck, he could even drill out a piece of steel bar and make his own cylinder and pin it up with a key of any design he wanted.

We wandered up and out through the backroom door, Zack with a screwdriver in hand. "Here, hold this for a second, and help me with the sign." He pulled a step ladder out of a side closet and started to climb. I handed him back the screw driver and in no time he had the sign off and down. The sign was about four feet long and four inches high. It was made of wood, and painted red with gold letters outlined in black.

"Pop-Pop's right," Zack said as we walked outside and onto the sidewalk. "This sign will look good over the garage side door. And it'll definitely remind us of the shop." He turned around to lock the door. "I'm really going to miss this place when it's gone," he said as we turned to leave.

Chapter 8 – Catholics

We lived next door to the Flahertys, who were what you might call a typical Irish Catholic family that made up a large portion of our town. Mrs. Flaherty was a heavy-duty housewife, who spent most of her waking hours picking up and caring for the family. Not that the house was always kept organized and tidy; something anybody with six children can attest to as pretty much an impossibility. My mother and Mrs. Flaherty grew to be very close, as they both learned from each other workable ways to raise and care for young children. These were not always the best ways, but at least they prevented premature fatalities. Mr. Flaherty was a soft spoken and kind man, and unlike the boisterous Irish stereotype, I never recall him in a foul mood or without a kind word or smile on his face. He worked for General Electric, GE as we would say, in Philadelphia. He worked long hours and I rarely saw him at home. He was a devout Christian, and it always amazed me when my mom told me he went to church every day of the week to pray before work. Mr. Flaherty was as bald as is humanly possible; I don't think he had even a single hair on his head. I don't recall him ever doing much home repair or yard maintenance, which is something that always preoccupied my father. I guess having six children left lots of alternate options for mowing the yard.

Tommy Flaherty was the oldest of the Flaherty children, at least twelve to fifteen years older than me. I can barely remember much about him, other than that he inherited his father's hairline at a young age. He had a tan Ford Galaxy 500 and was away most of the time at college. Jimmy was the next oldest, and was five or six years my senior. He was a little older than my brother, but they really weren't very close. Mary Anne was the lone daughter, and had red hair, freckles, and a big smile. As a kid she was as thin as a rail, and active in lots of school activities. Joey was next, followed by Michael. Joey was a year older than me, and Michael a year younger. They were the Flaherty children I spent most of my time with at an early age growing up. Daniel

Aloysius Flaherty was the youngest, about three years my junior, and was pretty much regarded by Joey, Michael, and I as a pest.

Our house and the Flaherty's were separated by a fence... well, two fences actually. The back part of our yards sported a galvanized wire fence. Up closer to the house, the fence was wooden, made up of white painted 2x4's in what looked like a series of six by three feet square boxes with diagonal wooden boards crisscrossing inside. As young children, the crisscrossing fence sections offered no resistance to us, as we could easily climb through the diagonal openings. As we grew older, after a quick climb onto the center of the diagonals, we could easily hop over the fence into the yard on the other side. Of course all this was preferred by kids to walking the thirty foot length of the wooden fence to the front of the house and around it to the neighboring yard.

Michael, Joey, and I were fairly close growing up until we reached first grade. The Flahertys had an enormous picnic table in their backyard that sat under a large multi-trunked maple tree. The table was easily large enough to fit the entire Flaherty family, plus three or four guests. The Flahertys would often eat at the table in the summer, as it offered a cooler alternative to the kitchen table in their house. When not being used for eating, the table served as a popular hiding spot, sitting spot, or general entertainment area for us kids. There was many a day that we imagined the table to be a sailing ship, with the attached benches serving as resting hammocks or perhaps our final passage when we were told to walk the plank.

The Flaherty house differed from our house as it had an enclosed front porch and no front entrance. Instead, the front door was on the side of the home facing our house. At the side, there were three steps with about a six foot square landing leading to the door. A three person deacon's chair sat on the landing, and this was another popular sitting spot when we were very young. When walking inside the Flaherty house, you were first met by the kitchen to the left and the dining room table to the right. On the wall of the dining room was a portrait of John F. Kennedy seated at a desk in front of the American flag. Traveling past the kitchen, you entered a large living room with a long continuous green couch which encompassed two walls and was joined by a curved section at the wall corner. Across from the couch was a TV with rabbit ear antennas, and in front of the couch was a mahogany coffee table that always seemed littered with empty glasses. Upstairs there were three bedrooms, one for Mr. and Mrs. Flaherty, one for Mary Anne, and one large bedroom shared by Jimmy, Joey, Michael, and Danny. The boys' bedroom, although large, left little space for walking with the four single beds positioned in an alternating zigzag across the room. In the hall, there were steps leading to the attic that roomed Tommy when he was home. The attic was only partially finished, with flooring boards only in the centermost section. This left open joists to the far sides of the "A" frame ceiling. I remember one time Jimmy happened too far to one side, and actually fell through the attic floor. Fortunately, he fell onto one of the beds in the boys' room. He didn't get hurt, and aside from the mess there was not much damage done, except for the hole in the ceiling and the plaster bits all over the bedroom. Nevertheless, following the accident, all of us except Tommy were forbidden from entry into the attic.

The Flahertys were proud of their Irish Catholic heritage, and took great pride in announcing their faith in everyday conversation, which I really didn't understand at a pre-school age. There was the fish on Fridays, the prayers before picnic meals outside, and the bird bath statue of the Virgin Mary that stood in the backyard just beyond the house. Of these, it seemed to the kids that making sure the birdbath was full of water was of the utmost importance, so Joey, Michael, and Danny would clamor to see who could get to the hose first and fill it whenever someone noticed it to be low on water. The birdbath sat in front of an enormous hydrangea bush, which bore large snowball-like flowers in various shades of blue and violet in the late spring to early summer. The hose was on the driveway side of the house, which bordered on the hydrangea bush. Because of the size of the bush,

however, it became necessary to walk in the driveway, which was a problem if you happened to be barefooted, which was the summer footwear of choice for us kids. The driveway was not paved, but consisted of a grey colored bed of trap rock. This amounted to a collection of pointed granite rock pieces about one inch in size. Walking on the trap rock in bare feet was a torture we all exposed ourselves to multiple times as a rite of
passage over the years. By the hose bib was a variety of yard implements, like shovels, rakes, hoes, and brooms that had never quite made their way back to the garage – a pretty common occurrence at the Flaherty house.

I remember one particular day when we were about seven years old and playing together one summer afternoon. The hydrangea bush was in full splendor with dozens of blue, pink, and lavender snowball shaped blooms. Flying in and out of the flowers was a variety of bees, flitting from blossom to blossom. We were fascinated with the bees, and studied them at first just from a distance. We called the plain honeybees, which were by far the most prevalent, "worker bees." The large black and yellow bumblebees we somehow labeled "queen bees," mistaking their size and alternate variety for importance. Although we were young, we enlisted ourselves to catch the bees in glass jars, something we had seen our older brothers do before, which was regarded as a feat that clearly showed a certain degree of courage.

The glass jars were preferably of the screw cap variety, which were commonly used with mayonnaise, coffee, or peanut butter. These could be readily found in the trash and could be cleaned out with the hose. Once armed with an appropriate jar, the trick was first to put a sprig of hydrangea flower into it, so the bee would feel at home, then to carefully follow a bee until it landed on a flower. Cupping the jar on the bee and swiftly placing on the lid trapped the bee inside for closer inspection. Of course being trapped in the jar infuriated the bees and caused them to violently thrash about the jar with an intense buzzing that would actually cause the jar to vibrate. Exactly why we did this as a source of entertainment, I can't fully explain. Why we did it in our bare feet made even less sense, and where our parents were while we performed the courageous ritual remains a mystery to me to this day.

On that particular afternoon, while Michael, Joey, Danny, and I all sat watching our bees, Joey's jar began to fog. This brought about the revelation that with a diminishing air supply the bees would surely die, so we set out to put holes in the jar lids to allow air in. We left our bee jars on the Flahertys' front step landing, and set out for the garage for the tools to make holes in the lids. This required a walk across the trap rock and into the garage. Joey being the oldest was the first into the garage, and he emerged with a thin rusty nail and a hammer. Joey's plan was to use the nail and hammer to puncture the metal lid to make about four air holes per jar. Joey started the hammering and the nail slipped, turning to one side and scratching his middle finger just below the knuckle which caused his finger to bleed.

Joey was alright until he saw the blood, then he started to cry. He rushed inside the house to Mrs. Flaherty, who promptly sprayed the cut with some Bactine and put a Band-Aid on it. In the meantime we had successfully used the hammer and nail combination to put air holes in all of our jar lids, plus Joey's. Joey came out of the house, with the Band-Aid on his finger and a Pop-Ice Popsicle in his hands. He immediately sat on the deacon's chair on the landing. Meanwhile Michael, Danny, and I continued to sit on the steps, staring at our air-refreshed but still infuriated bees as they buzzed inside the jars.

"How you feeling Joey; your finger stop bleeding?" I asked.

"A lot better. Mom says I'll be OK. It don't hurt. Thanks for poking the holes in the lids. Now the bees will be able to breathe," Joey replied.

He bent down to pick up the nail, and carefully put it in the lid hole, and then he pulled it out. His face curled and in a hushed voice he observed, "Did you notice the nail has rust on it. You know what that means?"

We all knew, but none of us had thought it until Joey brought it up.

"Lockjaw! You get a cut from something rusty and you get lockjaw, and then you die," Joey informed us. "I wonder how much time I got left?"

"Beats me? Does your mouth feel like it's lockin' up?" I asked.

"Nah, but it might still be ok because of the cold from the popsicle," he replied.

I looked again at my bee, then up at Joey on the chair. "Well, I'll miss you Joey. I wonder if you get lockjaw and die, if you can still talk when you go to heaven. It would really be crummy if you couldn't ever talk to me again."

Joey looked down at me from the deacon's chair and answered, "It doesn't matter anyway. You're a *Public* and not a Catholic. Everybody knows that you can only go to heaven if you're a Catholic."

I didn't know that, but somehow it didn't really bother me too much at the time. Dying for me seemed a long way off, and I was a lot happier not to be dying soon from lockjaw, than I was concerned with not going to heaven when I was older.

We all decided that we would leave Joey alone and get him a present before he died. We all left the landing, including Joey, leaving our bee jars under the chair so they wouldn't get knocked over. The three Flaherty kids went into their house, and I went back home to look for something. At home I found a glow in the dark cross I had gotten from my church Sunday school that I thought might be appropriate, but in looking for some wrapping paper, I lost interest in returning to Joey.

Besides, it was nearly suppertime, and my mom said I had to stay home.

The next morning, I remembered the cross, and headed over to the Flaherty's, wondering if it was too late. I climbed up the steps and rang the doorbell. While waiting, I looked down under the chair at the bees in the four jars. All of the bees were motionless, and most certainly dead. Ironically Joey answered the door, full of energy, and buzzing about the latest Sally Star show on TV. He had totally forgotten about lockjaw, dying, and the bees.

But I didn't forget the story, particularly the part about *Publics* not being allowed in heaven. It really didn't seem right to me, but I wasn't sure what to do about it. I could change, but figured I had plenty of time to consider a strategy. Besides, if the rest of my family wouldn't be there, I wasn't sure how much I wanted to be there anyway.

It was now about six years later, and the first day back to school for seventh grade. The Flahertys' still lived next door but Michael, Joey, and I had grown apart. We remained neighbors, but after kindergarten, we had entered different schools, which resulted in a completely different circle of friends and different interests. We would still acknowledge one and other with a hello when we passed, but we strangely grew apart, almost as if we had moved away to different towns.

There were two school systems in town. If attending the public school system, you went to the Mary A. Finney Elementary School from kindergarten to fifth grade, followed by the Harry S. Truman Middle school from sixth to eighth grades. Both of these schools were located across the Pike and at the end of West Clinton Avenue, about a fifteen minute walk from my house. The two schools were on separate properties, but within a stone's throw of each other. The town was not large enough to support a high school, so for grades nine through twelve, you went in the completely opposite direction to the neighboring town of Collingswood and its senior high school.

The other school system was parochial or *Catholic* as we called it. Following a year in kindergarten at Mary A. Finney Elementary, you switched to the Saint Aloysius School from first to eighth grade, followed by high school at Pope Pius VI. Saint Aloysius School, or St. Al's as we called it, was also located across the Pike, but was over on West Haddon Avenue, located between the Saint Aloysius Catholic Church and the church's rectory which housed the priests, and the convent which housed the church's nuns. It was a true parochial school in which only the priests and nuns served as school teachers. Fittingly, the church and school were named after Saint Aloysius, the patron saint of youth.

We *Publics* started school at the Harry S. Truman School at 8:15 AM, meaning that under normal circumstances I had to leave home a bit before 8:00 AM to get to school on time. There were no buses to any of the schools, so everybody walked. In the sixth and seventh grades both Zack and I were responsible enough to be chosen as school safetys. This meant I had to leave the house about fifteen minutes earlier than usual to go to my post. The idea of being a safety was that a group of students were each assigned a specific street corner on which to stand along the route to school. The safetys' job was to help the younger children cross the streets on the way to school to make sure they didn't dawdle or get hit by a car. There were certain perks to being a safety. We got to wear a white shoulder belt with a badge as part of our official uniform, and we got special permission to arrive at school up to ten minutes late in the morning and leave school ten minutes early at the end of the day. This was so that we could be in place at our corners before the other kids got there so we could help them cross the street. It was considered a great honor to be chosen as a safety, at least in the sixth and seventh grades, but by eighth grade the novelty had usually worn off, and it became uncool to hold the position.

Saint Aloysius School started at 8:00 AM and ended at 3:00 PM, a full fifteen minutes earlier then us *Publics* both coming and going, so they had their own set of safetys. Of course, as is often the case with differing cliques, there was a certain animosity between the two groups, and it was not unusual for me to hear "I'm Catholic and I don't need to listen to you *Public* safetys from the St. Al's stragglers.

As safetys we could change corners about four times a year if we wanted a change of scenery. On our side of the Pike there were fewer corners to choose from, so I usually picked the corner of Bettlewood and the Pike or Haddon and the Pike because they were closest to home. On this first day of school I had the Bettlewood corner, just up the street from Mausser's Locksmith Shop. The corner was not particularly busy as far as safety crossing guard duty was concerned due to the small number of kids that passed this way on the route to school. Since the Pike was considered a major highway, we allowed only crossings of Bettlewood Avenue, with the ultimate crossing of the Pike taking place two blocks south at the traffic light. So after a few crossings I had extra time to contemplate the new school year and the seventh grade. I had on my new first day school clothes which were dressier than usual having been selected by my mom. They felt uncomfortable, and I wondered how I had allowed her to talk me into getting them in the first place. There was no nervousness about the school year, just the anticipation of new teachers and new subjects, and the usual dread of starting over again. Across the Pike, I noticed my neighbor Joey Flaherty running alone towards St. Al's, obviously a bit late, and I thought about the episode with the bees and the lockjaw and wondered how we could have been so naïve back then.

Looking up to the corner of Haddon, I saw Jack Karaszkiewitz signal with waving arms that it was time to go off duty and leave the corner for school. I acknowledged the signal with a similar arm wave, then turned to face east and gave the same arm wave signal to Zack at the corner of Johnson and Bettlewood, which he acknowledged. Then I picked up my backpack, light and empty of books, and started on the trek to seventh grade.

Chapter 9 – The Route

The school day was over and it seemed like the seventh grade wouldn't be too bad. I had Mrs. Caprio for English and home room which wasn't great. The rumor was that she hated kids and gave even the best students a "C" just because she didn't believe anyone was more than satisfactory. But Mr. Baum in math and Mrs. Birkholder in science seemed like they lived to teach their classes and that they would keep things interesting and enjoyable. Zack was in my homeroom and gym class, and we sat together at lunch with Peter Gallagher, the Karaszkiewitz brothers, and Burnsy like usual. Today the lunch subject was our season ending ball game, which we relived like it was the World Series. Melanie Duffer at the next table had gotten glasses over the summer and Larry Dobbs moved to Haddonfield, and that was about the extent of the news since last spring. I left at the end of the school day for safety duty with a good feeling since there was no real homework for the night - just getting my English, math, science, and history books covered. On the walk to my corner, I saw Zack up ahead, and I ran to catch up with him. He was putting on his safety belt when I reached him, and I asked him why he hadn't worn his new school clothes that day. He said his mom still wasn't home in the morning but she should be back by the time he returned from school.

When we reached the Pike we saw the Catholic kids being let out from St. Al's. Those who lived on our side of the Pike formed a line, which was led by Sister Mary Evelyn Anne and backed by Sister Theresa Marie, both of whom were dressed in the traditional black and white nun habit with veil. All the Catholic kids were required to walk together double file in the line, from the school to the light on West Clinton Avenue and the Pike. There was no talking or straying from the line permitted until they crossed the Pike. Zack and I stopped and allowed the line to pass parade-like before us. The line was nearly a half of a block long, with everyone wearing the mandatory school uniforms. Long dark blue pants, black dress shoes, and a light blue button-down shirt for the boys; and a blue plaid skirt, knee high navy blue socks, black shoes, and a light blue button-down shirt for the girls. Once across the Pike, the line quickly broke up into small groups of friends, veering off in both directions up and down the street.

Once the entire line had crossed the Pike, we followed, and then we in turn curved off to assume our corner posts. After school, safety duty lasted about twenty minutes, crossing the same group of kids that had passed in the morning. The job was pretty much the same, but everyone tended to walk a bit slower and be a bit happier. When the kids stopped coming, Jack waved to end safety duty, and I passed the signal on to Zack. I walked home to drop off my books, change clothes, and get my bike to go to the paper station. Mom was there when I got home and she wanted to hear about school, so I didn't leave until she was updated on all of my new teachers. I got my bike and bag and started down the street, turning onto Johnson Avenue, when I caught sight of Zack on his ten-speed. I slowed down and he caught up to me in no time.

"My mom was there when I got home and she loved the garage and the sign," Zack said. "I got to pick whatever I wanted for supper, so I asked for meatloaf," he continued. "So I got to go to Nick's to pick up some ground meat."

Nick's was a small butcher shop and grocery store in the neighborhood, and many of us kids made frequent trips there at our mother's requests to pick up whatever was urgently needed for a last minute meal, be it bread, milk, eggs, or meat. Zack asked where the paper station was, and I said it wasn't that far away, so he decided to follow me. When we got to the McGuillans' house, there was a *Millar's Cyclery* van parked out front with the motor running, with a man and two boys inside. Just as we got near the driveway, the two boys got out of the van, and it pulled away. One of the boys was holding a paper bag, and had just thrown a cigarette down in the street. On closer inspection, both boys looked the same, with the one with the paper bag wearing jeans and a gray short sleeved sweatshirt. The other still had on his school clothes which I recognized immediately as a Saint Aloysius uniform.

Both boys were a lot bigger than me, fairly muscular, and both had shoulder length dusty blonde hair. From their identical size, looks, and build I figured they must be twins. Other than their clothes, they were hard to tell apart, until I noticed the one with the paper bag had a long scar extending from between his thumb and pointer finger to midway down his arm. I waved good bye to Zack and started up the driveway. Besides the two twins and me, there was no one else in the station.

"Who are you?" the boy in the gray sweatshirt asked.

"My name's Bill. I took over Jimmy Reeder's route," I replied.

"Aw, that Reeder's a punk!" he fired back. "He lives up my street and stole that Mrs. Dildine and Mrs. Welsh from me. Glad to see he's gone, he was a horse's arse. I always hated the kid."

"Yeah, I'd like to take him and that black bomb of a bike of his and run him down. Teach him a lesson," said the twin in the school uniform.

I didn't say anything. I didn't like these guys, so I just looked down at my papers.

"Can't you talk, kid? Cause I'm talking to you. Or are you a punk like Reeder?"

I kept looking down and stopped folding, deciding just to put all the unfolded papers directly into my bag.

"Who's that friend of yours with the red Continental ten-speed? The thing looks brand new."

I looked up. "His name is Zack. He just got it."

"Well it's sweet, so he better watch it," he laughed. "Say, where's he live?"

I really didn't like these kids, and I didn't want to talk to them. For some reason, I didn't want them to know where Zack lived, so I lied. "He lives on Clinton Avenue, up by the Pike."

The two boys seemed preoccupied, so I wasn't sure if they heard me or were no longer paying attention to me. I figured it was my chance to get out.

"Shit, there's only 52. I forgot about that bitch Mrs. A. Convey being back from vacation. I need an extra," the boy with the scar and the sweatshirt said.

"Take it from that pussy Louis the Torch Morrison," said the other, and I looked up to see him pull one of Alvin's papers from his pile and put it into his brother's bag.

"I'm out of here," I thought as I put my bag on my bike and began to ride away.

"See you later punk!" I heard off in the distance as I rode away.

I stopped at Coldspring Avenue and folded half of my papers and put them in my bag, while I sat on my bike. Serving the papers to the houses was getting easier and I found I could throw them pretty accurately, as long as I threw when the house was ahead of me and not on my side. At the Lightfoot's, I was feeling pretty confident, then let a paper sail into their front bush. Feeling guilty, I circled back and got off my bike, and leaned into the bush to retrieve it. After pulling it out of the bush, I noticed the cover page was ripped, so I put it into the front of my bag and pulled out another and placed it gently on the top step. "Guess I'll save this one for us at home," I thought. I threw one up on the McAleers' steps and it hit the silver galvanized metal door front a bit hard, making a loud bang. I was relieved to see the door was not dented, and resolved to myself to take things a bit slower. So the last few houses on my block I served with extra care, and then I threw the paper with the torn cover onto my porch.

"Almost done," I thought, as I turned back down the street and onto Johnson for the trek back to the four Smythville houses. About midway down Ormond Avenue, I saw one of the twin brothers on the lawn tinkering with his mini-bike, which was a small red gas powered motorcycle, which rode low to the ground, and had no fenders, front light, or turn signals.

As I got closer, I noted it was the brother without the scar, who had changed out of his school uniform and was tinkering with the mini-bike. He looked up at me as I rode by, and I pedaled faster. I got to the Smythville homes and dismounted from my bike, as it seemed easier to walk these last four papers than ride. When I got to the last house, Mrs. Mac Mullin was waiting on the porch. "Have a good Labor Day?" she asked.

"Yeah, I guess so. But it was back to school today," I joked.

"Sorry to bother you, but do you have time to take the banner down?" she begged.

I hopped onto the porch and the banner was untied and down in a minute.

"You're a saint. Wait, I got something for you." Then she motioned me to come into the door.

I followed her in and stood in the doorway. The room was small and dimly lit and had a musty, camphor smell. "Just be a minute," she called out.

I remained standing, and noticed an end table and side wall covered with framed black and white pictures from a time long past. There was one of a man in a military uniform, who I presumed could be her husband, and several other pictures probably from the early 1930's by the look of the cars. There was one picture of the house, in somewhat better shape, and of a young woman posing on the house front porch steps, with a fancy hat and a long dress, holding a bouquet of flowers. On the other wall of the house was a large pendulum clock that was stopped and frozen forever at 11:56. Nearby was a console television in front of a bulky brown easy chair with a basket full of old newspapers beside it. Past the dining room, I could see Mrs. Mac Mullin, moving about; then I saw her walk out with a smile and a small bag in her hand.

"Found it," she said, as she scuffled towards me. "Thanks for helping me. I think you should be able to use these."

She handed me a small bag filled with about 500 used rubber bands. I could tell by their appearance they were the same red rubber bands we used to wrap our papers, just blackened and stretched from use. I wondered how long she had been saving them, and if I would ever use them; after all, a new bag of 10,000 cost only a dollar. I thanked her for her kindness, and left out the front door before turning back for my bike.

It had somehow turned 5:00 as I headed back up Ormond and I wondered if those two twins would be outside. As I neared their house, I saw them both, one sitting on a front step and the other still messing with the mini-bike. "Nuts," I thought.

As I got closer, the one with the scar yelled out, "You horse's arse, you lied to me. That kid don't live on Clinton!" Then he threw a rock at me, which skipped off the street and narrowly missed my bike as I approached.

I began to pedal faster, and passed by the house. A second rock was thrown that grazed off my back tire. "Good one, Danny," the boy with the mini-bike laughed. "Should I give the punk a real scare?"

A second later, I heard the mini-bike start up. It sounded a bit like a cross between a motorcycle and a lawn mower, and it was moving fast.

"Get 'em Bobby," yelled the one with the scar, and the mini-bike motored closer. I didn't look back, and began pedaling while standing to get maximum speed. I could hear the engine whining louder as Bobby gunned the motor, and before I knew it he was next to me.

"Punk, you lied to us. Time to teach you a lesson. Don't be giving us any crap, or you won't know what hit you."

The mini-bike veered towards me, and I slammed on my brakes. It grazed my back tire, and Bobby laughed.

"Some tough guy, what you gonna do now?"

The mini-bike whined, and he began to circle me.

"Knock it off," I yelled back. "What is it you want from me?"

I was stopped and he continued to circle me, swerving closer and closer with each revolution. I pulled the paper bag off my handle bars, and swung it around my head, snapping it at him as he came on my right hand side. The bag hit the front mini-bike handlebars and knocked his hand from the throttle, causing the menacing machine to stop in mid-pace. When I pulled the bag back, it got stuck on the throttle cable and I heard something rip just before I saw the bike topple over. The bag came loose when the throttle cable pulled off from the handlebar. The cycle motor shrieked, and Bobby hit the ground.

"You horse's arse!" he screamed. "I'll flatten you for this."

The bike motor whined, then abruptly puttered out, creating a moment of silence. I was plenty scared, but seeing him slowly pulling himself up from the ground with his screaming made me feel like giving him another slug with the paper bag. When I saw his bloodied leg, reason caught up with me. "You need help?" I offered.

"Not from you!" he shouted. He pulled up the bike to restart it, but the throttle cable was detached from the handlebars and laying on the ground. I could now hear Danny, brother number two, yelling off in the distance.

"Get moving!" I thought, and my feet began pedaling again. I pumped as fast as I could until I reached Johnson Avenue. I turned to look back, and then coasted when I saw the brothers far behind, retreating back to their house. I slunk down to a slower pace but my heart was still pounding. Up the street I saw another kid with a paper bag, and recognized him to be Mike Gaines. He rode up alongside me and asked how I was. He said he heard the mini-bike, and saw me swing and knock off Bobby.

"I didn't mean it," I said. "I don't know what's with those guys. They just started after me."

"They're the Dobalo twins," Mike said. "It's not you; they don't get along with anybody. Ask anyone in the station. Danny's the tougher one, but they're at their worst when their together. I think they got a chip on their shoulder against the whole world. Don't take any crap from them. They won't mess with you near the station; they're only brave together on their own turf. Mrs. McGuillan already nailed 'em when they were messin' with that Alvin Morrison. Tell 'em you're a friend of mine, and that I said I would sock 'em if they gave you any crap. They'll leave you alone."

"Thanks, I really appreciate it. That makes me feel a lot better," I gratefully acknowledged.

"No problem," Mike said. "We newsboys got to stick together; besides, my little brother says you play one heck of a centerfield. Don't need to see you get hurt."

Mike rode off, and I felt a sigh of relief. "Heck, Mike Gaines knows who I am," I thought. "Those Dobalo kids sure ought to be afraid of him."

I had traveled past Collins and Clinton and turned up my street toward home. It was now quarter to six. "I still better talk to Zack and get his help," I supposed. "I gotta find another route over to those Smythville houses before those Dobalos knock my block off."

Chapter 10 – Smythville Dam

The next morning it was raining, not a downpour, but a continuous drizzle that made you wonder if it would ever stop. I left for my safety station, with a hooded green raincoat on, and my freshly covered books inside of my backpack. The raincoat was bulky, which made it difficult for me to pull my safety belt over it. With the rain, foot traffic to school was lighter than usual, with the lucky kids able to bum a ride to school to keep from getting wet. When Jack Karaszkiewitz signaled safety duty was over, I waited anxiously to talk to Zack about the events of last evening and my Smythville dilemma. Zack was certain he could help with a solution, but he wasn't sure how much help he could be today because he had a drum lesson in the afternoon at 4:30.

Besides the rain, the school day was uneventful. Each class seemed to be a review of what we had learned the previous year, followed by a review of upcoming expectations for the new year. By the end of the last period, I was anxious to go home, and I rushed out to my locker to drop off my books and pick up my raincoat. Going outside, I noticed Zack was waiting for me for the walk to our corners. Not surprisingly, it was still raining. Drizzling just enough to make it annoying.

"Stinkin' rain!" I commented to Zack. "Guess I'll have to get a plastic bag to keep my papers dry."

Zack nodded. He had on a baseball cap, and the water dripped down off the brim and fell to the ground in a rhythmic cascade which he timed with the kicking of his foot as he walked. As we approached the Pike, we again saw the Saint Aloysius procession before us. I quickly scanned the oncoming group, searching for the twins, but such a search was next to impossible because of the hoods, raincoats, and umbrellas which blocked the faces at least partially from sight. As we went to our corners, Zack said he would meet me at Coldspring Avenue, and could be there by 3:45.

I hustled home to change, get my paper bag, and find a plastic bag that was big enough to use to keep my papers dry. When I got to the station, it was full of carriers, but neither of the Dobalo brothers was there. Without hesitation, I picked up my stack of unfolded papers and placed them in the plastic bag which was inside my normal canvas bag. It was Wednesday, but the papers were light, and I left without folding to meet Zack at the corner on time. When I arrived, Zack was not yet there, so I parked my bike under a tree at the dead end of the street and delivered the four papers on Collins Avenue and the four papers on Coldspring Avenue by foot, climbing up each set of stairs and placing the paper between the storm door and permanent door on each house to keep them dry.

Zack rode up just as I finished and together we travelled back to my bike at the dead end of the street. Once there, we looked down the steps leading towards the creek. The drizzle seemed to intensify a bit, and I wondered out loud if today with our rushing and the rain if it was the best day to be conducting such a task.

"There's no time like the present," Zack said as he locked our two bikes together by the steps.

I readjusted the plastic bag to keep the papers dry, and then we both headed down the steps towards the creek and then on to the dam to the south. The grass at the bottom of the steps was overgrown and the ground was soggy and made a sloshing sound as we headed towards the high metal fence which separated us from the dam. Just past that point was an even larger adjoining fence that ran through the woods and isolated the four Smythville properties from foot traffic.

Near the intersection of the fences was a gate that allowed entrance to the area near the dam. Like the fence, the gate was about six feet high, made of black wrought iron, and topped with pointed bars, selected originally for either its decorative effect or more likely as a climbing deterrent. Zack examined the gate and its lock, then pulled out a paper and pen and asked me to read out the lock name and model number. The lock was a high security outdoor padlock with a polished stainless steel hinged shackle and a shrouded aluminum base. The lock was labeled Security Pro and the code 6421 was stamped into the base. Zack wrote the information down and stuffed the paper into his pocket. We stood looking through the gate together for a while, while the rain continued to fall on us.

"If you get past this gate it seems you would have access to the entire old factory grounds on this side of the creek," Zack said. If you follow the fence, it looks like there is a second gate which leads out and is not far from the Smythville homes."

I nodded in agreement. "That's what I thought too, looking from the other side."

"The way I see it," Zack explained, "is all we need to do is pick the locks on both sides and you'll have clear sailing to Smythville. It has lots of advantages. It will cut a lot of time from your daily delivery and you can avoid passing the Dobalos' house. You know it wouldn't surprise me if both this lock and the one on the other gate on the other side had the same key to open them both."

"Do you think you have the key?" I asked.

"No, I don't have the key. I bet my dad could have made one by looking in his books and referencing the number on the bottom, but I don't know how to do that," Zack replied.

"Well, maybe we could cut off the locks and replace them with different locks that we had the keys for," I offered.

"No, that wouldn't work," Zack theorized. "It would only be a matter of time before somebody from the county public works realized that they couldn't unlock the gates, and then they would replace them, and maybe get suspicious. I think the best bet here would be to find out if both locks are the same, then pick one and take it back to the shop and take it apart and build a key that would fit it and maybe the other one as well. Then you could have the key and the public works guy would never know."

"You think you can do that?" I asked.

"Yeah, I think we could figure it out, and if we ran into trouble probably Pop-Pop could help."

The rain continued to fall and Zack wiped his forehead, and then looked at his watch.

"I gotta go to my lesson, so we can't do too much more today," Zack supposed. "But when you head over to Smythville later today, you could check out the other lock and write down the name and lock number so we could at least see if they are the same."

"Sure," I said, "that'll be easy."

We started walking back up along the creek towards the steps and our bikes. When we got to the bikes, I checked and the papers were still dry. Both Zack and I climbed on our bikes, and we looked at each other just before we started to leave. Both of us were soaking wet.

"I think you'll be ok today," Zack laughed. "I don't think the Dobalo brothers are stupid enough to come after you in the pouring rain."

"Yeah, I think you're right," I answered, and we both left in different directions.

I finished serving the route. It took a while as I was careful to make sure each paper was either placed on a dry porch where it couldn't get wet, or between the front doors of homes having storm doors. When neither option was available, I rang the bell and handed the paper inside. It took a lot of extra time, but I knew how angry my dad got whenever he got a wet paper.

I finished my street and headed for Smythville and the now-dreaded Ormond Avenue where the Dobalo brothers lived. I pulled the drawstrings on my hood tightly into a knot, squinted my eyes, and pedaled as quickly as I could down the street onto Landing Street. Even though each of the four Smythville homes had a porch, I decided to drop the paper between the screened storm door and the wooden main door of each just to make sure it stayed dry.

I was thinking about the gate lock and number, when I opened Mrs. Mac Mullin's door, and was startled to see her standing there. "Oh, thank heavens you're here!" she whimpered. "I need your help again."

She opened the door for me to come in. I hesitated because I was soaked.

"Come in! Come in! You have to help me with my bedroom window. It's pouring in and I can't get it to shut. Just a few weeks ago I couldn't get it to stay open, and now I can't get it to close!" she continued.

I kicked off my shoes and pulled off the raincoat and left them on the porch, and then I walked inside. Mrs. MacMullin pointed to the stairs and told me to go on up.

"It's a mess up there. I moved the pictures from the nightstand to keep them from getting soaked, and hung a towel in front of the window. I tried to get the window down but I just can't," she said.

I went up the narrow staircase upstairs to where there were two bedrooms. The smaller room had a chair, a floor lamp, a small table, and a sewing machine. The other had a bed, a dresser, and a nightstand. Next to the nightstand was an open window. The towel Mrs. Mac Mullin had placed in front of it had fallen and there was a puddle of water on the floor and in the windowsill. The covers on the bed near the window were also damp. The pictures on the bed which had been moved from the nightstand seemed to be dry. I looked at the window and instantly saw the problem. Somebody had opened the window and placed a flat stick in the side casing to hold it up. As soon as I pulled out the stick, the window pretty much fell shut on its own.

I picked up the towel and wiped up the puddle on the floor and the sill as best as I could, then I wiped off the nightstand. I laid the stick flat on the window sill, and then turning, looked at the pictures on the bed for a moment. The pictures were actually framed black and white photos. There were three, and each one looked extremely old. One had a picture of a mustached man on an old fashioned bicycle, one of those ones with the huge wheel in back and the small wheel in front. The other picture was of a man in a military uniform; he was smiling, and his jacket was adorned with numerous medals and patches. Of these, the most notable medal looked to be a bronze castle on his jacket collar, and the most notable patch was a winged star over his left breast pocket. The last photograph was perhaps the oldest and was slightly blurred, but I'm not sure if that was due to its poor photo quality or just deterioration with age. In it, the mustached man now with a suit and top hat stood in front of a brick factory. Next to him was a beautiful dark haired woman in a long dress and elegantly veiled hat, holding the hand of a six or seven year old girl dressed in a ruffled dress and dark buttoned coat. The girl was holding a small doll, and all three were smiling under a sign reading H.B. Smyth Machine Company. I guessed these pictures could have been Mrs. Mac Mullin with her family, and figured if that was the case, then she must have lived here a pretty long time.

Taking the towel, I headed downstairs, bending my head as the staircase turned to make sure I didn't bump it on the low ceiling. Mrs.

Mac Mullin was at the bottom of the steps. "Is everything ok?" she asked.

"Yeah, there was a stick in the window on the side holding it up. I pulled it out and shut the window. You'll have to put the stick back in to hold it up if you want it to stay open later," I replied. "Oh yeah, I wiped up the water as best as I could with the towel," I added as I handed it to her, and she nodded approvingly.

"Oh thank you! Is there anything I can do for you?" she asked. "You're so wet. Do you want a towel to dry off a bit?"

"No, I'm ok, plus I'm only going to get wet again when I go out," I replied.

I started for the door and thought about the lock on the gate, and realized I had nothing to write down the number with. "Actually there is something I do need. Could I borrow a pen or pencil? I need to write something down from that sign by the creek for a school project."

She answered "of course" and ventured off, returning minutes later with a pencil and a piece of loose leaf paper for my "school report."

I thanked Mrs. Mac Mullin, went out on the porch and put on my shoes and raincoat, picked up the paper bag and ran down to the gate to record the lock information. The rain was still coming down and I struggled to write S-E-C-U-R-I-T-Y P-R-O 6-4-2-1 on the paper without it getting too wet.

"I'm pretty sure that is the same model as the lock on the other gate," I thought.

Looking up I again noticed the sign on the fence – "Former site of Benjamin Shreve Dam circa 1830. Replaced by Smythville Dam Circa 1937." Looking past the sign at the water roaring over the dam, I supposed, that the current dam must not have been the original. Then suddenly the roar of the water over the dam got louder than I recalled, and I realized the rain had begun coming down in a torrent, so I ran up the path and towards Mrs. Mac Mullin's house again.

I jumped up onto the sagging porch and wiped my face with my hands, then pulled down my hood and shook my hair to stop some of the dripping. Mrs. Mac Mullin heard me on the porch and came out with two towels. She handed me the first and I wiped my face and hair.

"Thanks for the pencil," I said as I handed it back to her. By now the rain was coming down so hard that I could barely hear her say "You're welcome."

Mrs. Mac Mullin gestured for me to sit down on a porch rocking chair, which I did; then she sat down in another right beside me.

"So you want to know a little history of this town?" she asked.

Chapter 11 – Smythville Town History[1]

The downpour continued as we sat down on the rocking chairs on the porch. Mrs. Mac Mullin took her towel and placed it over her shoulders as she settled into the chair.

"The town of Smythville was first settled in about 1835," she started. "It was founded by the Shreve brothers Jonathan and Samuel, who grew up in the town of Medford. The brothers came from a wealthy family and were well educated by their father, who owned and ran a grist mill to grind locally grown grains. The brothers traveled through the nearby woods on a trip with their father to Trenton in the early 1830's, when they noted the terrain of the area caused the creek to form several sets of falls in a short 100 foot long section. The Shreve brothers purchased the land, and taking advantage of the water flow, they constructed a dam and a water turbine to power a textile manufacturing facility on the property. Shreveville, as it was known then, prospered into the late 1850's, growing into a village with a population of more than 300. The Shreves built themselves a large home on the property, and soon Shreveville was a prospering community in the midst of the local farm country. The Shreves' successful business dissolved by the start of the 1860's, a result of sagging textile sales. About this time, Samuel Shreve fell ill, and the family found themselves unable to continue the business and they decided to sell.

Hezekiah Bradley Smyth grew up the youngest of six children, on a 60-acre farm in Woodstock, Vermont, where his father raised livestock and owned a tannery. Hezekiah helped his father with the tannery until age seventeen, but because of competition with his five older brothers, he left to apprentice in a woodworking machine shop in Lowell, Massachusetts. Hezekiah was a brilliant boy, and became a skilled craftsman by the age of twenty, specializing in the production of window sashes, shelves, and doors. Bored with his life, Hezekiah became convinced he could improve the woodworking machinery used in the trade. He researched and developed a machine which he patented in 1869 at the age of twenty-one. This was for a mortising machine used in the manufacture of blinds. In the fall of 1869, Hezekiah was traveling down from his home in Bridgeton, Vermont, to Philadelphia along with his fiancée, a young spinster named Eveline English, to market his invention. It was during this trip that he first came upon the Shreveville mill.

The mortising machine became extremely popular, but Hezekiah's profit potential was limited because he had to subcontract out work to various foundries to build the equipment. He continued to design, and within two years, he had designed five other wood working machines and applied for their patents. With the feeling that he could best achieve success by building and selling his own machines, Hezekiah set out to build his own factory. Hezekiah remembered the failing Shreveville textile mill, and in his mind he foresaw the possibilities of transforming it into a machine manufacturing site. So in 1871 at the age of twenty-four, Hezekiah, with the help of his father, purchased the mill, a village full of buildings, and its surrounding 45-acre site.

By this time, however, the Shreveville mill had been shut down, and the mill town was a scene of desolation. Hezekiah's first order of business was to change the town's name, and never known for his modesty, the name Smythville sounded right to him. He brought workers down from Lowell who helped him ready the factory on the property for occupancy. The original Shreve residence served as the dining and living quarters for Hezekiah and his employees until the employee homes on the site could be renovated. With that accomplished, the machine shops and the foundry were totally rebuilt, and the dam and the raceways which provided power for them were completely reconditioned.

Hezekiah's wife Eveline was not as captivated with the Shreveville mill as her husband so she expressed a preference to stay in New England with her more affluent friends and family members, at least until

Hezekiah could modernize the factory and restore the Shreve residence to the mansion style of home to which she had grown accustomed. During the next five years, the factory grew, and profits from manufactured woodworking equipment began to pour in. Hezekiah totally renovated the home to try to lure Eveline back to Smythville to stay, but she refused. Despite the distance, he continued to visit Eveline in New England, and in the spring of 1874, she bore him a daughter, Ella. Sadly, shortly thereafter, a scarlet fever epidemic broke out and the child died. Afterward, Eveline always partially blamed Hezekiah for the child's death since he was not home with her when the epidemic broke out and the baby died. Although the two would never live again together, Hezekiah continued to visit her over the next few years, fathering a son Elton two years later.

Despite his family troubles, Hezekiah saw business at the factory grew exponentially. As the numbers of employees grew, he upgraded the town with his own money, creating a public park at the center of the village and building a dormitory for unmarried factory mechanics, an opera house for entertainment, and a schoolhouse for village children. Never complacent, Hezekiah branched out into other areas of mechanical fabrication. The Star bicycle was developed and built in Smythville in 1881, and Hezekiah personally handled its production and marketing. The Star bicycle differed from typical bicycles by having the larger wheel at the rear, where the rider sat, and the smaller wheel up front. This allowed for greater control especially when traveling downhill. To illustrate this Hezekiah hired a professional rider to ride a Star bicycle down the steps of the United States Capitol to publicize its improved maneuverability. Hezekiah also arranged for bicycle races all over the country which the Star would often win. Both the marketing and design proved to be successful, and the Star bicycle became another moneymaker for the H.B. Smyth Machine Company."

It was obvious to me that Mrs. Mac Mullin had a love for the area and the history of this part of town. As the story began to wane, so did the downpour and the rain returned to a moderate drizzle.

"So what happened to Hezekiah?" I asked. "I mean, it seems like he ended up being extremely wealthy, but what about his family? Did he ever get back with his wife and his son?"

Mrs. Mac Mullin smiled and took off her glasses to wipe away some stray raindrops, "We'll leave that part of the story to another day," she promised.

Chapter 12 – Unlocked

The next day after school Zack was a man with a mission. Sort of like Hezekiah Smyth, once Zack had an idea in his mind there was no stopping him, especially when it related to anything mechanical or involving tools. The rain had stopped and after school Zack went over to the dead end at Collins and Coldspring Avenues, locked his bike to a tree, and went down the steps to the creek. He then continued further to the locked fence by the dam and the site of the old mill. He brought with him a small leather pouch containing what he considered to be the appropriate tools for the job. In the pouch he had placed some of his father's lock picks, a wrench, a hammer, and a new lock and key. He also brought three bump keys he had found in the shop for the general size and shape of the key typically used for the Security Pro type padlocks. He had researched this information in the lock shop manuals, and found the bump keys in a drawer labeled BUMPKEYS by his father. Interestingly enough, when the drawer was opened, it contained nearly fifty-five styles of bump keys, each one in a separate yellow envelope on which his father had written the lock codes and descriptions. In his search at the lock shop, Zack speculated that his father had likely supplied the locks and the keys for the fences at the mill, and that the records of the exact key code were likely still on file somewhere in the store. Unfortunately he didn't know where to look for them.

The idea of the bump key is that it is a special key which has been cut so that each peak of the key is equal and has been cut down to match the lowest groove in the key. When looking at such a key, it almost resembles a small saw blade. By placing the key in the lock, applying some torque, and striking the key sharply with a hammer, the force of the blow is carried down the length of the key, which forces the top pins of the lock to jump above the shear line leaving the bottom pins in place. With a little practice, and several bumps of the hammer, the lock can usually be opened pretty quickly.

Zack tried to insert the first of the bump keys into the lock. He could pretty much tell as he looked at the lock keyway on the bottom of the padlock and the key that there was no match, but he tried it anyway. As expected, the key didn't fit. The second bump key looked much closer in shape to the keyway. When it was inserted, it started to slide in properly. With Zack applying a bit of turning force and rapping the key a few times, he was able to get the lock to spring open.

"Wow, that was pretty easy," thought Zack as he took the lock off the gate and put it into his leather pouch. He then took the new padlock from the pouch and placed it on the gate.

"Hopefully somebody doesn't come to open the gate in the next two days," Zack thought.

He collected all his stuff and left for the stairs up from the creek ravine. Getting on his bike, Zack headed back to the lock shop.

At the lock shop, Zack went straight for the work bench, and then he pulled up a chair. He had already placed the Security Pro catalogue on the work bench where he was working. He pulled out the original gate padlock, which he had been careful to keep unlocked, and laid it on the bench top. Using a $7/64$ inch hexagonal wrench, he removed the mounting screw located in the toe-side shackle hole of the opened lock. Holding the trap door at the base of the lock in place, he then locked the shackle into the padlock body to relieve the pressure on the actuator. He then carefully removed the trap door and the nut at the base of the lock, at which time the lock cylinder and the actuator easily slipped out along with the two locking ball bearings.

The actuator easily disconnected from the lock cylinder, and Zack took this cylinder and examined it. The lock cylinder consisted of a cylindrical portion, where the key could be inserted, and an adjacent square portion of the cylinder shell which housed the six lock pins and springs. Zack remembered his father describing this part of the cylinder, which is called the bible, as being the most important and complex part of the lock. Each of the six pins is split into two different lengths forming six separate pin stacks which are spring-loaded in six cylindrical cavities. Each of the six lower pins are called the key pins because they contact the key. The six upper pins are spring driven and are called the driver pins. When the proper key is inserted into the lock, all of the key pins and driver pins align along the shear line. When the different length key pins are aligned at their tops by the insertion of the corresponding cut key at their bases, the tops of the key pins and the bases of the driver pins form a straight line, so that the cylinder can be turned, rotating the key pins away from the driver pins. When no key or the wrong key is in the lock, pin misalignment prevents the cylinder from turning.

Zack knew disassembly of the bible, although not difficult, had to be performed with great care to avoid losing the six key pins, the six driver pins, and the six springs. It was even more important to make sure all was kept in the proper order when the parts were removed if he was to accomplish his goal of making a replica key to match the original. Using great care, he removed the "E-Clip" at the base of the master cylinder. Then, by revolving the plug at the top of the cylinder exactly 90° counterclockwise, the plug containing the pins and springs could be removed from the cylinder shell.

Zack slowly rotated the cylinder and pulled out the plug, holding the entire assembly upside down to ensure the pins did not drop out. He then carefully removed the springs, driver pins, and key pins, and placed them in a magnetic dish that he had seen his father use in the past to keep things from rolling away. He was careful to place them in the exact order he had removed them. Concentrating on the key pins, he measured their height so as to know how deep to cut the six teeth in a new key. The shop had plenty of the proper style blanks, and he took one, placed it into the key cutting machine, and using the key coding feature, cut the key to the calculated depths from the key pin measurements. Once the key was cut, he positioned the key in the dish, placing the key pins so they just touched their respective key cuts to make sure when they were placed in line they formed a flat shear line.

'Looks good!' Zack thought to himself. 'Now it's time to put everything back together.'

So he took the springs, key pins, and driver pins and placed them back into the plug. Then he carefully pushed the plug back into the cylinder shell, rotated it 90°, and placed back on the "E clip" with a pair of needle-nose pliers. Holding the rebuilt cylinder by the bible side, he attached the actuator and then sat it down. He then placed the swivel side of the shackle back into the lock, turned the lock over and put in the two ball bearings, followed by the cylinder and actuator combination, and then the trap door. Placing the extended nut into the trap door, and turning in the mounting screw using the hexagonal allen wrench, he tightened the lock until it was snug.

"Done!" he said, "Now comes the real test!" And with that he closed the shackle by turning it and pushing it into the lock. Giving the now-closed lock a tug, he pulled harder and it would not budge.

"Fully locked and proper," he said to himself.

Then taking the key, he pushed it into the closed lock and turned it. Just like new, the lock sprung open, and Zack sat back with a triumphant smile. Likewise, somewhere far away, his father must have looked down and also smiled approvingly. The boy who could barely muster a "D" on his math exams in school had taken apart the old gate lock, figured the proper key cut arrangement, and cut a key to fit and work the lock!

Taking the freshly made key, he went back to the key cutting machine. Grabbing another key blank, he made a duplicate copy of the key. After a quick deburring, he took the second key and tested it. Just as expected, the key opened the lock. Zack took both keys over to an engraver, and punched the code "SM1" on each key head bow, short for Smythville mill key #1. One of the keys he put in his pocket, the other he took and put on his key chain, right next to the gold key given to him by his father.

Chapter 13 – The Old Factory

Friday came and went. In science we learned about single-celled organisms like the paramecium and the amoeba. The amoeba has a false foot called a pseudopod which seemed odd to me. Mrs. Birkholder even had one we could look at under a microscope, but it really didn't move much. In algebra we substituted letters for numbers, 3a +2a = 5a which everybody understood, and 3a x 2a = $6a^2$, which seemed a bit confusing. But overall, it was not really too big a deal. On the paper route I collected a second time and things went pretty well. I only missed 5 of the 42 houses. I paid my paper bill to Mrs. McGuillan, and made over a $10.00 profit for the week, so I was happy. On the walk home, Zack and I agreed that early on Saturday morning we would go down together to the locked gate by the Smythville Dam to check things out. We agreed I would meet Zack at his house at 7:30.

I was pretty excited Saturday morning and woke up about 6:15 without the need of an alarm. I slipped on my clothes, grabbed my paper money, and started into the hallway. I passed my dad who was on his way to the bathroom and he asked me where I was going. I told him I was going fishing with Zack and he wished me luck. I went out to the garage and got my Stingray. I was still feeling good, so I decided to stop at the town bakery, which was just up the street on the Pike, about a block passed the Esso station. To add to the adventure I figured I'd get some doughnuts for Zack and me. I arrived at the bakery about 6:55 and waited for it to open at 7:00. The owner, Mrs. Manual was the mother of Terry Manual who was in my class. Mrs. Manual was setting out some fresh pastries when she saw me through the plate glass storefront window. She walked over and unlocked the door so I could come in. A small bell on the door made a jingling sound when the door opened and closed to repetitiously announce my entrance. The smell of the bakery was almost as good as eating the doughnuts. The aroma made you want to stay there all day; and looking at all the types of doughnuts, cakes, and buns made the choice so difficult, I could have spent the rest of the day deciding. It was ninety cents for a half dozen doughnuts, so I decided to get that. Two chocolate frosted, two vanilla frosted, and two cream filled. Mrs. Manual lifted the doughnuts off each shelf with a piece of white tissue paper, and then put the doughnuts in a white bakery bag. If I had gotten a dozen, she would have put them in a box and had it tied with string using some tying machine they had, but I didn't think we could eat that many. I paid the ninety cents exactly in change and left the store, taking out a chocolate frosted as soon as I got outside. Holding the bag in my left hand with the top curled up on my bicycle handgrip, I rode my bicycle to Zacks while eating the chocolate doughnut which I held in my right hand.

Zack was waiting outside when I got to his house, and we decided to walk to the dam. We took the longer route down to the Bettlewood Avenue Bridge, turning off the sidewalk just before it, and heading south along the side of the creek. We each ate our three doughnuts and argued over which type was best, finally agreeing it was the cream filled. I crushed the bag into a ball and pushed it into my pocket. It was still early and we passed no one on our trip to the bridge or along the creek. Zack had brought his pouch of tools with him, and when I asked him what was in it, he took out the original gate lock along with the key.

Handing them to me he said, "Wait until you see this. Just try it."

I took the lock and inserted the key and turned it, and it immediately popped opened.

"And the best part," Zack beamed, "Is that's the original gate lock! I was able take it apart and made a key that fit and could open it."

"How'd you do it?" I asked. "Did you need Pop-Pop's help?"

"Nah, I just tried until I figured it out," Zack replied. Then he told me, "The key's yours to keep; I made another for myself."

The day had started out great and was getting even better. I locked and unlocked the padlock a dozen times as we walked along. It opened easily, just like it was new. We continued to walk along the creek, past where it bended, and the grass began to get higher and the path was less traveled. Looking to my right I saw we were approaching the steps that descended down from the dead end of Collins Avenue. To the left was the creek, rapidly getting wider, and the lake which had formed from its damming. Ahead on our side, we could see what remained of the original old brick factory. Just up past that was the dam.

When we reached the gate, Zack pulled out his keychain, and selecting the correct key, he opened the lock that held it shut. "You see, I put a temporary new lock on the gate when I took off the old one so I could make the key," he said.

He then opened the gate and we both walked inside. After putting the temporary lock into his tool pouch, he asked me for the original lock, and he put it on the gate and locked it, essentially locking us inside and preventing any others who might pass by from entering. Once inside the fence, what remained of a stone path led to the factory, branching off in several directions around it. Another path continued southward along the fence towards the dam, along which was the other locked gate close to the four Smythville homes. The stone paths had not been traveled in some time, as indicated by the weeds growing in them. We imagined that the only visitors to the area now were probably county public works men, who would regulate the dam level, if there was a reason to do so.

We both started towards the abandoned factory, and as we got closer its appearance worsened. All of the windows had been broken some time ago and were now completely missing. One path headed towards a door, and next to it was a swinging garage type door. It was positioned about three feet off the ground with an elevated berm of dirt in front of it that looked like it was once used for loading and unloading items from the back of trucks or carriages. High above the berm was a network of rusted steel rails which held a sliding wheeled lift. This, we speculated, was likely used for lifting heavy machinery. Zack went straight for the door next to the berm and tried to open it, but it wouldn't budge. He fumbled through his pouch and pulled out his lock picks and began the task of trying to unlock the door. I walked around past the berm, and then continued around the side of the building, only to realize as I turned past the corner that a good portion of the side brick wall had fallen down and was completely open. The wall had likely fallen many years ago, as there was no trace of the missing wall, with only a few stray red bricks on the ground nearby. Inside the factory, a good portion of the roof was also missing. In assessing its state, what was left appeared to be stable, and I cautiously walked inside the open area. Once inside and feeling a bit braver, I ventured inside the roofed section and over towards the door that Zack was still working to unlock. Going over to the door, I noticed a deadbolt and unlatched it, then turned the knob and opened the door to Zack's surprise.

"What the heck? How did you get in there?" he asked in a startled fashion.

"Sometimes you don't need to have the key to get in if you follow the right path," I answered.

Zack followed me in and shut the door. We both turned around and looked at what remained of the immense room, and at the contents of the inside of the factory. For the most part the factory floor plan was open, with only two real rooms inside. Like the outside of the building, the floor was brick, except the color was a darker brown, maybe from years of wear, or maybe due to a different composition. The factory had windows on all four walls, with the wall facing the creek having the largest ones, with interior frames that seemed to be a bit more ornate than their side wall counterparts. The ceiling looked to be at least twenty feet high at the front and back walls, being at least another eight feet higher at its vaulted center. Along the center of the ceiling there were at least three evenly spaced risers which were vented, presumably to allow hot air to escape when opened. Most notable of all when looking up was a huge steel shaft which ran the entire length of the building. It appeared to be bolted together in about ten-foot intervals, and it was ruggedly held in place by numerous heavy sets of bearing blocks supporting the shaft about every six feet. The shaft had a series of sprockets attached to it, some teethed, and some pullied; and it seemed clear to us that the shaft had at one time served as a sort of master transmission of spinning power to the various machines that ran in the factory below.

Aside from a few wooden frames, which had for the most part been stripped of their cast iron or steel mechanics, the factory was pretty much devoid of any old machinery. Looking up at the huge drive shaft, Zack instinctively walked over towards the side of the factory which faced the creek, and I followed. Once there, we could see near floor level a heavy steel shaft that entered through the wall, with a large sprocket at its end and the remnants of an adjustable gear system which could engage or disengage power. This Zack said was likely to have been used to shift the shaft speed and torque, sort of like the derailleur on his ten-speed bike. A door with a top window was nearby this floor level shaft, which opened to the outside.

In the corner of the front of the factory there was a small walled-off room which looked like an office. We walked inside and saw it was paneled in wood, with detailed floor and ceiling moldings. A heavy old oak desk sat in the room, pushed to one side. The desk looked to be made of solid wood and had probably not been removed over the years because of its weight. The desk had four drawers, a narrow top drawer which was locked, and three side drawers, one of which was missing. There were no chairs in the room and the walls were stripped of any decoration. In usual fashion, Zack focused on the locked top drawer of the desk, and I went back out into the factory near the main power shaft with what Zack called the derailleur mechanism. I looked at the mechanism and tried to visualize its operation but was mystified.

There were numerous gears meshed together and several levers, but pulling on them they seemed to be immovable. I turned to look outside through the door towards the creek and noticed that on the other side of the power shaft was a second door that I figured to be a closet. I walked over and gave the door a good tug and it opened, revealing a dark room about six feet square. It was hard to see in the room because there appeared to be no windows. There were things hanging from the wall, but not being able to see I was taking no chances, so I quickly exited to go get Zack.

When I got back to Zack in the office, he had opened the desk drawer, and was now trying to pull it completely out.

"Did you find anything in the drawer?" I asked.

"No it was empty, but when I tried to pull it completely open, the drawer got stuck," Zack replied. "I think there is something lodged inside that is jamming it from being pulled out."

Zack continued to pull and push on the drawer; then he grabbed one of the longer picks from his pouch and stuck it inside the drawer and partially shut it and pushed with the pick. After a couple of tries, whatever was lodged in the drawer came loose, and Zack pulled the drawer until it was completely open. Tilting the drawer at an upward angle, he pulled hard and it popped out completely from the desk. Looking into the drawer cavity, he reached inside with his hand and pulled out the offending item. We both examined the article, which consisted of a wooden handle with a cast iron circular top, about the diameter of a quarter, but probably three times as thick. Looking at the top of the circular iron piece were the initials HBS, with the words *H. B. Smyth Machine Company* printed around the disk circumference. We each took turns examining the piece and determined it might have been a stamp used in the early days to seal envelopes with hot wax. Turn over an envelope, pour on some colored wax from a candle, then push the stamp in it before it solidifies to seal the letter with a monogrammed inscription. Both Zack and I agreed the stamp was an excellent find and Zack put it in his pouch.

"Oh, I found something else," I explained. "I found a tool closet or something over by the power sprocket, but it's so dark that I can't see what's inside."

We both walked over, and Zack pulled a small flashlight from his pouch and shined it into the room. The room looked to be filled with ropes and chains, hanging from pegs in the room. Zack shined the light up to the ceiling, and we saw some kind of shuttered window, high up in the roof. Running down the wall from the shutter was a coiled rope which was tied to a winch with a crank. Zack released the winch lock and slowly turned the crank and two window shutters high up ahead began to open, and the closet was bathed in light from the outside window. As he continued to crank the winch, the shutters reached their maximum open position, and then began to close. Zack continued to crank and the shutters, after closing, again began to reopen, so Zack continued to crank until they were again at their maximum open position. He then pushed down the wench lock to hold them in the open position.

We looked about this closet, now fully illuminated, and could clearly see how the pullied shutter system operated. We could also see that the closet was full of a series of ropes, chains, and belts of various sizes that hung down from its walls. The chains were metal, and some of the belts were leather. Lower on the walls were hooks that must have held at one time a large variety of sprockets and pulleys. A few of the sprockets and three pulleys were still hanging in place, along with a rusted saw, pick-ax, crowbar, and shovel. It was clear from the number of hooks that quite a large assortment of other tools must have been present in the room in the factory's heyday. We decided to leave the closet intact, so this time I unlocked the winch, and turned it until the shutters closed, and flipped the gear striker to hold the closed position in place. We then shut the door, leaving the room and its contents in its 1870's state.

With nothing much else to see inside the factory, we headed out the back door to follow the transmission shaft to its former source of power. The shaft ran to three separate gear systems, each in varied states of deterioration. Each gear system was connected to a turbine blade that sat in a concrete water raceway. The water raceway followed around the factory side. It started out to be about ten feet wide and at least two feet deep. Near the turbines, it split into three separate smaller raceways, each of which was about three feet wide and two feet deep. Each of these three smaller raceways had a guillotine type valve that could be opened and closed by turning a steel "T" shaped crank to raise and lower the guillotine via a screw mechanism on both sides. Using the valves, water flow could be adjusted individually to each turbine. The turbines were about five feet in diameter, and water from each of the smaller raceways allowed water to hit one side, causing it to spin. Following the turbines, the water flow dropped several feet to another common raceway, and then fed down to the creek which was still at least another seven feet lower.

Looking at the set-up, it was hard for us to tell whether they ran all the turbines at once or whether they were operated separately. Zack seemed to think that maybe they had started out with just a single turbine, but as the power demand grew greater, they added the others to provide additional torque to power the increasing amount of equipment. We speculated that back in the 1830's when Benjamin Shreve first built the complex, he built the first dam on the creek just a short distance from where the ten-foot raceway diverted the water to the turbines. The dam was wooden and its height adjustable so that the majority of the creek's water continued to flow over the dam, while a small amount could be diverted to the raceway and the turbines. Shutting off both the dam and raceway caused the water to cease flowing downstream completely and pool into a large multi-acre pond, still at a higher elevation than the creek drop-off, which we later referred to as the

Smythville Lake. In this manner, even when the summer months came, rainfall dropped off, and the creek began to dry up, there was still plenty of reserve water to power the turbines.

Zack and I sat on the sides of the first turbine and marveled at what we called ancient technology. We talked about how great it would be to see everything running. Of course now that would all be impossible. First of all, no water presently ran over the turbines, the water level equalizing to its present level based on how the system was left when it was shut down. Secondly, what was left of the turbines was severely corroded, and efforts by Zack and me to revolve them around by pushing against them with our feet couldn't even muster up a fraction of an inch of movement. The guillotine valves were corroded in their final resting position, and sections of them were totally missing. The water in the raceway was a muddy brown color that was completely opaque, so that the only way we could determine how deep the raceway was in sections was to put a stick in them to see how far it could be pushed before it hit bottom. But the final blow to its functionality was the wreckage of the Shreve Dam itself. When Zack and I walked upstream to view it, its fifteen feet of wooden locks and adjustment tiers were just an ancient memory, and now just a few pilings and waterlogged wood planks remained.

The Shreve Dam had been replaced by another dam, about thirty feet down river, which effectively rendered the original useless. Although not built by Hezekiah Smyth, the new Smythville dam built during the Depression in 1937 still bore his name and continues to function to this day. As Zack and I walked towards this newer dam, the roar of the water grew louder, and the speed of the water in the creek began moving faster. Even now more than thirty years old, the Smythville Dam was a sight to behold up close to the two of us. The dam was over 40 feet across and consisted of two sections. The first of these sections, which was about 25-feet across, dammed water which flowed directly from the creek. Its level was pretty much set by an 18- inch wide concrete weir that ran its entire 25-foot length. Water dropping over this weir fell over ten feet down to the basin of the creek below. The remaining 15 feet dammed water from the connecting section of the lake. The ends of this structure were made of concrete, but also contained four sets of adjustable metal weir plates, which could be used to adjust the water level in the lake. Each of these plates was about two feet in length and could be lowered by almost three feet of water level if necessary. The plates were operated manually by a series of screw adjusters with large 6 inch diameter wheels on their positioning stems which could be turned to adjust the height to achieve the desired water level. To access these screw adjusters it was necessary to climb above the metal plates and onto a metal catwalk that crossed over the second dam section.

The two sections pulled water from the two independent streams, but under the present operation, water was only flowing over the wider creek side section. Looking at the dam, water was flowing at a pretty good rate from the 25-foot creek side, but because of the long width of the section, the water passing over the 18-inch wide dam weir looked to be only about an inch deep. Due to the position of the weir, water would flow over it, falling down in an arced fashion to the creek basin below.

Because of its width, it was possible, although dangerous, to walk across the 25-foot creek weir if the water level was low enough. On that day, the strength of the one inch stream of water wouldn't knock a surefooted walker off the concrete weir and down into the creek bed below. Zack put down his tool pouch and took off his shoes and socks, eager to cross over to the middle section of the dam, where he could then climb up onto the metal catwalk to look at the lake side of the dam. I pleaded with him not to do it, but he was off before I could finish.

"It's easy!" he yelled as he walked across the 18-inch wide concrete dam surface, while the cold redwood colored water ran over his toes.

Before I knew it, he was at the catwalk, beckoning me to come with him.

Reluctantly, I took off my shoes and did the same, finding the feel of the cool water pleasant on my feet. Once I started onto the ledge, my fear of falling dissipated and I continued over to the ladder up to the catwalk. When I got to the center I joined Zack on the catwalk, and we both peered into the water on either side below, marveling at this attraction which we had seen from a distance so many times before, but had never truly understood. Based on its design, it was clear now that the new dam was meant only to control the level of water in the lake, in order to preserve it for recreational use and aesthetic reasons. It really had nothing to do anymore with creating a source of power. It could be argued that the dam could help prevent surges in the creek's level, and flooding during periods of long intense rains. But we still heard of instances of flooding along the creek occasionally, and flow over the largest section of the dam was going to flow over it uncontrollably anyway should its volume be greater than its present level.

We stood on the catwalk for about twenty minutes, fascinated by the continuous stream of cascading water, watching as occasional sticks floated downstream and were temporarily caught by the concrete weir. Eventually they would become dislodged by the passing water and crash to the creek bed below. With time the novelty of the event wore off, and we both ventured back across to the safety of the river bank and our sunbaked shoes and socks.

Feeling a sense of fulfillment from our adventure we both decided we had seen enough for the day and would start towards home. Zack picked up his tool pouch and we started back past the old factory and the fence. Once at the fence, we remembered the supreme purpose of the day's events, changed direction, and started towards the locked gate on the Smythville side of the dam. When we reached the second gate, Zack said, "You take the honors!"

I reached into my pocket and pulled out the key Zack had made and tried it on this second lock. I slowly pushed the key in the keyway and it slipped in like a hot knife into butter. Turning the key, the lock popped open.

"Sweet!" Zack yelled. "The key works both locks, just like I thought. Both of the locks had to have been keyed together!"

The look of happiness on Zack's face was contagious, and we both slapped hands together.

"I'll bet my dad made them keys originally for the county when they decided to put these fences up," he insisted. Then he stood a while thinking about his father, and the smile disappeared and was replaced by a quivering lip. "I wonder if he'd approve of all this," he finished.

After a few moments of silence, I spoke up. "I don't think we're doing anything wrong with the locks and keys. Thanks Zack for helping me. You're the best friend I ever had."

Zack took his fist and pumped it into my shoulder. "Knock it off, cause you know you're only my second best friend. That Peter Gallagher has got you beat." Then he slurped like he was eating soup and we both laughed. I'm not positive, but I think he even momentarily put his arm around me.

We both turned around to head home. The space between the two gates was less than a mere eighty feet but would save me nearly forty minutes each day, not to mention random encounters with those Dobalo twins.

We walked back to the gate nearest to home. Zack took out his keys to unlock the gate. The gold key given to him by his father glistened in the early afternoon sun. The gate opened, and he pulled the key from the lock, and we both walked through. Then we both turned back. I shut the gate and Zack put the lock back on and pushed the shackle shut. Gazing through the gate Zack said "I guess you're right, we aren't doing anything wrong. We're just making you a paper trail."

Chapter 14 – The Stolen Stingray

When we got back to Zack's house he mentioned that I would need one thing more. He went into the garage and pulled out an old chain from a swing. Then finding an old bicycle tire inner tube, he cut it and slipped the chain inside. Taking the lock and key from his tool pouch, he placed the lock through one end of the chain, then wrapped the chain on the frame of my bicycle under my seat. Placing the other end of the chain in the lock, he closed it and handed me the key.

"Now you have two keys to carry around. Before you know it, you'll be just like me and need a key chain. I don't think you'll be taking your bike down those steps each day when you go down on the paper trail, so remember to lock your bike before you leave it," he said. "And keep the chain in the tube to keep it from scratching the paint off your bike."

I offered to pay him for the lock and chain, but he refused. It was getting late so I left to go pick up my paper bag and to go to the paper station. When I rode up to Collins Avenue I noticed the Millar's Cyclery van out front of the McGuillans' house again. The van was idling and the passenger door was open. I pulled up in the driveway to see Danny Dobalo walking towards me, a full load of papers in his bag. He was wearing shorts and a tank top shirt, exposing his more than adequate biceps.

"Long time no see," he grimaced as I rode by him.

'That kid really is a creep,' I thought. And reaching the garage, I turned to see him get into the van and slam the door shut. Shortly after, I thought I heard some snickering from the van, and then it drove off.

I grabbed my stuff and started into the station. There was considerable laughter coming from inside. Entering I saw Alvin Morrison, Jon Shelly, and Joey Gilmore. Jon Shelly had his short sleeves rolled up and was parading about, holding up his arms and showing his muscles. Giggling, Alvin and Joey were shooting rubber bands at him.

"How dare you! You punks!" Shelly joked, clearly doing an exaggerated imitation of Danny Dobalo. It was hilarious.

I found my paper pile, sat down, and pulled out a rubber band, and shot it at Shelly. Then when he was turning, I shot him again, hitting him on his backside.

"I hit you in the arse!" I teased, and laughed so hard that my side began to hurt.

When the laughter ceased, Shelly sat down. In his best Danny Dobalo imitation said to me, "Hey you, long time no see!"

It seemed I wasn't the only one preoccupied with thoughts of Danny Dobalo. When things quieted again, Alvin asked me how I was making out with the new route. I answered that things were fine.

"How about those Smythville houses. Isn't that's a bit of a hike for you?" Alvin inquired.

"It's not too bad," I answered. "Some of the old women in the homes are kinda interesting," I added.

"I'd stay away from them," Joey Gilmore chimed in. "I hear they're crazy. And at night, the rats climb up from the creek and the old ladies catch 'em and eat 'em."

"I doubt it," I answered. "They're old, but not crazy. And some of them have some remarkable stories to tell."

"I heard that that Mrs. Mac Mullin's lived in her house pretty much her whole life. My mom's friend says she heard that she is related to that H.B. Smyth guy that built the mill and the factory."

"Well she's plenty old," I replied, "but I don't think that Hezekiah Smyth guy had much of a family, at least none around here."

Our conversation was interrupted when Jon Shelly walked by on his way out with his papers.

"That Hezekiah Smyth guy is a punk!" Shelly squawked. "He had two wives and two sets of kids."

Shelly went out the door with his papers and left. I didn't know if he was serious about his comment on Hezekiah or if he was still imitating Danny Dobalo.

All three of us, Alvin, Joey, and I then simultaneously got up with our folded papers to leave. I took the familiar route to Coldspring, remembering that I would use the paper trail for official business for the first time. I patted my pocket as I rode down the street, and the jingle of both keys confirmed in my mind that I had not misplaced them. I served the first eight houses, and then rode down to the dead end to lock up my bike. There was a medium size tree by the steps sufficiently large enough to allow me to string the lock around it and through my bike frame, so I chose this spot to secure my bike.

"I'd better take all the papers," I thought, so I pulled off the bag, and slung it over my shoulder and headed down the steps. The walk to the gate was short, and as usual, not a soul was in the area. I unlocked the gate, and walked about 25-feet to a spot by an overgrown mound of weeds. Then I dropped my paper bag there, where it was concealed by the weeds, and traveled on with only four papers. Two minutes later I was at the second gate, which I unlocked, and headed for the Smythville houses. Four swift throws and the job was done, and I returned through the gate and back to my paper bag. I glanced over to the dam, remembering the cool feel of the water over my toes, and then picked up the sack and went out through the gate and off the shortcut trail.

"The whole thing couldn't have taken more than ten minutes," I thought as I relocked the gate, feeling proud of this small but major accomplishment.

I headed up the stairs with the bag, eager to finish serving and get home for a rest. It was only about 3:00, but the day had been a long adventure and I was feeling a bit tired and hungry. When I got to the top of the steps, I looked around, but my bicycle was nowhere to be found.

"Am I losing my mind?" I thought. "I'm sure I locked it to that tree." I stood dumbfounded for a minute and set down the paper bag and looked around, but there was no bicycle anywhere to be seen and not a soul in the area. I looked down in the weeds and the trees going down the hill towards the creek and spotted the rubber tire tube and chain, about half the distance to the creek. I hiked down to pick it up and found the lock and chain ends still bound, but the chain broken in half, with the remains of the center cut and twisted broken link still attached to one end.

"Who would want to steal my bike?" was my original thought, followed by, "Once I get home, my dad will know what to do."

I decided it was best to continue to serve the papers on foot while I walked home, since I assumed whoever took the bike was now long gone. Serving on foot was not a problem, but the more I thought of telling my dad about the bike's disappearance, the more difficult the explanation got.

"I can't tell him the bike got stolen while I was walking through the trail. He'll ask about the locks and the keys."

I reasoned that the details of the paper trail were not necessary, and I'd just say I went down in the woods because I had to go to pee, and when I came up the bike was missing.

When I got home, my father was changing the oil in our car, and I called to him as he lay beneath it.

"Dad, my bike was stolen! I had it when I was serving papers, I had to pee, so I locked it and went down in the woods, and when I came back the chain was cut and the bike was missing!"

My dad pulled himself out from under the car. His right hand had oil on it, and he had a smudge of grease on his forehead. My dad was a good father. He never yelled and I don't believe I ever heard him say an unkind word about anyone, let alone utter a curse word. He was in his early 50's, and spent the majority of his time working so that he could provide a good life for the family. At home he was always busy keeping up the yard, or maintaining the house, or fixing something that my brother or sister or I had broken. He rarely spent time on anything I would consider to be fun, or satisfy some personal hobby or interest. Instead he quietly did all the little fatherly things to help his children on the proper route to adulthood. I once heard him explain his philosophy on handling children. He said raising children is a lot like fishing; the tricky part is knowing exactly how much line to let out, and when it's time to start winding back in. Once you find the proper balance, you both will achieve success. And here I was today, again testing the rig of his reel.

"What's that you said?" he asked as he wiped the grease from his head, his blue eyes staring back at me as only a loving father could.

"My bike was stolen," I repeated. I was serving my papers at the end of Collins Avenue, when I had to go pee. I hadn't gone since this morning before I went over to Zack's house. So I locked my bike onto a tree, and went down the steps towards the creek to go in the woods, and when I came back up, my bike was missing and the chain I used to lock it up was cut."

I took the chain and lock out of my paper bag and showed it to my dad. He examined the chain and lock carefully, paying particular attention to the broken, twisted link.

"Where did you get the lock and chain?" he asked.

"Zack gave it to me. He got the chain from an old swing in his garage, same with the tire tube. He has lots of locks from his dad's old shop."

My dad liked Zack. He and Mr. Mausser had been friends for years through our church.

"Well, it looks like whoever took the bike really wanted it," he reasoned. "You have to have a pretty powerful chain cutter to break that link. Do you have any idea who might have wanted to do something like this?"

"Not really, and whoever took it did it fast. I couldn't have been gone more than a few minutes."

"Well, I'm really not sure how much I can do," my father fretted. "Whoever wanted it went to a lot of trouble to get it. It wasn't just some passerby that happened to have chain cutters. Let me finish up here and we'll go report it to the police. In the meantime, you go in and get something to eat and drink. I don't think we saw you at lunchtime."

I went in and made myself a peanut butter sandwich. My dad came in as I was eating it, and he washed his hands and waited for me to finish.

"Let's take the car," he said as I finished. "Then afterward we can go over to Collins Avenue for me to see where this happened."

We got into the car, a 1967 blue Chevrolet Impala with blue vinyl seats. I sat up front next to my dad. The police station was only about two blocks away, so the drive was fast. We went into the station and my father talked to his friend Sergeant Tony Sniztches, who happened to be in the station on duty at the time.

"You'll have to fill out a police report," he said. "There have been a lot of stolen bikes lately, but this is a bit unusual because it was an older stingray. Most of the recent stolen bikes had been the newer ten-speeds."

My father and I sat at a table and he had me fill out the police report, prodding me to fill it out completely and accurately in a helping way by asking me questions.

"What was the type of bike, what was its color, anything that would make it easily recognizable?"

I filled out the form, writing down the story of the woods and the cut lock, then ended it with my signature and my phone number and address. I had told the story of having to go pee so many times now that I was beginning to believe it myself. We left the police station, and my dad drove me down to the site of the crime. Along the way I pointed out the paper station and several of the houses on my route. He parked the car at the end of the street and we got out. He looked at the woods, the hill, and then down the stairs towards the creek, and he asked which tree the lock was placed on.

"That one," I replied, showing him the medium sized tree trunk I had selected. "And I found the cut chain and lock down there in the woods."

My father took in the surroundings and looked up and down the street. He shook his head and started back for the car. "I'm sorry," he said. "But there's really not much more we can do about this except to see what materializes. These types of things sometimes have a way of working themselves out."

On the drive back home, my dad started asking me more about the paper route. Did I like it, was it hard, did the people I served seem to be nice, general things like that. He ended by asking me, "Will you be able to continue without your bike?"

"I think I'll be ok," I said. "I walked off the back end of the route today and it wasn't too bad."

"Well, let's wait a few days to see what transpires," he replied. "Maybe we can help you out, and with some of your paper money, get you a new bike."

"Well, I kind of would like to eventually get a ten-speed like Zack's," I countered, "but I'm really not sure how practical that is for delivering papers."

At that, we pulled up into the driveway. My brother was standing there and he wanted to hear the story of the bike, so I repeated the story for what now seemed like the thousandth time.

That night after dinner, I was sitting in the house watching TV, when there was a knock at the door. My father answered and it was Detective Hebner from the police department. He asked if he could ask a few questions, and my father said fine, and called for me.

"Why don't we all sit on the front porch together and go over the police report again," my father said.

Once we all got seated, Detective Hebner started.

"So you're a paperboy. I used to serve papers when I was your age son. It's hard work. What paper do you serve?"

"Well I serve *The Courier-Post*," I replied. "I pick up the papers on Collins Avenue, and the route runs for the most part from the end of Collins Avenue, over on Coldspring to Haddon, and up to the Pike."

Detective Hebner nodded, and wrote something down on the notepad he was holding. "You know, there have been quite a lot of stolen bikes in the neighborhood in the last few months - - nearly two a month. This one's odd though because it doesn't fit the pattern. Almost all the other stolen bikes have been high end bikes like ten-speeds. From the sound of it, your bike was an older Stingray, with really no special features like a five-speed, or one of those Stingray Crate type bikes with the custom wheels and racing design."

I nodded my head and he continued. "Do you know anybody who would have liked to take your bike, or anybody that you have had a fight with recently, or somebody who lived nearby on the street who might want your bike?"

"No sir, I really can't think of anyone who would particularly want it," I replied back.

"Why do you say it like that ...particularly want it?"

"Well, like you said," I continued, "It was pretty old, and not a ten-speed."

"Do you like the new ten-speeds?" the detective asked.

"Yes, some of my friends have them and they're fast. I'm saving my paper money to get one."

"Oh, really?" he observed. "You're saving up your paper route money to get one?"

"Yeah," I answered. "But with my bike stolen, my dad said that he might help me by chipping in some to help."

"Is that so?" the detective quipped. "You know son, there is one thing I don't quite understand. You're a big boy, and I bet if you had to pee as bad as you said, that you could have made it down the steps and done your business in a matter of minutes. I guess I don't understand how somebody can appear out of nowhere so fast, cut the chain, throw it in the woods, and then make off clear with the bike, without you seeing or hearing anything. At the least you think you would have heard him throw the lock and chain into the woods which were right near where you were standing!"

I looked at the detective, and then I looked at my father. "I didn't see or hear anything," I stammered back.

"And one other thing, I talked to some of the neighbors on the street, and at least a couple said they saw your bike parked on the street several times in the last few weeks, without you nearby, and without it locked. Have you been in need of several restroom breaks in the past couple of weeks? Maybe you..."

My father stopped the detective in mid-sentence and said he didn't like where this was leading.

"Detective," he said, "We came to the police for help, and to warn others of a potential problem in the town. We did not come to hear any half-baked accusations. Is your plan to chastise the victim or to pursue the criminal?"

"Of course it's the latter of the two, sir," the detective replied. "I'd like to thank you both for your time." And with that he took his notepad and headed off the porch to his unmarked squad car.

"It's men like him," my father said, "that keep law-abiding citizens from seeking help from the police. All caught up in their own self-importance and cleverness. He'll outthink us all, instead of looking for some facts. I think he's been watching too much Perry Mason! Unfortunately, I wouldn't expect much of a chance of him helping us find your bike. You go on back to the TV, and don't bother yourself thinking more about our friend the detective."

Chapter 15 – Hezekiah Smyth's Family[1]

September came and went. Work at school became more intense with biology projects and history assignments, not to mention Mrs. Caprio's weekly essays on Great American Literature. After school, the days were getting shorter and colder. Lately I was serving with a sweatshirt on, and it was starting to get dark by the time I got home from delivering papers. I had now grown accustom to serving the route by walking instead of by bicycle. It took a bit longer to walk to the station, but I could make up time by folding the papers as I walked along the route. My paper bag was especially heavy on days like Wednesdays when the papers ran about thirty to a bundle. On days like that I had to shift the paper bag strap from shoulder to shoulder about every block until I made it midway through Haddon Avenue, when my load lightened. Trips along the paper trail were now commonplace, and no more difficult than remembering to bring my paper bag or sack of rubber bands. I had been using this path for at least three weeks and had yet to see anyone in the area of the mill; and as the season grew colder and darker, I figured the odds of being questioned by any passerby on the use of the trail would be even more remote.

One particular Tuesday in mid-October, after arriving at the Smythville homes, I saw Mrs. Mac Mullin out on her porch. The day was particularly chilly, and walking along the woods it seemed like the color of the leaves had changed from their usual green to vivid shades of red and yellow almost overnight. As I walked towards the porch, she stood up from her chair, wrapped in a white sweater, and began to talk to me.

"I've noticed lately that you have been coming a bit earlier with the paper," she said. "I've been meaning to catch you the last couple of days but I keep missing you."

"Oh, my bicycle was stolen," I answered. "And now I have to get around on foot. I've changed the order I serve my route a bit to avoid some backtracking, so now your house is one of the first I serve instead of one of the last."

"Oh," she nodded. "I'm sorry to hear about your bike."

"Well, there's nothing I can do about it now," I commented. "I'm saving up my paper money to get a new one."

"I guess you need to be moving on to get to the other houses. But do you think you could help me for a short time in the next few days? It's starting to get chilly outside, and I need some help bringing up my winter clothes from in the cellar, and moving my summer clothes back down."

"Sure, I can come back when I'm done this afternoon, if you would like," I answered. "I could be back in less than an hour."

"That would be great, I'll go inside and start getting things ready," she countered.

I finished off the Smythville homes and started back for the rest of the route, wondering about Mrs. Mac Mullin along the way, and how older people were a bit strange. "Winter clothes / summer clothes - what's the difference?"

I finished the route, stopping home for a snack to take back with me. Seeing my mom, I mentioned that one of the old ladies on my route asked for some help, and recited the story of the summer and winter clothes. "I might be a bit late for dinner, but I'm not positive," I concluded.

"Well, that's nice of you to help. I'll keep your plate warm; we're having beef stew tonight."

I headed out the door with three Oreos. The sun had begun to set as I neared the old mill. Mrs. Mac Mullin was waiting by the door when I got there, and let me in when I arrived.

"I'm afraid there's no entrance to the basement through the house," Mrs. Mac Mullin explained. You'll have to go around to the back of the house. There you'll find a set of Bilco doors to the cellar. Here's the key that unlocks them. There's no light in the basement so you might need this flashlight. Unlock the doors, and go down the steps, and in the basement you'll see an old gray steamer trunk. There's a wheeled dolly near it you can use to help bring it up and into the house."

I headed out the door and around to the slanted Bilco doors. Shining the flashlight on the lock, I opened it, and pulled the two heavy wooden doors open one at a time. I started into the basement a bit tentatively, thinking of Joey Gilmore and his comments about the rats coming up to the houses from the creek. Getting to the bottom of the steps, I shined the flashlight all around the basement before I entered, stomping my feet intentionally when I got the courage to go in to scare away any rats that might be in the vicinity. The basement ceiling was low, and I had to crouch a bit when I entered to avoid hitting my head. Looking over to the right corner, I saw an old trunk like Mrs. Mac Mullin described and next to it the hand dolly. Making my way over to the trunk, I noticed that it was made of tin and had a circular insignia embossed into the side with the initials HBS, very similar to the wax stamp Zack had found in the factory desk. The dolly was angular, with two wheels on the bottom and two long green handles. It had two leather straps, one on each handle that buckled like a belt, and I fastened them after I positioned the trunk standing up on one side on the dolly.

Tilting the dolly and pulling, it moved quite easily across the hard dirt basement floor. Surprisingly, despite the trunk's weight, it also was pulled easily up the Bilco door steps and onto the porch. Mrs. Mac Mullin got the porch door, and I wheeled the steamer trunk into the living room. Laying it on its bottom, I unbuckled the straps, and Mrs. Mac Mullin pulled out a long skeleton key to open it and expose its contents. As the trunk was low on the floor, Mrs. Mac Mullin asked me to help pull things out. So one by one I pulled out the items and laid them on a pile on the couch. I was surprised that the contents were clean and not musty. Among the items was a heavy patchwork quilt, a woolen dark green blanket, several pairs of long brown, black, and blue pants, several button-down and pullover sweaters, a heavy winter coat, several pairs of gloves and socks, and several cotton pullover hats.

When the trunk was empty, Mrs. Mac Mullin pointed to the dining room table, and asked if I could load the summer clothes on it into the trunk, which I did. With all loaded, she locked the trunk, and I took it back to the basement with the dolly. Locking the Bilco doors, I returned to the front porch to see if there was anything else left to be done. She invited me back in, and told me to sit and rest a spell. As I sat, she went through the clothes and shook them out and refolded each item. As she folded, I asked her to continue the story about Hezekiah Smyth and his family.

"A friend of mine said something about Hezekiah having two families?" I asked. "Is any of that true?"

"Well," she started, "Hezekiah's first wife Eveline never returned to Smythville after baby Ella had died from the fever. As I mentioned, she always blamed Hezekiah in part for the death because he was not present at the baby's deathbed. Even though Eveline later bore him a son in 1876, Hezekiah grew apart from the family and pretty much stopped visiting them by 1880, although he continued to support them by sending money. In the summer of 1881, Hezekiah was introduced to a sixteen year old mill girl named Agnes Mitilda Gilikson who worked nearby in a textile factory and was living in a boarding house. Hezekiah immediately took a liking to the girl, who was smart and athletic and loved to walk down by the creek with him and watch the water run. Hezekiah always said the creek had the power to nurture the seed of true love to blossom.

Agnes had a good head for numbers and figures, and before long she was hired as a confidential secretary. The two had a secret affair and Agnes became pregnant with a daughter. The baby was born nine months later, and Agnes named her *Enola* because it was the word *alone* spelled backward. Naturally, because Hezekiah was 35 and Agnes was barely 17, there would have been a scandal, so Hezekiah sent Agnes to live with the family of his Philadelphia sales manager. The family helped raise Enola. In the meantime, Hezekiah furthered Agnes' education, and she eventually attended Penn Medical School.

Hezekiah visited Agnes in Philadelphia regularly and their love grew even more as she became older. In the summer of 1884, when Agnes became 18, he told her of his intent to marry her. So he returned to Lowell, Massachusetts, and demanded a divorce from his first wife Eveline, but she refused. In a fit of anger, he took all the letters he had written to her over the years and burned them in her stove. Then he went to the town clerk's office and transferred the house deed in Lowell to Eveline's maiden name of English, and set up a bank account of several thousand dollars for her and their son. Finally, he went to his sister's house and using his pocketknife, he cut out all references to his marriage to Eveline and any references to the two children born in Lowell, burning the paper scraps in her fireplace. In his mind, these actions annulled his first marriage.

Hezekiah and Agnes married in 1885, although she did not officially come to live with him in the Smythville Mansion until four years later when she completed her degree. When she moved in, she brought six year old Enola with her, but Hezekiah and Agnes referred to the child as their niece, to keep their earlier relationship a secret from the workers and townsfolk of Smythville, who regarded Hezekiah at this point as the epitome of the local social upper class. The three lived together in a very loving relationship, and enjoyed the finer things in life, as well as social status. Hezekiah ended up with over forty patents, and Agnes practiced medicine in town and made and sold herbal remedies. Hezekiah also published the *New Jersey Mechanic Trade Journal*, which Agnes edited and in which she advertised her herbal medicines. Enola grew up to be smart like her mother. She attended the Drexel Institute of Art, Science, and Industry in Philadelphia where she studied design and fell in love with a fellow student who was interested in the fabrication of biplanes. All was fine until the spring of 1912, when Agnes developed cancer. Enola returned home to stay and care for her sick mother, who died in December of the year at the young age of 46. Grief stricken, Hezekiah who was now 65, commissioned a near life-size Italian marble statue of Agnes and stood it on a granite pedestal under an iron canopy among the formal gardens of the Smythville Mansion. Enola, who was now thirty, stayed at the mansion in Smythville, where she assisted her father with his patent work, while her husband worked nearby with a design firm that manufactured war planes. Several years later her husband enlisted to serve with the Allied troops during World War I; but he died during the war, the victim of an aerial mishap.

In 1922, five years after the death of Enola's husband, Hezekiah died from complications from pneumonia at the age of 75. Immediately upon hearing of his father's death, Elton Smyth, Hezekiah's son by his first marriage, set out for Smythville to claim what he considered to be his inheritance. Arriving in Smythville, he ordered Enola to be thrown from the Mansion, and he had the marble statue of Agnes destroyed and thrown into the creek. Hezekiah's will was never found. It was thought to have been stolen from the mansion safe boxes by Elton and destroyed when he was not included as a beneficiary. Because of his past, no birth records for any of Hezekiah's children were available, so his land, factory, and mansion fell into a state-held trust, with all eventually becoming part of a state park. Hezekiah was buried next to Agnes in the St. Andrews section of the Pine Street Cemetery, where their remains lie to this day with but a simple common marking stone."

Mrs. Mac Mullin had finished her folding, and all the winter items were all now neatly stacked on the couch. "But what happened to Enola?" I asked. "Did she ever return to the mansion? Is she buried with her father and mother on Pine Street?"

"Well some secrets are best left untold, especially if they serve no purpose other than destroying otherwise happy lives," she replied. "Enola's identity as the daughter of Hezekiah and Agnes was never officially documented, although many familiar with the story at the time suspected she was. Enola never sought legal restitution, but trustees of the state did eventually cite circumstantial evidence as to her relation to Hezekiah and Agnes, and they granted permission for her to maintain a free residence in one of the homes in Smythville until her death."

Mrs. Mac Mullin looked at the clock on the wall and exclaimed, "Oh, my, how quickly the time has passed."

I looked up and nodded.

"You'll need to be getting home for your dinner," she said. "But if you could do one more thing before you leave, and please carry these winter items upstairs to my bedroom. You can leave them on the chair up there. What will take you but a few minutes will save me hours of trips up and down those stairs."

I replied "sure" and headed upstairs carrying half the load. I placed the clothes on the chair and went back downstairs for the second half of the load. Filling up the chair, I put the quilt and the heavy winter coat on the bed, not far from the nightstand that I had wiped down from rain when I had last entered the bedroom nearly a month ago. Before leaving, I looked again at the bedroom photos, especially the one of the man, woman, and girl in front of the factory. It had seemed old and blurry before, but today, the old photo was much clearer than the last time I viewed it, and I realized that some secrets are also puzzles left to be solved.

Leaving the room and heading down the steps I thought of how depressing it could be to live most of your life alone, and I felt a bit sad for Mrs. Mac Mullin. But when I got downstairs, my sadness was lightened as I watched her moving towards me, with a smile on her face and even a slight hop in her elderly gait.

"I have something for you!" she exclaimed. "I know it's not much, and cannot replace your stolen bicycle, but perhaps it will brighten your memories of this place when you think about it in the future."

She handed me a white cardboard box and she smiled and thanked me for my help. I opened the lid and pulled out a thin layer of cotton, and inside was a small three- inch pocket knife, clearly very old, but still in pristine condition. It's outside casing appeared to be made of ivory or scrimshaw, and on one side were the initials EBS, and on the other side was an engraving of the big-wheeled Star bicycle, held in place by a figure standing near the mill by the creek. At the base of the pocketknife was a bronze key chain about another three inches long. I gasped as I held it in my hand, and carefully folded out the knife, which was small, but extremely sharp and gleaming, even in the dull lighting of the room.

"Now be careful with that," Mrs. Mac Mullin said as I turned the knife back into its ornate handle.

"Oh I will, I will," I exclaimed. Then she opened the door and I headed again for home, attaching my two keys to the pocketknife key chain on the way.

Chapter 16 – Deanna Kolakowski

November blew cold that year, and as Mrs. Mac Mullin had observed earlier, it was the time to break out winter coats and hats. Once the frost fell over the area, the summer weeds along the creek turned brown and the leaves disappeared from the trees, creating naked sentinels along the paper trail. A heavy coat served as a better cushion against the bite of the paper bag strap on your shoulder, but the coat's bulk caused a tighter fit of the bag against your body, requiring numerous adjustments before walking became comfortable without the strained bag pulling against your neck and side. The Wednesday before Thanksgiving was particularly bad, with papers running twenty to a bundle and six inserts signaling the start of holiday shopping. I arrived at the paper station a bit earlier than usual, due to a half-day early dismissal from school. The day called for a teacher in-service afternoon, which I believe was some sort of fancy way of saying all the teachers were having a meeting with the school principal and superintendent to discuss the progression of the school year. So school let out just before lunch, but we still got to bring in a snack. Even crazier was that the Catholic school kids also got out early, even though their teachers didn't have an in-service afternoon. Not to be denied, the Catholics had gotten out early for some kind of special Thanksgiving service.

When I arrived at the station, Jon Shelly and Joey Gilmore were already there. As usual, Shelly and Joey were fussing and arguing, but in a pestering way – more like you treat a brother than an enemy. They were arguing over the origins of the Hulk, a comic book character of the time, whose picture happened to be on one of the pages of the paper. It seems the Hulk was appearing as a special balloon float in the upcoming Philadelphia Thanksgiving Day Parade. The two were arguing over the Hulk's origins, as though he were some type of historical figure.

"Dr. Bruce Banner became the Hulk when some chemicals he was mixing in his lab exploded," Jon Shelly insisted.

"You're so wrong," Joey retorted. "The Hulk became exposed to cosmic rays when the space ship he was piloting went through some kind of space storm and crashed back into earth."

"How could he have survived a crash into earth from outer space?" Shelly shot back.

"He turned into rock, you idiot, remember...It's crumbling time!" said Joey.

"That's the Thing, not the Hulk. The Hulk is green and is just a human that gets bigger and stronger when he gets mad. The Thing was made of bricks and is red. He is part of the Furious Five."

In walked Alvin Morrison, who had been intently listening to the argument.

"You're all wrong," he said. "The Thing was part of the Fantastic Four". There were Mr. Fantastic, who could stretch his body into any shape, the Invisible Woman, the Human Torch, and the Thing. They were all flying together as humans in space when their ship was exposed to cosmic rays and they became superheroes."

"Well we know which superhero you would be, huh, Louie. The Human Torch!" shouted Shelly.

Then I jumped into the conversation. "So Dr. Doom, who's the Hulk?" I asked.

"The Hulk is Bruce Banner," started Alvin. "He built a bomb that exploded and produced gamma rays that turned him into the Hulk.

Whenever he gets mad, he turns green, and the madder he gets, the stronger he gets."

"Well then how does he become normal again? None of this stuff makes any sense," said Shelly.

Just then, up the driveway walked two girls. One girl was tall and thin, with long black hair and pointed features. She was holding a newspaper bag. The second girl was about four inches shorter, and her body was firm and developed. She had long curly brown hair, and was wearing a heavy blue coat, with white fuzzy trimming at the sleeves and inside the hood. She didn't have on the hood, but instead had on a blue and white ski cap, with a white tassel on the end. The hat sat on top of her hair, but her bangs hung out and flipped up from under the hat in the front, and the rest of her hair flowed out from the back and sides of the hat and fell in curled ringlets down her back.

"Who's that?" I asked.

"The skinny one is Kathy Milano; she's Christine Milano's younger sister, and she's a loud mouth. Don't get her started or she'll never shut up. The good-looking one is Deanna Kolakowski. She lives over a block on Greenbriar Avenue. I'm pretty sure both of her parents are deaf. Both girls go to St. Al's and are in my class," Joey said.

"You said Deanna's parents are deaf? What about her; can she hear?" I asked.

"Of course, you knucklehead," Joey answered. "I told you she was in my class at school."

The two girls came into the station. Both looked a bit out of place among the boys, particularly Deanna, who acted very shy and said very little.

Kathy, recognizing Joey, spoke first, "Hey, Joey, I'm here to pick up the papers for my sister Christine's route. She's playing a solo at church and practicing for the holiday service. We need to pick up her papers and serve them."

She talked as she pulled out a paper from her pocket with the house numbers and showed it to Joey. Christine Milano was at least a year older than me. I rarely saw her because most of the time she picked up her papers long before I got to the station. Christine had the smallest route in the station, only 22 papers. She delivered down on East Oakland Avenue. Christine looked a lot like her sister Kathy, who was closer to my age. Similar, except Christine wore aviator-type wire-rimmed glasses that were popular around the time. I remember they had Photo Gray transition-type lenses that got darker like sunglasses when they were exposed to light.

"Well, her papers are over there in that corner stack," Joey said, pointing. "You'll need to put one of each of those six circulars in each paper before you serve them."

With that Joey and Shelly got up with their papers folded, and boarded their bikes to depart.

"See you later, Human Torch!" Shelly yelled out as he rode away.

"See you later, Hulk. Take care, Mr. Fantastic!" Joey yelled out. "It's clobberin' time!"

The girls looked at each other and smiled. Kathy pointed her finger to her open mouth, silently gesturing that she wanted to gag.

"I think I know who the Torch is," said Kathy Milano. "Who's Dr. Fantastic?"

"Well, Joey and Shelly keep confusing the Hulk and the Thing," Alvin said matter-of-factly. "So, Mr. Fantastic must be Bill here!"

Deanna looked at me with her big brown eyes, and they seemed to twinkle. She smiled and our eyes met briefly for a second, then she looked down. I suddenly felt flush with embarrassment, and I quickly looked away too.

"Christine didn't say anything about these circulars," Kathy said. "Put one in each?"

"Yes, one in each," I mumbled.

"She didn't say anything about the circulars...because we don't get inserts that...often," I added a bit louder, after clearing my throat. I was trying to sound intelligent and helpful, but the more I said, the more tongue tied and stupid I felt.

"Oh, is that it?" Kathy answered. "Crap! I forgot the bands! Say Dr. Fantastic, could you shoot me over about 25 rubber bands as a loaner? Looks like you got plenty and Christine didn't leave me any in the bag."

"That's Mr. Fantastic," Deanna corrected in a tittering manner, looking me in the eye again and winking.

"Sure, I said," feeling even more embarrassed, but trying to retain my cool.

As I leaned to pass the bands to the girls, the stack of papers I had been sitting on slipped out from under me, and I toppled to the floor.

"It seems like Mr. Fantastic has lost his super powers," Kathy laughed as she picked up the bands.

I raised myself up and straightened the pile of papers I had knocked over.

"Yep, that's no stretch, back to Mr. Ordinary," I said. "Nobody can stay fantastic forever."

Hastily I picked up my bag and papers, before I could make a bigger fool of myself.

"See you later," I said. "You too, Alvin."

"Nice meeting you," said Deanna as I left. "Hope to see you again sometime."

I walked out into the driveway, going a bit further down it before I stopped to adjust my bag, which was much heavier than normal and already biting into my shoulder.

"What's up with you?" I heard Kathy ask inside the garage.

"I think he's cute," was Deanna's tiptoed response to Kathy, as I plodded off.

Chapter 17 – The Holiday Season

December came bringing the Christmas season and even colder weather. It also brought several revelations. The first was the most pleasant. Speaking with Mike Gaines and Conrad Stipp one Tuesday in the station, they both mentioned how much they were looking forward to Christmas tips. When I asked what they were talking about, Mike said that each year at Christmas, most patrons give their carrier a Christmas card with some extra money in it.

"Most people will give you between $1.00 to $2.00 each. With your route, you should make an extra $50 to $75," he said.

"You're kidding," I responded. "That's more than I normally make in over a month."

"Of course that depends if the people like you," Mike said. "If they do, the tips should begin to come a week or two before Christmas when you collect."

The thought of the extra money excited me. I had been saving my money for a new bike, but I really only had managed to accumulate about $55, and I still needed to buy Christmas gifts for my mom and dad and brother and sister.

The second revelation wasn't really so great. Zack and I were part of the Youth Group at our church. We gathered nearly every Sunday night in the church parish hall for a couple of hours with other kids our age and generally goofed off. Our church, St. Mark's Lutheran, which was just up the street from my house, had a parish hall connected to it which contained a very large multipurpose room. The multipurpose room had a polished concrete floor, which had an elevated stage at one end. The stage was carpeted with a plush maroon colored rug and had a small movable altar and cross, a podium, and a piano on caster wheels for use during Sunday school. There was a kitchen beside the multipurpose room, which opened up to it just before the stage through a large serving window with a pull-down accordion blind. And tucked by the back walls were racks of chairs and folding tables that could be set up alone or together to form an assembly area for Sunday school, movie watching, arts and crafts, or a dining room for special church dinners or funeral lunches. The ceiling in the multipurpose room was over two stories high and contained two fold down basketball backboards and rims at both sides that could be lowered with a steel rope crank assembly. During Youth Group, after a short period of church chat and some related religious activity, the boys generally broke out into a basketball game, while the girls sat around and talked.

One of the main responsibilities of the Youth Group each year was to hold a Christmas play, which was usually held the last Sunday night before Christmas. It was part of a Christmas pageant where all the children of the church gathered to celebrate the season, which usually consisted of singing by the cherub and youth choirs, a few readings and prayers, offering, and the play. Afterwards there were snacks of Dixie ice cream cups and pretzel rods, and everybody got a box of red and green foiled Hershey kisses when they left for home. The play was usually some shortened version of Dickens' *A Christmas Carol*, or some playful variation on the story of the birth of Christ including shepherds in the field, a star at night, no room at the inn, birth in the stable, and the three wise men. I had gone to the play every Christmas season for as long as I could remember, seeing my sister, and then my brother perform. I had a bit part as the inn-keeper the previous year, but this year since I was older, I was expected to take on a larger role.

This year, a major variation of the play was planned. It was written and would be directed by Lisa Parker, who was the older sister of Dave Parker, who had the largest paper route in our station. The play was about a sheep and his shepherd who kind of get lost and stumble upon the manger and the Savior's birth. There were lots of talking animals, shepherds, the angel, the inn-keeper and his wife, and of course Mary and Joseph. Lisa was a senior in high school and was taking the production seriously. Youth Group usually started promptly at 7:00, and most of us got there about fifteen minutes early and shot baskets until the nights' activity officially started. On that night, Lisa walked onto the court promptly at 7:00 and took the ball from me and Scott Anderson, telling us to meet immediately with everybody else on the stage.

"We have a lot of work to do, and less than three weeks to get it all done," she started. "Altogether, there are nine speaking characters in the play, and we need people to help make the set and work the lights. So, we need volunteers or I'll start nominating."

Zack immediately said he wanted no part of the speaking roles, but he would gladly be responsible for making the sets and manning the lights. Although this sounded like a lot of responsibility, it really wasn't as bad as it seemed. The hardware store on the Pike sold appliances and always had at least two refrigerator boxes by the curb for disposal on Tuesdays, and cutting the boxes down and doing a quick paint job of a stable and an inn had usually sufficed in prior years. As far as lighting, there really wasn't much, just maybe a small light for the inn and the manger and the operation of the spotlight. Zack had done spotlight duty before, which was really not much more than focusing down the slide projector to a small screen size and shining the resulting beam on whoever was talking.

Costume design was quickly taken by Terry Manual and Lisa Ott, who were familiar with the power of a few bathrobes and towels to clothe the shepherds and the wise men. Speaking parts were next, with the role of the inn-keeper, and his wife, and the three wise men going quickly to Billy Armstong, Diane Bender, Scott Schaeffer, Bob Bansky, and Dave Parker. Mary was to be played by Lisa, and Joseph, who never had any speaking lines, by Bruce Hendry. That left the six major talking roles of the shepherd, his talking sheep, the angel, the talking donkey, the talking wolf, and the talking dog. Gwen Waring took the angel's role, which doubled as the narrator, Mark Chrenowski took the wolf, Paul Slason chose the mule, and Mike Gayman took the dog.

Lisa had a big smile on her face and pointed at me and Scott Anderson, saying "That leaves the two largest speaking roles left: Shep the wayward shepherd, and Blacky, his perpetually lost sheep."

I looked at Scott Anderson and Lisa, and then spoke up. "Hey, there's something fishy going on here. How did everybody know to swipe the minor roles so fast? It's almost like you planned this out in advance."

Lisa laughed and joked, "Everybody knows that all biblical stories are a bit fishy. You had ample opportunity to volunteer, but you didn't. That leaves Scott to play Shep, and you to play Blacky. Case closed, and thanks for your support!"

Scott and I reluctantly agreed, and Lisa handed out copies of the play to each of us, along with yellow colored markers to highlight our lines. We practiced our lines by reading through the play in its entirety the first time, with comments by Lisa on how she envisioned us to act. The second time we read through to see what we had remembered. The night ended with Lisa gathering us together and asking us to try to practice and learn our lines in the next week.

"We really only have a couple more weeks to practice," she implored. "Remember, if you don't learn your lines, you'll be letting the whole group down, besides making yourself look like a fool!"

After her speech, we broke down into small groups, and filed out the door. Zack and I walked out together and he asked if I could help him on Tuesday to get a couple of refrigerator boxes from the hardware store. He said that Pastor Heft had given him a key to the parish hall so that he could bring in the boxes, cut them down, and start working on the scenery. I told him no problem and that I could also help him cut up the boxes and paint the scenes.

Monday came, with a harsh wind and some light snow flurries, and although the calendar had not yet announced the start of winter, we knew it was already here. Zack talked about his plans for constructing the inn, the grass fields, and the manger scenes on the way to and from school, changing his plans a bit in the afternoon to include a large cardboard star covered with aluminum foil which was to be hung from the ceiling. I told him his plan sounded great, and he said he was going to look in his basement and garage for some paint for the scenes, and dig up some drop cloths to make sure he didn't mark up the floor in the parish hall while he was painting. Feeling a bit guilty because of Zack's exuberance for the play, I decided to bring my lines with me to practice and memorize while I served my route.

When I reached the station, there was a buzz of conversation among the carriers, due to December's biggest surprise, which was posted on the bulletin board in the corner of the station, just above the table that held the wire cutters and forms for new paper customer applicants, and vacation & stop delivery requests. There in bold print was a note from Mrs. McGuillan stating that the last day of paper pickup from her garage would be Friday December 17th, with money collection being performed as usual prior to 6:00 PM. Her note went on to say that although she loved the time she had spent with each of us, she was moving on to a full time job and would be unable to continue the job of running the station.

As of Saturday, December 18th, the station would be moving a block south to the corner of 28 East Greenbriar Avenue, with papers to be picked up from the garage beside the house which faced onto Johnson Avenue. All paper payments after December 18th should be made through the new station managers – Irene and Deanna Kolakowski.

I wasn't sure how to feel about the change in location of the station. The extra block walk really wasn't really a big deal. But just the thought of Deanna Kolakowski made me a bit nervous for reasons I could not clearly understand. I left to walk to my route, and took out the script for the play, but I was having a hard time staying concentrated on the lines. I kept thinking of Deanna's brown eyes and the curl of her hair from under the ski cap. The harder I tried not to think of her, the more I couldn't get her out of my mind.

I finished my route still in an enamored frame of mind, when I passed by St. Mark's and noticed Zack's bike locked up by the railing of the steps to the parish hall door. I checked the door knob, and it was unlocked, so I walked in to find Zack.

Having gone to this church my entire life, and with it being located just a few doors up the street, I knew it well. When you walked into the parish hall from its outside door entrance, there was a short hallway. Entering and going straight, there was a staircase that went up to two different levels. Going up to the first level brought you to a small alcove that led into the church. In the small alcove is where we changed into our acolyte robes, which were stored in a closet in the room. On the upper shelf of the closet was a record player on a timer, which was attached to an outside speaker. Every day at 6:00, the record would play a one minute song of bell chimes of some familiar Christian song like *It Came Upon A Midnight Clear*. From outside, everyone thought the church had an intricate bell tower, even though none was visible. Interestingly, even the occasional sound of slight scratches in the record refused to dissuade the public that the bells were not real.

Going up to the second level took you to a floor with three rooms. The first of these rooms was Pastor Heft's office, the second was a small Sunday school room for elementary school children, and the third room was large and contained four sets of tables in a square arrangement. This was where the church board met, but the room also doubled as a classroom for Catechism. Because of the single set of stairs to this upper floor, there was an emergency exit that led outside to a steel fire escape out the back of the building.

Not thinking Zack was upstairs, I turned left when I entered the door and walked about ten feet down the parish hall corridor which branched out into three directions: to the kitchen, to another Sunday school wing, and into the multipurpose room. Looking inside, I saw Zack, laying out some drop cloths.

"Hey, glad to see you," Zack said. "I just came back from the hardware store and they already had two refrigerator boxes outside by the curb and they said I could have them. You want to go get them now?"

I checked my watch and it was only 5:00 and we didn't eat until at least 6:00. "Sure, let's go!" I said.

The walk to the hardware store was only a little more than a block down the Pike. In less than five minutes, we were standing next to the huge cardboard boxes. Altogether there were three boxes, two refrigerators and one washer. Zack tipped over the first refrigerator box and pulled out small assorted cardboard pieces and ties and instructions, and threw them into the washer box. We then lifted the empty refrigerator box and carried it to the church. The box was not heavy, but it was cumbersome, and we had to stop about three times on the way back to adjust our grip. Once at the church, Zack unlocked both of the double doors and propped them open, and we easily carried the box inside and stood it up in the back corner of the multipurpose room.

"Are you ready for the second, or do you need to rest?" Zack asked.

I said ok, and we left to get the second box. This second box contained a bit more waste packing material, including four heavy cardboard corner guards, and Zack decided to keep these in case he needed them for additional scenery support. Making our way back to the Parish Hall was even quicker the second time since we now had practice with our grip. Once in the parish hall, Zack looked at his watch, then took off his coat and said he was going to stay a bit longer to take some measurements and look for some extension cords. I had to get home, but was still thinking a bit about Deanna, so I asked Zack if I could borrow his bike for about fifteen minutes, telling him I needed to check something on my route. Zack said sure and gave me the key to the bike lock. Once I got riding, I shifted into high gear and started pedaling down the street, turning on Johnson Avenue and continuing past Collins Avenue. Slowing up as I approached Greenbriar Avenue, I looked at the house numbers. Sure enough, number 28 was on the corner. Passing the house, I looked at the garage, then rode on past. The wind felt cold on my face and hands, but the rest of my body felt warm and my heart was pounding. Riding a few blocks further, and with my mind sidetracked, I suddenly realized I was at Ormond Avenue.

Not wanting to turn there, I rode on past about a half block, and turned to head back to the church. As I came up to Ormond Avenue a second time, I noticed the white Millar's Cyclery van stopped at the corner. I ducked down my head and pedaled by, traveling at least a block before turning to look back. The van was still in place at the corner, with its white lights beaming across Johnson. Feeling a bit more relaxed, I continued on towards Greenbriar Avenue, when I noticed two figures turning from Oakland Avenue onto Johnson. As I got closer, I squinted through the cold wind, and then recognized the jackets as belonging to Deanna and Kathy. Without thinking, I rode up alongside them both and said hello, stopping them momentarily. Stopping the bike a few feet forward, I ran my fingers quickly through my hair to adjust it from the wind, and said, "Nice seein' you both again. I guess we'll be seein' each other a bit more in a few weeks."

"Well, if it ain't Captain Fantastic," said Kathy.

Deanna laughed. "She'll get it right eventually," she said. Then she added, "I've been thinking about you."

My heart began fluttering again, and any sense of confidence I felt began to flee. "Yeah, I've been thinking about you to…well, er… you know, with the station moving and all."

As I spoke, the white Millar's Cyclery van drove by, slowing up a bit as it passed. While passing it honked its horn twice and then quickly sped up again.

"There go those Dobalo boys," said Kathy.

"Yeah them and their creepy friend," said Deanna.

"Speaking of creepy people, I gotta be getting home. Me and my mom have to pick up my sister from St. Als," said Kathy. "See you two later." And she left.

I looked at Deanna and she looked back at me. Her eyes sparkled in the moonlight. Both of us seemed to want to talk, but instead there was an awkward silent pause.

"Yeah, I guess we will be seeing each other more once you're picking up you papers from my garage. "

"The news was a big surprise," I said. "And two weeks will be here before you know it."

With that, a car drove up into the driveway of her garage, which was just a few houses up the street.

"That would be my dad," she said. "I really gotta be going. It was fantastic seeing you again."

"Yeah, you too! See you in a couple of weeks," I replied, and I started back for the church.

"Well, that was a little better than last time," I thought. "She even said that she was thinking about me."

I pedaled onto Haddon Avenue, and waiting by the corner of Haddon and Johnson, I again saw the van.

"If it is those Dobalo brothers, they can't do anything to me around here," I thought. And I rode up on the sidewalk and into my driveway. Once the van passed, I rode out and up the street to the church.

Getting back to the church, I locked the bike back up and went in to see Zack.

"Finish what you needed to do?" asked Zack.

"Yeah, just what I wanted to do," I answered. "But I saw those Dobalo kids again. They're starting to creep me out. I don't trust them."

"Why, what did they do?"

"Well, I think they were in a van with somebody else," I said. "And they drove by me real slow a couple of times and sort of followed me home."

"They drove slowly behind you and followed you home?"

"Not exactly."

"Did they say anything?

"Not really."

"I think you might be imagining too much," Zack supposed.

With that he walked over near the serving window to the kitchen, and opening a switch box on the wall, he shut off the lights to the parish hall. The room went dark, with only the red glow of the exit lights to guide us to the door.

"Think you can stop by tomorrow night about the same time? I could use your help laying out the manger and the inn," Zack asked.

"Sure, soon as I get done my route I'll be right over," I replied.

We walked out the door and Zack pulled out his key ring. Despite the dark, he had no trouble discerning the keys, locking the church door, and unlocking his bike.

Tuesday there was still a buzz at the station about its movement to Greenbriar Avenue. It was confirmed by Donald Elfrith that Deanna Kolakowski's parents were both deaf, and he wasn't sure how he was going to be able to communicate with them when he was paying the paper bill on Fridays.

"I think that Deanna will really be the one running the station," Alvin Morrison observed, "And her mother is in charge in name only."

"Well what does Deanna know about running a paper station?" Donald questioned.

"I think the only thing you really need to know is that each carrier gets charged 57 cents a week per paper. And I believe knowing how to count is also important, but not necessarily a must," joked Alvin.

I wanted to stay and hear more about the Kolakowski family, but I had promised Zack I would help him when I was through with my deliveries, so I reluctantly picked up my papers and rushed out.

It was still cold and windy out, and a blast of wind hit me when I got down to the bottom of the steps on my way to the Smythville houses. A thin layer of ice was forming on the creek surface in the area near the bottom of the steps where the water ran slower, but further up near the fence where the water ran faster, there was no trace of ice.

I unlocked the gates and walked the trail, and saw Mrs. Mac Mullin waiting by the door as I approached her front steps. I walked up on the porch, and she opened the door. Luckily I was standing right there as she opened it or the wind might have ripped it right out of her hands.

"My, it's windy," she said. "Pull down that hat or you'll be catching yourself a nasty cold."

I pulled my hat down and handed her the paper.

"I hate to trouble you, but I was hoping you could help me again. It's getting near Christmas, and well, my Christmas lights are in a trunk in the basement."

"Sure," I answered. "How about I bring it up tomorrow?"

"That would be great!" she said.

I ran off the steps and back to the paper trail through the stiff wind by the creek. Exiting, I scrambled up the steps onto Collins Avenue. Interestingly the wind was less noticeable there, possibly because it was blocked by the more densely positioned houses.

I served Haddon Avenue alternating side to side, even in the area by my house so I didn't need to backtrack. As I got near the end of the street, I could see Zack's bike, again locked up against the parish hall railing. When I got to the church, the door was unlocked and I went in. Once through the hallway, I saw Zack at work on the inn. The box was laid out as a large rectangle, with one large window and a swinging door. He had used a permanent marker to draw details on the cardboard, like a windowsill, a doorknob, and a mailbox, and he was thinking of adding a sign.

"How about calling it The Bethlehem Inn," I suggested, and he agreed that the name seemed fine.

"I found some red and black paint for the inn," Zack remarked. "And I found some yellow, green, and gold paint for the manger scene. Course I'm still not exactly sure how to best do the manger."

I took a scrap of cardboard and did a rough sketch of a manger. It was just pretty much an 'A' frame of timbers, with what looked like wood planks in the lower half, then two big windows in the back.

"But you don't need to cut the windows out, just draw them like they're windows in the back, and you can even draw some animal faces, like they're behind the manger and looking inside at the birth."

Zack liked the idea, and we began cutting the second box. Zack was cutting using a razor knife, and I assisted using my pocketknife. In no time the box was gutted into a flat rectangle, then I drew on the simulated wooden beams and pointed roof, complete with two windows with the face of a horse, a cow, a goat, and a sheep looking in. Zack said he couldn't tell from my drawing which was the goat and which was the lamb, but I said it really didn't matter. We then carefully began cutting along the roof line, with Zack performing the left side and me doing the right. Zack finished a bit before me, and watched as I completed my cut into his at the peak of the roof.

Just as I finished cutting, Zack said, "That is so cool!" And I stood back to admire our handiwork.

"Not the manger," he said. "Your knife. That is one of the coolest knives in the world. Let me see it again."

I handed him the pocketknife, with my former bike lock key and the Smythville gate key hanging from its key clip end. He once again admired the scrimshaw carving, just as he had done the first time I showed it to him.

"It's excellent, and it's so sharp," he said, as he closed it and handed it back to me.

We stood up the manger and admired it. We had cut it so the box would be standing vertically in its final position, so it held its shape very well when it was erect. We picked up the bits of paper that had been cut from the boxes and placed them into a large trash can, saving the bottom piece from one of the boxes to use for the star. While I picked up the last few pieces, Zack drew the star on the cardboard and began to cut it out. When done, the star looked surprisingly good, and was nearly three feet in height and width from tip to tip.

"That's excellent progress for two nights. All I need to do now is paint these up a little and get some tin foil on the star and my job will be done. Er... well, except for the lights," Zack said.

"Yeah, well I haven't even started on my lines yet," I said, feeling a bit guilty.

"You're smart," Zack said, "you'll know those lines in no time."

We carried the cut boxes to the back of the room and propped them up against the wall, holding them in place with the trash can and a rack of chairs. We then put on our jackets and hats. I started towards the door but Zack was looking around.

"Did you see my other glove?" he asked. "It's really freezing on your hands riding without it."

I saw the glove over by the second chair rack and pointed it out to Zack. It was for his right hand and he kept it off as he walked over to the switch box and opened it.

"Wait for me," I said, "I want to see which of the switches you are flipping."

I looked into the switch box and there must have been twenty switches. Of these about half were on.

"It's these four switches," said Zack. "Numbers 4, 6, 8, and 10. They turn off the overhead lights to the room."

I pushed all four switches to the off position, and the lights went out. Like the night before, the room was filled only with the red glow of the exit signs.

We walked out the door, me first, then Zack so he could lock the door. When Zack finished, he looked up and said, "Where's my bike?"

Sure enough the bike was gone from the railing, with no trace of the lock or chain. We walked around the outside of the church but saw nothing. Walking around a second time, I spotted the chain. In similar fashion to when my stingray was stolen, the lock was still intact, but the chain had been cut and was bent at the cut link. The lock and chain were thrown up on an old bench that sat below the fire escape in an alleyway behind the church. Our guess was that the robbers snuck around the church, looked in through a side window to the multipurpose room where they saw us working, then cut the chain, and took off again around the back of the church, throwing the chain on the bench below the fire escape. If it were my new ten-speed bike that had been stolen, I think I would have cried, but Zack remained stoic.

"There's something going on here that's not right. It's almost like somebody's been watching us, then when they knew the coast was clear, they cut the chain and ran off with the bike. This stinks! Whoever it is better hope that I don't find them, 'cause they're going to pay!" Zack exclaimed.

Chapter 18 – Clued In

The following morning, after safety duty, Zack and I talked about his stolen bike on the way to school. Considering it was a new bike, he was taking the loss fairly well, but he was still pretty mad.

"So what did your mom say when you told her about your bike?" I asked.

"At first she was kind of mad, but it almost seemed like she was mad at me," he said. "She said I really needed to be more careful about where I left it, and make sure it was in a safe place. But for crying out loud, I told her it was locked up, and right in front of the church. Heck, what could be safer than that? What'd she want me to do, bring it inside the church?"

"I told my dad about it," I replied. "He got pretty mad about the whole thing too. He was irked again with that Detective Hebner. He said he ought to be out catching the crook stealing the bikes instead of grilling the kids that had them stolen. By the way, my dad said to tell you he would take you to the police station if you wanted to fill out a report. He said he'd be glad to; he wanted to give those guys at the station a piece of his mind anyway."

"Tell him thanks," Zack said. "My mom called the police to tell them what happened, and they said a squad car would be over as soon as they could make it, but when I went to bed last night, we still hadn't seen anybody. And I didn't see my mom this morning when I got up because she had already left for work."

"Well, my dad gets home about six o'clock; just stop by any time after that and he'll go with you to the station if you want," I said.

"Ok, I'll probably be in the neighborhood anyway tonight," Zack said. "I guess I'll be back at church painting the scenes."

"Yeah," I replied. "So what do you think you'll do to get around?"

"I've been thinking that maybe I should try to get a job or something. I'm pretty handy at fixing things even though I'm only thirteen. Maybe I'll try to get a paper route like you. Let me know if you hear if any are available. I remember when I got my bike that they had some used ten-speed bikes down at Jippo's bike shop for around $60; maybe I could save up for something like that. Pop-Pop said he might be able to help out with a little money."

As usual the day at school was pretty uneventful. Things were slowing up a bit already with Christmas only about a week and a half away. After school I went to the paper station and when I got there, Jon Shelly and Kevin Leahy were there. I hadn't seen Kevin there for a while. He went to the Catholic school and was usually a pretty quiet kid.

"Hey guys." I said as I walked in, "not too long before we move to the new station."

"Won't bother me a bit," Shelly said, "It's actually a bit closer for me. But I guess it's a bit worse for you; you got an extra block there and back to walk."

"You're walking now?" asked Kevin, "I thought I remembered you riding your Stingray when you delivered."

"I was but it got stolen," I said. "Stole it right on my route. I had it locked up, but they broke the lock where I had it parked and threw the lock and chain down into the woods."

"That sucks," said Kevin.

"You can say that again," I replied. "And just yesterday my friend Zack had his ten-speed stolen from right in front of the Lutheran church where he had it locked up."

Shelly got up to leave, and as he did he mentioned, "I heard that Jim Celento had his stolen about three weeks ago from in front of the Shop 'N Bag. But his wasn't locked up."

Shelly rode off, and I started to pick up my bag.

"Hey, did you or your friend notice anything strange before the bikes were stolen, like if somebody was watching you or anything like that?" Kevin whispered in a confidential tone.

"Not really," I replied, "what do you mean by *anything strange*?"

"Heck, I'm not really sure," Kevin said. "And I don't like to make accusations, but right before my bike got stolen, I remember seeing that Millar Bike van riding around. And I saw Danny and Bobby Dobalo in the van. I really don't like either of them that much from school, so I guess that's why I remember. Anyway, I left my bike outside and went inside the Quick Shop for only about five minutes to get a bottle of Coke, and when I came out the bike was gone and so was the van. Of course I can't prove anything; I'm just speculating."

"That's weird," I replied. "I saw the van shortly before my bike was stolen. And I was riding my friend Zack's bike just the night before it was stolen, when I saw those brothers in the van. I remember it kind of felt like they were following me. I really don't like those guys either. It does make you wonder."

I left the station, thinking about the van and those Dobalo brothers. The more I thought about it, the more suspicious I became that they had something to do with the robberies. Then trying to get them out of my mind, I pulled out the play lines again and fumbled through them as I walked my route. The more I reread the play, the dumber the story seemed to get. As I got to Coldspring Avenue, I remembered that I had promised Mrs. Mac Mullin I would help her with her Christmas lights.

"So much stuff to do - homework, play lines, papers, Christmas shopping, Mrs. Mac Mullin's lights."

I decided to skip the path, serve the rest of the route, then return to Smythville with their papers. That way I could get the trunk with Mrs. Mac Mullin's lights when I was there and put them up. I figured the lights might take a while, and I didn't want to piss off my other customers around Christmas tip time. I put the play lines back into my pocket and picked up the pace. The afternoon didn't feel quite as cold as the few days before. Finishing the route, I returned to the end of Collins and down the trail, unlocking the gates in the dark. I served each of the four Smythville houses and went up to Mrs. Mac Mullin's house last and knocked at the door.

"Great, you remembered," Mrs. Mac Mullin said. "The Christmas lights are in the basement in a second trunk, with some other decorations. The trunk is green. You remember how to get into the basement, right?"

She handed me the key and a flashlight, and I went around the back of the house and unlocked the Bilco doors to the basement. I shined the light inside and noticed there were actually four trunks in the cellar. It seemed a bit odd, since I didn't recall seeing them all before. The tan one I had moved before was directly across from the doors, which is why it must have stood out before. The green one and two brown ones were located over to the left side of the basement. I grabbed the trunk dolly, and positioned it on the green trunk. The trunk was lighter than the one with the winter clothes, and it wasn't in as good a shape. I dragged the dolly across the dirt floor and up the Bilco steps, then onto the porch. Then I pulled the trunk and dolly into the living room.

The trunk was latched shut but not locked, and I opened it up. Inside was a small artificial tree in two pieces, as well as a stand, some wrapped boxes, a string of Christmas lights, a revolving light, and an extension cord.

"If you could just get the lights and put them up around the door outside," Mrs. Mac Mullin requested.

With that I pulled the strand of Christmas lights and the extension cord from the trunk. I originally had thought the lights were for the tree, but their size was too large. The fifteen or so bulbs on the string were each about $1^1/_2$ inches tall and in multiple colors of blue, green, red, yellow, and white. Each light was shaped in a pointed fashion, and the glass of the bulb was molded with a waved texture so it resembled the flame of a candle. My father had a few bulbs like this at home that were originally his father's, so I knew they were very old. Taking the lights out on the porch I noted a series of small bent nails at about one foot intervals around the door. Hooking the wire about nails took only a couple of minutes and the strand was hung, with its length almost perfectly matching the outline of the front door molding. I plugged the lights into the extension cord and into an outlet on the side of the porch. The lights illuminated, and I walked over to inspect them. One of the red bulbs along the door top was blown out, so I unscrewed it and replaced it with a different red bulb that happened to be at the lower right hand corner of the door. I then screwed the burnt out bulb in the empty lower socket as there were no spare bulbs of which I was aware. Going back in the house, I looked again inside the trunk just to make sure I had not missed any spare bulbs.

"Oh, one hundred thanks," said Mrs. Mac Mullin. "With the cold weather and my arthritis, I would never have been able to do that."

"That's it?" I exclaimed. "What about the tree and everything else in the trunk?"

"Oh, that's so much effort; you needn't do anything with those. You can just take the trunk back down the basement."

"What? The majority of this work is just bringing up the trunk from the cellar," I said. "Let's put up the tree."

"Well I'm not sure whether all the parts for the tree are even there," Mrs. Mac Mullin said. "The tree hasn't been put up for quite a long time. But I guess if the spirit is willing!"

Under Mrs. Mac Mullin's direction, I began to move the couch closer to the side of the room, opening some space in the corner for the tree. I then took the tree and put the base in the stand and tightened the three large wing nuts on the stand that held it in place. Then I put on the top piece. Altogether, the tree was not much more than four feet tall. What's more, its color was white, not green, and it was covered with shiny plastic needles which were relatively sparse and really not lifelike at all. After moving the tree to its corner resting spot, I went back for the revolving light. It was one of those spotlights that consisted of a white light, with a revolving disk in front of it, sectioned in four quarters of blue, red, yellow, and green transparent plastic. I plugged in the light and flipped the switch and the light came on and the disk began to revolve, and a stream of alternating blue, red, yellow, and green light shown on the tree, seeming to transform its very color with each quarter revolution. It was just like the saying," if a man wants a green coat, turn on the green light."

"It's just wonderful," said Mrs. Mac Mullin. "It really puts the room into the Christmas spirit."

"Since you've gone this far with things, could you also please pull out the boxes from the trunk?" she said. "They're not really presents, just boxes for the ornaments. After I put up the Christmas balls I can just put the empty wrapped boxes under the tree to make it look more festive."

She took the lids off two of the boxes, revealing that their bases and lids had been wrapped separately. One box contained red glass Christmas balls, and the other contained blue glass balls. She covered the boxes again with the lids and pushed them under the tree.

"What's in the third box?" I asked.

"Oh, that's the old star for the tree top, but it's broken," she replied. She took the lid off the box to reveal that the uppermost point on the star had broken off. "Just put the box back in the trunk. I believe it broke over twenty years ago, but my late husband and I bought it during our first Christmas together and I just don't have the heart to throw it out."

I put the box with the star back in the trunk.

Other than the box with the star, the trunk was now empty, save for a few loose Christmas cards from prior years. I pulled out the cards and noticed the bottom of the trunk, which was made of tin, was rusted on one side. This trunk was not nearly as nice as the other trunk which had held the clothes, and it had no embossed initials. Oddly, although the inside appeared clearly rusted through on the bottom in several places, there were no holes through the trunk bottom, as if it had a second metal bottom, and the rusted bottom were just an insert.

I asked Mrs. Mac Mullin if she wanted the trunk back in the basement and she said yes. So I closed the lid and put it back onto the dolly to take it outside. I walked past the Christmas tree just as the yellow light was shining upon it, and I noticed that the wall and ceiling behind the tree were stained. It was likely a watermark. Judging by its position, it may have been due to water which had dripped from upstairs, possibly from the bedroom window. I pulled the trunk outside and returned it to the basement, then returned to the living room to give Mrs. Mac Mullin back her basement key.

"Oh thank you," she said. "You're so nice to help me."

"No problem," I said.

As I started to leave I pointed out the stain on the wall behind the tree.

"It looks like it might be a water stain." I remarked. "Is everything ok with that bedroom window upstairs? It's shut, right? Maybe some water dripped down here and got on the wall?"

"Oh, the window is fine and shut, but thanks for asking," she said. "But your right about it being a water stain. It's been there for years. I'd love to get the wall repainted, but I can't do it, and I really can't afford to pay a painter."

"Well I have a friend who might be interested in a small job like that," I commented. "I'm sure he wouldn't charge much, and I know he's looking to make a little bit of money."

"I don't think I could afford much more than $20 for the job," she remarked.

"If you're interested, I could ask him," I said. "He's basically about the same age as me. But he's painted a lot before for his mom, and he does a good job."

"Well ask him, and if he's interested, maybe we could work something out for after Christmas," she said.

I left the house and started back for home. By the time I got there it was 6:15. By coincidence, Zack was walking up to my house from the church, just as I was walking down from the opposite direction.

"I finished painting the inn, and I'm about halfway through the manger," Zack said. "And I decided to take up your father's offer on filling out a police report."

"Great," I said.

Then I told him about the possible painting job with Mrs. Mac Mullin.

"Twenty dollars would be ok as long as she pays for the paint," he said as we walked into the house.

We both came into the kitchen.

"Good timing," said my mom, "We were just getting ready to sit down for dinner."

"How you doing, Zack?" asked my father. "Sorry to hear about your bike. Care to join us for dinner?"

Chapter 19 – The Dobalo Brothers

Danny and Bobby Dobalo were two identical twins, the only sons of Ellen and David Dobalo. Danny was the older of the two, born precisely 4 minutes and 31 seconds before Bobby. To look at the two side by side, you could barely tell them apart. Both had long curly blond hair, a tanned ruggedly handsome complexion, and were built well for their age with broad shoulders and a muscular body tone. But looking carefully at their hands it was possible to notice a difference between them, as Danny had a large scar on the back of his right hand in the area below his thumb and index finger. The scar was all that remained of a childhood accident which occurred when his brother Bobby grabbed for his mother's cup of hot coffee and it spilled on Danny's hand and burned away a part of his skin so that it hung from the bone like melted chewing gum.

Yet while the two boys looked virtually identical, a brief conversation with the two revealed they were different as night and day. Danny was very bright and expressive. Bobby was not. It seems in those brief 4 minutes and 31 seconds, some oxygen must have been cut off to his brain, which altered his personality. He wasn't retarded or disabled, but somehow he was a bit slow-witted.

The Dobalos grew up with their mother and father in the Heather Glen section of town, which was a bit more high class than in other areas. Their house in particular was custom built and had an in-ground pool, tennis court, and parking area for their father's boat and trailer. Their father David was a successful stock broker who worked in New York on Wall Street. Because it would have taken David over two hours to commute each way to work, he stayed in New York quite often, and was frequently away from home. Ellen, the boy's mother was beautiful, and she spoiled the boys in the same fashion her husband spoiled her, with the best clothes, toys, and gifts that money could buy.

As the boys grew, the differences in their demeanor became more apparent. In second grade, the school advised that Bobby be left behind to repeat a year, but Ellen insisted the two boys be kept together, so the decision was made to have both boys repeat the grade. This only seemed to make matters worse, since Danny who was extremely bright, became bored and disruptive in class. Add to this that the boys were both already very large for their age, and now were also a year older than their classmates, and it is no wonder that they eclipsed their classmates in size, strength, and agility. As the boys grew, they became bullies to other children, especially Danny, who regularly encouraged Bobby to do his dirty work for him. Bobby, being a bit slow, did anything his older brother told him, without question or moral.

After several years went by, the boy's father David grew tired of his commute and his spoiled wife and children, and left them. The house was sold, David moved to a Co-op in New York, and Ellen and the boys moved to a smaller house on Ormond Avenue. Alimony and child support payments from David allowed the boys and their mother to continue to enjoy some of the finer things in life; however, their lifestyle sometimes caused them to overstep their means. As the boys began to age, Ellen began to step out more with other men, and the boys became more independent and resentful.

As if almost a paradox, by junior high age, the boys had both become two of the most handsome and most athletic boys at the Saint Aloysius School, while also becoming two of the most disliked children by their classmates because of their arrogant and bullying personalities. Interestingly enough, however, the nuns and the priests at the school did not see the bullying, partially because Danny was clever enough to always show his ultimate respect to them and only carry out his bullying when adult authority figures were absent from the area. Bobby followed whatever command Danny dictated, but the orders were not to be carried out unless the adults were out of sight. As a result, the school officials attributed the boy's lack of popularity to petty jealousy over their size and age. After all, the boy's size and athletic prowess was a bit of a boon to the small school, bringing in extra sports notoriety to its otherwise dying parochial program. It was rumored that Father Lubbecci once went so far as to dismiss all talk of the boy's stealing a gallon of communion wine, despite the fact that he caught them red handed, in order to preserve their good personal and academic stature. The reason cited was always that Danny shouldn't be disciplined for the transgressions of Bobby because "...well ... we all know how that Bobby can be sometimes!"

Like their father and mother, the Dobalo boys always seemed preoccupied with flashy playthings. Both their father and mother had convertible sport cars, so why shouldn't the boys have glitzy bicycles with all the bells and whistles? There was a bicycle store in town, up on the Pike between Collins and Greenbriar Avenues, between the laundromat and Kara's Pizza. It was owned by Charles "Chip" Millar. The store was officially a bicycle and hobby store, selling both new and used bicycles. The hobby part of the shop was small, with a few odds and ends which could be perceived for hobbyists, the majority of which were car and truck model kits which were popular at the time. Teenage car enthusiasts could customize their vehicles by painting the plastic parts to their liking, then assembling and gluing the parts together with stripes and decals which were also supplied with the kits. A quality model vehicle was usually complete with detailed engines, white walled tires, and doors, hoods, and trunks that could be opened and closed. Once the model was made, you displayed it on a shelf, as they were really too fragile to play with.

Chip Millar was very into building car models, and he displayed an extensive collection which he had built right there in the store in the front window. In this manner, he could entice young wannabe car builders to buy them, showing ample expert examples of just how well the kits could be assembled. We always slowed down when passing Millar's to look at his window display, occasionally going inside to price out the kits. Of course, the bicycle portion of the store was much more profitable and Chip exclusively sold Schwinn bicycles that as far as we knew were the best bicycles available. Of course, Chip also sold lower quality used bicycles which were relegated to two racks he kept locked up outside the front of the store. Stories were told that you could sell your old bicycle to Chip at 9:00 AM in the morning for $5.00 and by 10:00 AM it would be out in the front rack with a $30.00 price tag. Chip's reputation for this practice was so well known in town that his name had morphed over the years from Chip into Jip, so that his store was often referred to by locals as Jippo's.

While his used bike prices were usually regarded as extreme, his new bike prices were considered to be fairly priced, so when buying a new bicycle, no one thought of going anywhere but Jippo's. This may have been due to the times, as superstores were really not available as an alternative. After all, everybody in town also bought their household appliances like washers, dryers, TVs, and refrigerators from the local hardware store.

One of Schwinn's most popular bicycles for young riders at the time was the Stingray, known for its high arching handlebars and banana seat. The most deluxe Stingray bicycle offering by Schwinn was their "Krate" series, whose model names varied by the color of the bike. This series of Stingray bikes was distinguished by its five-speed shifter, chrome fenders, small front tire and shock absorber, hand brakes, and color matched banana seat with a racing stripe. The bicycles were extremely expensive, and by age ten Bobby Dobalo had the red Apple Peeler model, and Danny Dobalo had the yellow Lemon Peeler model. Thus the boys' love affair with slick transportation had begun. As they matured and became dissatisfied, they graduated to the ten-speed style of bicycle, and eventually moved onward to the world of mopeds and mini-bikes, all of which were soon to be supplanted by the world of adult cars and hot rods.

Now at age fifteen and going on sixteen, Danny was preoccupied with the idea of having his own car, or "rod" as he called them. Through his association with Millar's bikes, he had befriended Billy Proudst, who had worked at the bike shop since his late teens and now was also into working on cars. Billy stuttered when he talked, but he could assemble a bike or rebuild a carburetor in a matter of minutes. Billy's job at Jippo's included picking up the bikes in cartons from the local Schwinn distribution center using the store van and driving them back to the shop where he would assemble them. Because of the nature of his job, he knew quite a few of the other bicycle store mechanics and owners in the neighboring towns. Billy owned a new 1968 Camaro that he had bought for $3800 with his store earnings, and Danny was currently in the market for something similar, since he would soon be getting his driver's permit; besides, he really already knew how to drive. To make money, he had embarked on a scheme to lift late model bicycles with Bobby and Billy, which they could sell either to unsuspecting Chip Millar or other out of town bicycle dealers through Billy's connections.

The three canvassed for bicycles in Millar's van, and then while one of the trio watched the unsuspecting owner in an alternate location, the other would ride off with the bike, eventually loading it into Millar's van. The trio had acquired over 25 bikes in the past year, generally averaging about one every other week. Danny usually masterminded each acquisition with Bobby performing the snitch and Billy fencing the stolen merchandise. The money for each job was split evenly in thirds, with Danny generally keeping Bobby's portion and putting it in the *kitty,* as he called it, for their new car. To date Danny had amassed over $1800 towards his goal and was branching out the business beyond our town to neighboring communities. Danny felt no remorse for the acquisitions and had no intentions of stopping until his monetary goal was met. Of the three, he was in the best shape should anyone get caught, as Bobby technically did the stealing and Billy did the selling. Bobby could easily be sold out, and Billy was an adult by age and would suffer the most severe consequences by law should they be caught. Danny had surely masterminded this plan to his benefit. Usually, he wasn't even present with the bikes when they were stolen or loaded in the van, as he was generally busy doing surveillance on the owner. Danny knew that he could never be held responsible for the others' actions, and in his mind, that, plus the money was the only thing that mattered.

Chapter 20 – The Station Moves

Friday, December 17th was here, amid the bustle of Christmas preparations. Although still over one week away, Christmas was on everybody's mind. The threat of snow made the mood even more complete. The weathermen had called for some heavy snow in the form of a Nor'easter for the morning, but the weather stalled somewhere over Virginia, and we were now told the worst of the storm would be delayed until Saturday and possibly into Sunday. With the anticipation of the snow and Christmas, it was difficult to concentrate in school, but fortunately, it worked the same for the teachers as the students. We watched a movie in science about Albert Einstein and his theory of relativity, which had nothing to do with our curriculum subject matter, but it served as a welcome diversion during the school day morning. In English we studied Robert Frost and Walt Whitman with the fervor that we would all someday become poets. But the highlight of the school day came in gym, where I scored our team's winning goal in crab soccer, a game where we all crawled on our hands and feet in an upright fashion and kicked a five foot diameter ball around the gym to see who could get it over the other team's goal line the most times.

Once the school day ended, I was anxious to get outside and wait on the weather. Zack and I walked together to our corners, talking of the impending snowstorm and whether or not it still would come. My mom had made me bring my boots to school in a bag, and I was bringing them home the same way. Zack, on the other hand, seemingly wore his work boots to bed, so he was already prepared. The air walking home from school was crisp, but calm. The clouds overhead were dense and grey and we couldn't help but feel that a storm was definitely on the way.

Arriving at the station, there was a large thank-you note posted on the garage bulletin board, thanking us all for being special workmates over the past months or years, and reminding us that starting tomorrow the station would be moving to 28 East Greenbriar Avenue. Betty McGuillan was sitting on the station table, talking to Conrad Stipp and Donald Elfrith, and I wondered if she was happy to see the station and all the boisterous boys leave her garage for the last time, or if she was really sad to see them go. I packed up my stuff, said goodbye to Betty, and started for my route. I collected from all but four of my houses and got Christmas cards from five of the homes, with Christmas gifts totaling $16. I decided to keep the Christmas money separate from my regular paper money, and stashed it in one of the cards from Mrs. Boyd. Collecting during the past couple of weeks seemed a bit more pleasant than usual because of the glow of the houses with their Christmas lights. Everyone genuinely seemed to be a little bit happier when they answered their doors, even the teenagers who usually seemed annoyed when I collected.

Passing St. Mark's, I decided to stop by to see if Zack was in the parish hall. Tonight at 7:30 we were having a dress rehearsal for the play which was now only two nights away. As expected, Zack was inside, tinkering with his spotlight and the two lights he had placed behind the inn and the manger. His painting of the scenery had come out quite good, but he still had to affix the foil star to a string and tie it up to the ceiling of the stage. He asked if I could stay a few minutes to help, so I took off my jacket and helped him put the ladder in place. We both agreed that tying the string to the star would look awkward, and we decided the best thing was to affix the string to the back of the star with duct tape, running the string from the middle of the star to its pointed top. Then the duct tape and string could be covered with foil to hide all their traces. With the string attached, all that was left was to tie the string around a stage rafter, which proved to be a bit more difficult than we had anticipated. We finally resorted to tying one of my sneakers to the string so that we could throw it over the curtain beam that ran across the stage. As per Murphy's Law, my sneaker got snarled in the string and would not slide downward, so we had to get the long candle snifters from the stage altar for assistance. With his prodding and my directing, Zack managed to hit my shoe and pull it down low enough that it was reachable. By cutting my shoe loose, it was now possible for us to secure the string by tying a slip knot in it and pulling both sides until the knot worked its way up to the top of the ceiling. We then retied the string to itself just above the star and cut off the excess. In the end, the job was successful, and the star looked great, but we knew that we would have a difficult time later cutting the string down from the rafter.

Finishing with the star, I looked at my watch and the time was already past 5:30, leaving me a little less than a half hour to get back to the station to pay my last paper bill to Mrs. McGuillan. I swiftly put on my missing sneaker and coat and headed for the station, telling Zack I would see him later that night for the dress rehearsal. As I started for the station, I could see flakes starting to fall, glistening in the air near the streetlights and the colored house decorations. I arrived at the station about 5:40 and climbed up the McGuillans' back kitchen doorsteps. Looking inside I could see Dave Parker inside paying his bill.

"Good grief," I thought. "I must be really late because everyone knows Dave Parker is always the last to do anything."

Mrs. McGuillan saw me at the door and motioned me to come inside out of the cold. I opened the door to a rush of warm air and the smell of the McGuillans' chicken dinner. At the table was Mrs. McGuillan with her paperwork and her cashbox. To her right was Dave Parker, pulling out wads of dollar bills from random pockets of his coat, and placing them next to the pile of coins he had already pulled out of his pants pockets. Seated to Mrs. McGuillan's left was Deanna Kolakowski, who had come to learn the bill paying process and learn the identity of the various carriers with whom she would soon be dealing.

Deanna looked glowing, with her dark curly hair spilling out over her head in tender ringlets, and the trace of a silver hoop earring peeking out from under her left ear. She wore a blue turtleneck sweater and tight jeans which were tucked inside her boots. She was helping Dave arrange his coins into dollar stacks to make counting his money easier. When she saw me enter the kitchen, she looked up right away and smiled, and her brown eyes twinkled in the reflection from the kitchen light.

"Hi!" she said from behind the stacks of coins. "Always saving the best for last."

My cold body began to feel flush from her gracious greeting as well as the warmth of the kitchen, and I apologized to Mrs. McGuillan for being so late on her last night of work.

"No problem, Bill. Dave just got here himself," she chuckled. "I guess you already know your new station manager Deanna Kolakowski."

"Yes, I do," I answered. "We've met before. Hopefully she can continue to meet the high standards you set for the job."

Both Deanna and Mrs. McGuillan laughed and went back to their counting. As they did, I looked at each of them, contrasting how different they both were. Mrs. McGuillan's hair was short, straight, and white. Deanna's was long, curly, and brown. Deanna's skin looked soft and radiated warmth, and her eyes were always animated. Mrs. McGuillan's skin was like leather, wrinkled and cracked in places, the results of a hard life, numerous children, and countless drags on her cigarettes. What's more, behind her glasses, her eyes appeared swollen and lifeless. Finally, Mrs. McGuillan wore an old yellow T-shirt under a brown plaid unbuttoned flannel shirt that draped her thin body while she counted coins with her weathered fingers. Deanna wore a tight sweater that accentuated her shapely physique while she positioned the coins with small, dainty fingers with polished silver nails.

"Let's see that's 20... 25... 30... 31... 32... 33... 34... 35 dollars and 34 cents," said Mrs. McGuillan. "Thanks, Dave for your years of service. You're the quiet kid that eventually always got the job done."

"You're welcome, I think," answered Dave. "Thanks for your help over the years. I know you had to wait for me a few times and I appreciate you putting up with me."

"Good luck in the future, Dave," she answered back, and handed him a small chocolate Santa figure wrapped in cellophane. "I hope to see you again sometime."

Dave started for the door, and nodded his head at me as he passed. "You're going to rehearsal tonight right? Is that at 7:00 or 7:30?"

"I'm pretty sure it's 7:30," I replied. "I'll be there; as a matter of fact I was just there with Zack putting up the Christmas star!"

"What's all the rehearsing for?" asked Mrs. McGuillan.

"Oh, it's for our church Youth Group Christmas play," I replied. "We're having a dress rehearsal tonight. The show is on Sunday at 7:00."

"Bill's the star of the show," said Dave. "He's the lost sheep that finds Jesus in the manger."

I rolled my eyes, and Mrs. McGuillan remarked, "Well that's something everyone should see. I certainly hope it doesn't snow on your parade!"

Deanna looked at me again and wrinkled her nose, "Mr. Fantastic the manger sheep? Personally, I think you're more of the lamb type."

"No," I said. "I'm definitely not a lamb. The part specifically says black sheep."

"Oh, that it explains it," Deanna joked.

"Alright black sheep, let's get on with the money counting; I gotta get to the bank before the blizzard starts," said Mrs. McGuillan.

Dave left out the door, and I sat down at the table. I pulled out my money, which I had in a blue sack, and piled the coins in dollar stacks, then pulled out the bills. "There's 23 dollars and 94 cents," I said.

Mrs. McGuillan thanked me for the money and the time I spent with her on the job. Then she handed me the last chocolate Santa.

"Well that's that," smiled Mrs. McGuillan. "My last collection!"

She then explained to Deanna that she normally would take all the collected money to the bank and get a cashier's check for the total amount of all the routes combined. Mrs. Galinskie would usually stop by Saturday morning before 9:00 to pick it up. "The cashier's check will cost you 35 cents. You are welcome to come to the bank with me tonight, but I'm not going until after dinner, so if you want to come back in about another hour, you can go with me then."

"That's ok," Deanna replied. "I think I got it. Thanks for the help. Wish me luck; I'm sure I'll need it."

"You'll do fine," answered Mrs. McGuillan. "See you too, Bill. Good luck with the play."

Deanna put on her blue jacket and a pair of blue mittens with fur at the wrists.

"Is it snowing out there yet?"

"Yeah, it's flurrying a little." I replied. And she put on her ski hat and adjusted it so her hair hung out the back and front in the desired flip, and we started out the door together.

The flurries were definitely a bit heavier than before, but the snow had barely even begun to cover the grass. Besides the snowfall, the air was still and it didn't feel that cold. We walked down the driveway and to the sidewalk. I didn't have any gloves on, and I was holding the chocolate Santa in my hands, so I pushed the Santa and my hands into my coat pocket, making the cellophane wrapper crinkle.

"That was nice of Mrs. McGuillan to give everybody a chocolate Santa... that is, everybody except me," she joked.

"Well, I'd give you mine if I didn't like chocolate so much," I kidded.

She playfully punched my shoulder and continued, "and here I thought you were kind of nice."

We continued up the street, walking side by side, and she asked me more about the play.

"So are you set for the rehearsal... you know... all your lines and stuff?"

"Well I think I know most of my lines by heart, but there are some of the longer ones at the end of the play I still stumble around with. I figure if I have to I can write the long lines on my hand and I can read them from there," I conjectured. "But I guess that all depends on my costume, since I really don't know if I have hands or hoofs yet."

"Well, so what are you going to do for tonight's rehearsal?" she asked.

"Oh, that's easy, I've got the script right here in my pocket." I reached into my pants' back pocket and pulled out the play script. It was pretty well folded and crinkled since I had been carrying it around for the past two weeks. "The lines highlighted with yellow are mine."

She took the script from my hands and began to look at it, first flipping through the pages to get a sense of its length, and then actually reading some of the lines. We reached the corner, and stopped. Going to the left went to her house, and going to the right went to the church. I knew which way I wanted to go, but I also knew I had a responsibility to the guys in the play.

"Did you want to take a quick look at the new paper station?" Deanna asked. "We could practice some of your lines while we walked over."

"Sure," I said, grateful that she had made my decision. "It's only 6:25, and I could really use the practice before the rehearsal."

The walk over to her house took no time. Her house was on the corner of Greenbriar and Johnson Avenues, while the garage which was completely on Johnson. The garage was in better shape than the McGuillans'. It was a single car garage with a roll up door. The driveway was paved with concrete and was only about thirty feet long and pretty much level with the street. Above the roll up door was a basketball backboard and rim. Since it looked like a relatively new net, I figured someone had been playing basketball there recently, although there were no signs of broken or missing windows. Deanna pulled up the garage door and we walked inside.

"Well here it is," she said, turning on the light switch. "The new *paperboy playpen* as Kathy Milano calls it."

I looked around and noted it was remarkably clean, and relatively empty. Unlike the garage at home, at Zack's, the Flahertys', or even the McGuillans', it wasn't filled with old paintbrushes, or stacks of lumber, ladders, car parts, or broken lawn mowers and bicycles. I saw one spade and a snow shovel on one wall, a lawn mower in the back to one side, and a rolled up hose hanging above it. In the front right corner was a trash can and broom, and in the front left corner was a narrow table with a bulletin board hanging above it – similar to the one at the old paper station. Next to the table, at about the middle of the side wall was a window that looked over to the back steps of the house. And at the back of the garage, just beyond the window was a door that opened to a path that led to the back of the house.

"Well, what do you think?" Deanna asked proudly. "The Milanos gave me the table and the bulletin board from their basement. Kathy and I carried them both over here all by ourselves."

"It's great," I remarked. "I don't think I ever saw a garage so clean and uncluttered. Heck, you can even park a car in here."

"Well my dad doesn't really do a lot of handy work," Deanna said, taking off her hat and laying it on the table. "And he does park his car in here, but you don't have to worry about getting run over tonight because he's working at my grandpa's in Philly. He usually works with him during busy times and over the weekends."

"What does he do?" I asked.

"Normally he works at the University of Pennsylvania, but during busy times he helps my grandfather at his bake shop. But hey, it's getting late and you gotta get going soon to the rehearsal, so let's practice those lines." And with that she pulled down the garage door, and hopped up and sat on the table with the script in her hands.

She began to read aloud, *"Say look above at the star; it grows brighter every second and is causing the sheep to become frightened and crowd together. That is, all the sheep except Blacky, who seems to be* roaming towards the star. I need to tell the other shepherds to keep watch of the flock while I chase after him."

I grinned and recited my line. *"But Shep, there is nothing to fear. The star is a sign of great things to come. An Angel from Heaven has said that a new King is to be borne tonight. Come with me and follow the star so that we may find him."*

She looked down and read Shep's next line, *"But I must stay with the flock to protect them from harm. I cannot leave with you."*

I continued, *"This is a special night. No harm will come to anyone on this most holy of nights. I must go."*

She flipped through some pages. "So what do you say to the hungry wolf?" she asked.

"Well first I say, *"Mr. Wolf, why do you follow me on this most sacred night? Are you traveling with me to see the birth of God's son, or are you following me because I would make a delicious meal?"* Then later I say, *"Well then let me continue my journey, and I will return later for you to dine on."*

"This is kind of lame," she said.

"Yeah, but remember it's really for the little kids. Plus, my acting will be a lot better when I'm in costume," I replied, as I hopped up on the table and sat next to her.

She continued to flip through the pages, and we covered the lines to the sheep dog, the angel, the donkey, and the inn-keepers. I whizzed through them all without a problem.

"Who are you kidding," she said. "You got this down cold." Then she looked over at me with her sparkling eyes and snickered, "Hey, you're not peeking are you?"

Just to make sure she then hopped off the table, and turned her back to me, pretending to hide the script from my view. Then flipping to the end of the story she read Shep's last lines, *"I'm so happy you are here Blacky. When I returned to look for you I thought you were eaten by the wolf, but you are safe. How could you have made such a long journey alone?"*

I sat back to concentrate. These last lines were part of the big ending, and it was the part I always got mixed up on.

I began, *"When first I saw the star, an Angel appeared and said not to be afraid. So I ..."*

I stopped in mid-sentence. Deanna looked down at the script to help me out.

"So I took off," she hinted.

"So I took off through the woods. First I saw the wolf who wanted a meal, but he was impressed by my bravery, so he let me go. Then I saw the donkey..."

I stopped again, confused with the lines. Deanna, still with her back to me read again, and gently leaned up against my legs that were hanging over the side of the table.

"Then I saw the dog..." she said.

Her backside snuggled softly against my legs and the back of her head inched in front of me, and I could smell the fragrance of her hair wisp faintly past my nose.

"Then I saw the dog," I continued, *"and he said it was dangerous for me to be out at night and that I should continue my search tomorrow, but I carried on getting lost only once. Then the star..."*

"the Angel reappeared and said to follow," she whispered.

I leaned forward and put my nose up to her hair. She didn't move away and continued to cuddle back against my legs and my chin. I whispered back, *"... to follow the straight and narrow path to the donkey who told me of the wondrous tale of carrying Mary and the Baby to the manger. Then seeing the star above the manger, I entered to find God's gift to the world – his only Son our Savior!"*

Deanna finished with the last line which was to be spoken by Shep. *"Oh, my little sheep, I thought you were lost and confused, but I was wrong. I should have followed you. This truly is a wondrous night!"*

The lines were over, and we both remained motionless, silently enjoying the moment. I swear I wanted to stay there forever. But the quiet was interrupted by the sound of the house back door opening and Deanna's mother sweeping the snow from the back steps.

I looked at my watch. It was 7:15. Deanna turned around and whispered, "That was fun."

I thanked her for her help with the lines, and we opened the garage door together. The snow had begun to accumulate on the grass, the sidewalk, and the street. Its intensity had stepped up quite a bit and looking up at the streetlight, there seemed to be no end in sight.

"I'll see you tomorrow, on your big first day!" I said as I left.

"I'm looking forward to it," she responded. "Hopefully we all don't get snowed in. Good luck with the rehearsal!"

The rehearsal went fairly well, and I knew my lines better than anyone else. The scenery looked great and Zack worked his usual magic with the spotlight. The costumes were still not completed, and Terry Manual and Linda Ott told me to bring two pair of black socks, a black sweatshirt, and black sweatpants. They would supply the rest Sunday night. There was a lot of talk about the snow, but Pastor Heft reassured us that if Blacky could find his way to the manger, then people would find their way to the church for the play regardless of the weather. When we left the church, it was still snowing hard, with about four inches already accumulated in the street. The weather forecast called for the storm to continue through Sunday, and when I woke up Saturday morning it was still snowing and there were at least eight inches on the ground.

My brother, father, and I went out early Saturday morning to shovel our sidewalk and our driveway, but by the time we finished, you could barely tell where we had started. The snow continued to fall at its steady pace, without letting up once. I was concerned about Deanna and decided to leave early at about 2:00 to see if I could help her. My mom made me bundle up more than usual and wear my boots, even though they were still wet from the morning. I grabbed my paper bag and a plastic bag to keep my papers dry, and I trudged off to 28 East Greenbriar through the snow. At the station, Deanna and her mother were outside shoveling, and I dropped off my paper bag in the garage and asked if I could help. Deanna asked her mother for her shovel, and together Deanna and I shoveled her entire driveway and the sidewalk around the whole house. Deanna seemed to be a workhorse, and despite her small size, she easily kept pace with my shoveling. By 3:00 we had finished clearing the snow, and some of the boys had arrived to pick up their papers, but the truck had yet to get there. Alvin Morrison and Shelly remarked that they had both heard we were due for twenty plus inches of snow, and no one disagreed with the prospects of such a forecast.

When the truck appeared at 3:30, the driver apologized, blaming a shortage of printing employees at the paper for his delay. Alvin and I helped Deanna open the bundles and count out the papers, making sure to keep the stacks near the back of the garage so they didn't get wet from the snow. The bundles were extremely thin at sixty to a bundle, and our thinking was that this was more likely the result of a lean printing day than a slow news day. Deanna thanked me profusely for my help, and by 4:00 I set out to deliver in the snow. I was lucky enough to hand papers to at least half my customers who were shoveling their walks. I placed the papers of the others inside their doors to keep them dry. I walked the paper trail to the houses in Smythville, wondering if anyone would notice my footprints through the fenced area. At Smythville the houses seemed empty, and the snow covered sections of the dam and the ice near it made for a memorable winter's image.

When I got home, it felt good to take off my heavy wet boots and change into dry clothes. The weather completed the transformation of our house to the Christmas season. My mom even baked cookies while we decorated the tree that my father had put up while I was serving my route. Everybody was home, including my brother and sister, and instead of watching TV that night or going out, we all sat together by the fireplace and listened to my father's Christmas albums by Nat King Cole, Frank Sinatra, and Glen Campbell. Other than the light from the tree and the fireplace, the room was dim, and out the back door you could still see the snow come down. By 8:30 I felt tired and I laid down on the couch closest to the fireplace and curled my legs up under the afghan, taking in the warmth from the fire, the sounds of the season, and the pleasant memories from the night before.

Chapter 21 – The Christmas Pageant

The night of the Christmas Play was a huge success. The snow stopped coming down about 4:30 and unofficially we received about sixteen inches. The Youth Group was to meet at the church at 5:00 so that we would all be ready and dressed in time for the 7:00 start of the Christmas pageant. My father walked over to the church with me. He was staying for the show, but he also said he was going to help some of the men shovel the sidewalks around the church and spread down some salt so nobody would fall. Theresa Manual and Linda Ott finally finished everybody's costumes. My costume and the wolves were best. Mark Crenowski, who played the wolf, wore a brown sweatshirt, brown corduroy pants, and brown socks on his feet and hands, along with a large brown snout and tail that Linda had made out of fabric and stuffed with cotton. My costume consisted of black sweatpants and black sweatshirt, with black socks on my feet and hands, along with a little black tail with a red bow on the end that they pinned to my sweatpants. Linda had taken a large mop head and dyed it black and sewed it onto a black ski cap, which I was to wear on my head to take on a fuzzy sheep appearance. Zack said I looked more like Bob Marley than a sheep. Theresa then took a burnt cork, and drew a large black triangle over my nose to complete the masquerade. To this I added the cheat sheet of my last line, which I wrote on paper in small letters and cut out into a circle and taped to the sock covering the inside of my hand. I then added a second blank circle to my other hand, so it would look like the white papers were supposed to represent the pads of my paws.

Despite the snow, the parish hall was packed with people for the pageant, and the program started right on time. Following three songs each by the cherub and children's choirs, the play began. The kids and adults all seemed to get a big kick out of our costumes and acting. I even ad-libbed a few baaaas into my lines to make me seem a bit more like a sheep, which got a few laughs. I miscalculated the brightness of Zack's spotlight, however, which really made it difficult to see anything in the dark room, including my hands. Luckily I remembered my lines, because when I looked down at my cheat sheet, the combination of the light in my eyes and the darkness of my hands made it virtually impossible to read. When the play was over, there was a lot of applause from the audience, and Pastor Heft gave Lisa Parker a small Christmas bouquet of flowers.

It felt good when the play was over, not that I ever really felt a lot of stress, but it was one less thing to be concerned about before the holidays. As usual, Mr. and Mrs. Strekis served everybody a Breyer's Dixie cup of half chocolate and half vanilla ice cream. Everybody also got a pretzel rod. For some reason, eating from the Dixie cup always made the ice cream taste a little bit better. Maybe it was due to the combination of the pretzel with the ice cream, or maybe it was because we got to eat the ice cream with those little flat wooden spoons.

As I sat on the stage, still in costume and eating my ice cream and pretzel, I saw Deanna Kolakowski, coming towards me with a large grin on her face. She was dressed in a red V-neck sweater, over a white buttoned shirt, with black pants and boots. A short gold necklace hugged her neck. She seemed extra happy to see me and raved that I was clearly the star of the show. I introduced her to several of my friends in the Youth Group, and she immediately fit right in, talking to Zack about the scenery, Linda and Theresa about the costumes, and Lisa about the play. I got Deanna a Dixie Cup and pretzel, but they were out of spoons, and she said it was ok and that she could use mine. Some of the kids said they were going over to Theresa's after we left church, and I asked her if she would like to go. She said maybe, so I left her with Zack for a few minutes while I went into a back room to change out of my sheep costume.

Deanna got her coat, scarf and gloves. I picked up my coat as well, which really consisted of a zip up sweatshirt with hood, over which I wore a maroon Harvard snap up jacket that my father had acquired from someone at work. My mother hated the jacket, saying it was ugly and provided no warmth, but I had taken a liking to it. We started for the door, where a small line formed to pick up a departing treat which consisted of a small box of silver, red, and green foiled Hershey kisses. Coincidently, the boxes were being handed out by none other than my father. When our turn in line came, I introduced him and Deanna to each other.

"Hey Dad," I said. "This is my friend Deanna. She now runs the station where I pick up my papers."

"Well I'm really pleased to meet you Deanna," my dad replied. "That's a pretty important job you have. It's really great that you could make it to the play. I think old Blacky here did a real nice job in the show tonight."

"Oh I agree, sir. He did a great job! I especially liked the shaggy mop top."

My dad laughed and pulled out two boxes of Hershey kisses and handed one to each of us. "Don't leave without your Christmas treat," he said.

"Thanks, Dad, I think we're going over to Theresa Manual's house. She is having a get together for the people in the play."

"Sure, have a great time," my dad said. "Be careful walking on the streets, though; they're still pretty slick."

With that we walked out the door and outside into the winter wonderland. The snow on the pavement leading from the parish hall had been cleared pretty well, and at least there the footing was not slippery. In the rush to get changed from my costume and leave the church, I had forgotten my gloves in the back room, but it didn't seem to matter. The weather outside had become calm and it didn't feel cold at all. The storm had completely cleared, and the sky was cloudless and partially illuminated by a waning crescent moon. We continued on, following the others exiting the church property. The plows had given the street a once-through, which pushed the snow on both sides of the street several feet high. Since most people on the block had yet to complete shoveling their sidewalks, it was easier to walk in the plowed portion of the street. We turned from the church and traveled down Haddon Avenue, with no real destination decided. While we were walking in the snow, it seemed unusually quiet outside. The drifts of snow on the rooftops of the houses, combined with the illumination of their Christmas lights, made for a festive scene.

"Your father seems real nice," Deanna said. "And his eyes are a deep shade of blue, just like yours."

"Really," I remarked. "My father, brother, sister, and I all have blue eyes. Only my mom has brown eyes."

"Oh, so you only have just one brother and sister?" she asked.

"Yeah, we're all five years apart. I'm 12, my brother's 17, and my sister's 22."

"You're only 12? I got you beat. I turned 13 in October," she said.

"I'll be 13 in February. So how about your family? Do you have any brothers and sisters?"

"Just one brother named Joe who is 19, but he moved out of the house a year ago."

"Did he leave for college?" I asked.

"No, he just couldn't take any more of my parents. My father is very set in his ways, and my mother makes a big deal about everything. Both my parents are deaf and dumb you know."

"I'm sorry to hear that. How did it happen?" I asked.

"Nothing tragic or anything, they were just both born that way. They met each other at a school for the deaf in Philadelphia."

"So how did you learn to talk?"

"I don't know," she replied. "How did you learn to talk?"

"Well, you speak very well," I said. "Did you go to a special school?"

"No, my nana, who was my mother's mom, lived with us up until I was eight. She sort of helped raise my brother and me. After she died, things became more difficult around the house. My father's not home much, and when he is, he is very restrictive, and this used to drive my brother crazy. So as soon as he turned 18 and graduated from high school he got a job and moved to get away from him. Since then, things have changed a lot around the house. Sometimes it's very quiet, and I feel so alone."

We had walked down Haddon to Johnson Avenue and turned onto Clinton Avenue walking towards the creek. Theresa Manual's house was up on the left, and I asked Deanna if she had decided if she wanted to go in or not.

"Well, if you would like to we can," she said. But if it's just up to me, I kinda would prefer just to be with you tonight. It's so gorgeous outside. I would be happy just to keep walking and getting to know you better. I can stay out tonight until 10:30 before I get yelled at. I told my mother I was going over to Kathy Milano's to help her with a school project."

"Sounds good to me," I replied. So we walked past the Manual's house, and continued down Clinton Avenue, turning right onto Coldspring.

"I didn't do this on purpose," I said. "But this is part of my paper route here. I serve mostly on Haddon Avenue, Coldspring Avenue, and the dead end on Collin's. And I also have four houses over near the mill in Smythville."

"Smythville?" she remarked. "I went there a few times with my brother to go fishing. Isn't that quite a long hike from here?"

"Not really," I answered. "But that's because I know a shortcut."

Not really knowing why, we walked down Coldsping to Collins, and to the dead end and the steps down to the creek.

"Do you want to see something neat?" I asked. "But you have to promise not to tell my secret."

"Sure," she said, and she held her right arm up and then made a crisscross motion over her chest.

We headed down the steps, towards the creek. Once down the steps, it seemed the snow wasn't quite as deep. Maybe it was due to the trees, or maybe a lot of the snow had blown onto the creek. In either case, the view of the creek in the moonlight with the snow was stunning. Nearly all of the lake and a large part of the creek was covered with snow that had fallen on the surface ice. The area where the water flowed fastest was not frozen. In the dark, against the white backdrop of the snow, the running water looked black like oil. The moonlight reflected off this black water, and it glistened as it bubbled onward. We continued walking until we reached the gate, and I told Deanna to shut her eyes, make a wish, and say a magic word.

"Abracadabra," she said, as I quickly pulled the key from my pocket and unlocked and opened the gate.

"Hey, how did you do that," she asked.

"A good magician never reveals his tricks," I responded.

I pushed the gate open, which was more difficult than usual because of the snow, and we walked in. The factory, which looked so old and abandoned in the daylight, now looked renewed and clean in the snow and the moonlight. We continued over near the dam, and stopped before its rushing waters. A large four foot chunk of ice had accumulated on the dam's concrete weir, and despite the rushing water, the ice slab remained unmelted and protruding about $2^1/_2$ feet over the edge.

"There's something you don't see every day," I remarked.

"The way the moon shines over the water kind of gives everything a greyish hue," Deanna said, "Sort of like in those old black and white movies."

Turning around I told her to look over the fence and up the hill at the houses.

"See the house with the lights up around the door," I said. "That's one of my customers named Mrs. Mac Mullin. I put up the lights for her."

The houses were barely visible up on the hill because of the poor illumination provided by the streetlight in the distance, but the colored Christmas lights were easy to see as they reflected against the snow covering the house roof and porch.

"It's amazing how such a small string of lights can light up the whole house." Deanna said.

Then I told Deanna a shortened version of the history of the mill and the story of H.B. Smyth. She had never heard the story before.

"Do you really think that Mrs. MacMullin is the daughter of H.B. Smyth?" she asked.

"Well, that would put her in her late 80's," I reasoned, "and that seems about right."

We both turned back to look at the water running over the dam. The slab of ice was still trapped on the edge despite the rush of flowing water. It seemed odd to me that the water from the creek had once provided the power for two factories, helping to spur on the industrial revolution, and bring together a girl in her teens and a man nearly twice her age. Now nearly one hundred years later, its force was not sufficient to push a four foot slab of ice over the dam's weir. Still looking at the ice, I bent down and picked up a wad of snow into my bare hands and fashioned it into a ball. Then taking my best aim, I threw the snowball at the chunk of ice, narrowly hitting its edge, but barely causing it to waver. I wiped my cold, wet hands on my pants as I watched Deanna attempt to equal my throw. Pulling off her gloves and putting them in her pocket, she took some snow and made a ball, throwing it in the general area of the ice, but missing it by a wide margin, which resulted in a small splash of water in the vicinity. Suddenly with a turning motion, the ice began to move and slide further over the weir, until its weight caused it to crash down into the water below. Deanna wiped her hands on her pants, and took a half step closer to my side. Then while we were both looking at the rushing water, she softly slipped her bare hand into mine, and intertwined our fingers together. Just the feel of her bare hand seemed to speak louder than words, and I believe at least for a moment that our hearts became one. We must have stood there silently, watching the moonlit flowing water for five minutes, captivated by its beauty and by our thoughts of each other.

Warmed by our entwined hands, we stood frozen in time, neither one of us wanting the moment to end. Then through the corner of my eye I noticed the lights around Mrs. MacMullin's door had gone out.

"Did you see that?" I whispered. "The Christmas lights up on the house just went out. I guess old Mrs. McMullin has gone to bed." I looked down at my watch. "Yep, 10:00 on the dial."

"Oh, jeez," Deanna whimpered. "As much as I hate to, we better be going. I told my mother I'd be home by 10:30."

So we started on our way back, the same way we had come. I hadn't relocked the gate when we had entered, so as we left, I took the lock and pushing it shut, locked the gate until my next passage. Then we walked along the creek to the steps, and climbed back into our individual lives. Together we walked slowly up Collins, both talking of Christmas which was now only six days away. When we got to the corner of Collins and Johnson, where we had stood only two nights earlier, we looked over a block to Deanna's house and could see her father busy re-shoveling the sidewalk and driveway. Deanna cautioned that she felt, at least for tonight, that we should say goodnight here, so her father would not know we had been out together. So we crossed to the other side of Johnson Avenue, where we stood together, partially hidden from view by the trunk of a large buttonwood tree.

"Thank you for the most wonderful night," she said as she retook my hand into hers. "I really had a fantastic time."

"Me too," I replied. Then she quickly inched closer and gave me a quick kiss on the cheek.

"I'll be thinking about you all night and until I see you again," she said, than she started off for home.

I stayed behind the tree and watched as she made way her back to her house. When her father turned his back to shovel in the opposite direction, she made a quick dash up the front steps and through the front door. She was definitely clever; her father hadn't even noticed her enter the house. Now alone, I looked down at my watch.

"She just made it," I thought. It was exactly 10:30.

Chapter 22 – O' Holy Night

Monday morning I awoke at 6:50 to the sound of my mother and brother talking. Our house had only three bedrooms, one for my mom and dad, one for my sister, and one for me and my brother. My brother was insisting that his sources had told him that we would not be having school because of the snow. My mother knew better than to trust my brother's sources. In our town, everybody lived within walking distance to the school, so there was no busing. What's more, our school superintendent, Mr. Thompson, hated giving snow days. On snowy days Mr. Thompson would get up early and walk to the school, and if he didn't slip or get stuck, he would rationalize a school opening. He really didn't care about the teachers. They got paid to get to school on time, and if their commute was to be delayed by the weather, he was known to say, they should just leave the house a bit earlier.

Those were the days before the Internet, cable TV, and phone trees. The town had an easy way of telling everyone if school was cancelled due to snow. If the fire siren that sat atop the Borough Hall went off at 7:00 and 7:30, then school was cancelled. That included all schools - Elementary, Junior High, High School, or Catholic. By 6:58, I was wide awake, and my mother, brother, and I all sat on the bed listening for the telltale pulsing sound. The clock next to the bed ticked to 7:00, but there was no sound. My brother said maybe our clock was fast, but when we had still hadn't heard anything at 7:05, my mom patted us both on the head and said, "Time to get up."

We both reluctantly got out of bed, me immediately taking off my pajamas and getting dressed, while my brother opted for a quick shower first. By 7:30, we were both downstairs at the breakfast table, hoping for a reprieve from the 7:30 siren. Again, there was nothing. My brother chomped down his peanut butter toast, then immediately left for high school. Even on the way out the door, he was complaining about the crummy schools not being closed due to the snow. I didn't really see it being such a big deal. We already were scheduled to have off this coming Friday since it was Christmas Eve, plus the whole next week. Five minutes later, I was done with my breakfast, and I went to put on my boots.

On our front porch each winter, my father put up a small 3 foot by 6 foot room that we called the enclosure. The room consisted of four sections that attached to the porch floor and ceiling. Each of the sections was solid wood at the bottom, and windowed at the top. The two side sections jutted out perpendicular to the front of the house. The front two sections then connected to the sides at right angles and ran parallel to the front of the house. One of these front sections also contained a door. The small enclosure provided a small, unheated room which you entered prior to entering our living room. Its purpose was to prevent a gust of cold air from entering the house every time the front door was opened, providing a windbreak on the other side of the door. We used to sit on the front doorstep as kids and pull off our snow covered boots in the enclosure before entering the house. Being young, we usually left our boots in the enclosure overnight, which didn't do much for warming them up or drying them out in the cold enclosure air. Last night, of course, had been no exception, and when I picked up my boots, they were still wet and partially covered with snow. My mother yelled at me for not bringing the boots inside and placing them in the kitchen next to a register to dry. So she brought me an extra pair of socks and my sneakers in a bag to carry to school to change into once I got there. While she got the socks and sneakers, I struggled with the boot laces, which were wet and cold, and still had chunks of frozen ice and snow embedded in them.

Armed with my books and bag, I headed for my safety corner. Most of the sidewalks were now shoveled, but on the ones that weren't, the snow was now crunchy as opposed to powdery. Following safety duty, I waited for Zack, and we walked to school and talked about last night's play. Zack concluded that it had gone pretty well and he wondered how we would be able to untie the star. He said he noticed that I didn't stop over at Theresa Manual's house after the play, but figured I had better things to do.

"We really didn't do much at Theresa's house anyway," he said. "They had some good snacks, but mostly everybody was concerned about the snow and didn't stay too long. Everybody had a good word to say about your friend Deanna. She seemed cute, and all the guys agreed she's a keeper. The girls said you should have her join us regularly at Youth Group if she's interested."

We continued to walk on to school, and I shuffled my books and the bag with the shoes between hands. The morning wind had whipped up a bit and my exposed hand kept getting cold and cramped from carrying the books and the bag.

"Didn't you wear any gloves?" Zack asked.

"No, I left them at church last night after the play," I answered. "Funny that it didn't seem quite as cold and windy last night."

Zack took off his glove and reached into his pocket, pulling out his ring of keys. He removed a brass one from his key ring and gave it to me. "Here," he said. "This is the key to the parish hall door; stop in after school and get your gloves, but remember to give me the key back, it's the only one I have and I have to return it to Pastor Heft."

I took the key and put it on my key ring with the pocketknife. There were now three keys on its chain. "Thanks, Zack. I promise to give it right back after I pick up my gloves."

School went by quickly, and on the way home I looked hard and long at the line of Catholic kids as they paraded out of school and along the Pike before crossing. I didn't see Deanna, but I did see Kathy Milano and got a brief glimpse of one of the Dobalo brothers, although I wasn't sure which one it was.

When I got to the paper station, the papers were already out, and I waited a few minutes to see if Deanna would appear but she didn't. Serving papers went fine despite the extra block of walking, and I was surprised to notice when I reached the Smythville houses, that the street was cleanly plowed and the sidewalks and porches for all the houses were neatly shoveled. Having some extra time after delivering, I decided I better get started on my Christmas shopping, since I had yet to buy anything for anybody in my family. There was a limited selection of stores along the Pike to shop, but they would have to do. I walked down four blocks to the Save More Pharmacy, which sold this stuff my sister liked called Jean Naté Friction Pour Le Bain, which was some kind of after-bath lotion or perfume oil. In the same aisle, on the men's side, I picked up a bottle of cologne called English Leather for my brother. In another aisle of the store they had an assortment of gloves, and although I had no intention of spending my money to buy myself a new pair, I went over to look at them. Seeing a large assortment for women, and recalling that just the day before I had heard my mother complaining how she could never find her gloves, I decided that might make a good Christmas gift for her. After looking through the selection, I decided on a black leather pair of women's gloves in a size medium, although the size differential between the large and small sizes seemed virtually indistinguishable to me.

That left only my dad. As I walked past Millar's bike and hobby shop, I glanced in the window to look at the new car models, staring predominantly at one called the Hot Heap, which was an old Ford Model T Roadster with exposed engine. The kit was obviously taking advantage of the popularity of a similarly named Hot Wheels car that we still couldn't find in local stores. After a few minutes of browsing, I decided to look in the store, and once inside, I noticed some White Ace Stamp mounts that they sold in various sizes that I knew my father would like. My dad collected stamps, and the White Ace Stamp mounts allowed a collector to place a mint stamp inside the mount, then into his collection books. Unlike hinged mounts, this type of mount prevented damage to the gummed back portion of the stamp, protecting the front of the stamp while on display. The mounts seemed overpriced, but I had the money, so I bought him three sets, each which could be cut and used for stamps of different sizes. On the way to the counter, I checked out the Schwinn ten-speed models, like the Varsity, the Continental, the Super-Sport, the Sports Tourer, and the Paramount. Their prices ranged from about $90 to $350, and I carefully inspected the differences between each. At the counter was Billy Proudst, who I had seen before and had heard my brother talk about. I asked him about the different models of ten-speeds, and he seemed to think the Super-Sport model was the best value for the money. I paid for the stamp mounts, and picked up a free brochure that was on the counter explaining all the Schwinn bicycle models. I felt good about all my purchases. I had spent roughly $15 and completed all my required Christmas shopping.

As I walked up the Pike towards home, I began thinking of Deanna and the night before. As I passed by Utches Candy shop, I decided to stop and take a look around. Mr. Utches owned a boat marina down the shore near Cape May. His candy store was closed most of the summer, but around Christmas time his store was filled with freshly made candies and chocolate. In the back, beyond the candy counter, he also sold greeting cards and other types of knick-knacks. I looked at the solid chocolate figures on sale, remembering how Deanna had commented that she didn't get a chocolate Santa from Mrs. McGuillan. Sure enough, I saw the exact Santas on sale, wrapped in cellophane and tied at the top with a ribbon. I was about to purchase a Santa when I noticed a similar sized chocolate sheep for sale. I decided this would be an even better gift, so I picked it up from the counter and began looking at the cards. I saw one card I liked with a cartoonish picture of the Manger scene, complete with animals, that said "I never realized there was a second Christmas star until I met you" and I picked it up for Deanna. I was also drawn to a second card showing a snowy winter scene at an old water mill. On the cover it said "Thinking of You at Christmas," and inside it said "Remembering Friends and the Spirit of the Season Reminds Us We Are Never Alone." I decided I wanted to get this for Mrs. MacMullin.

With the three additional purchases, I again started for home, only to again be interrupted, this time by the hardware store. Remembering Mrs. MacMullin's burnt out bulb, I stopped in to buy a replacement. Once inside and looking at the Christmas gear, I also saw a gold colored glass star for a treetop. It only cost 75 cents, so I picked it up along with the six cent replacement bulb. By the counter, in the tools section, I also noted a set of heavyweight wire cutters for $3.79, and I decided to purchase these for Deanna, before she broke her hands cutting off the wire bands on the paper bundles in the station. The cutters she had were old and dull, and the new cutter was a practical gift that I really thought she would need.

Tuesday brought a cold drizzle of rain that lasted the whole day and compressed our sixteen inches of snow down to four inches and created a lot of slush in the streets. On the trip home from school and to the station, I pulled my hood up tight to keep the rain off my head. Entering the station I saw Deanna, sitting on the table and in a much happier and drier mood then me.

"Long time, no see, Blacky," she said. "I missed you yesterday."

I walked over to my papers, pulled down my hood, and wiped my brow. Then looking up at her I asked, "By missing me, do you mean you just weren't in the station when I was here, or do you mean you missed me because you really wanted to see me?"

She looked at me strangely for a second, then smirking, she picked up a rubber band off the table and shot it at me. As it whizzed past me she said, "Neither of the two and I just missed you again."

We both laughed, and then she whispered, "Actually I had to lay a bit low yesterday. I thought for sure we would have off because of the snow, so I just told my mom that I heard the fire siren at 7:00."

"Aren't you the sly one," I commented.

"Ah, I didn't really miss anything, and Kathy brought my homework from school anyway. Hey, speaking of St. Al's, I was hoping...err...wondering, if maybe you would like to come with me to church this Friday, you know, Christmas Eve. I'd really like to go, but my mom and dad don't like to go because they can't hear anything, and Kathy and her family are going away, and I really don't want to go alone."

"Sure I'll join you; with an invitation that good who could resist?" I replied. Then thinking about it a bit more, I said "But wait, my family and I always go to our church for the 11:00 Christmas service. In fact I think I have to be an acolyte. What time would we be going to your church?"

"Oh, we would be at the 7:30 to 8:30 service. My mother and father would never let me go any later than that alone. The way I figure it, I should finish getting everybody's paper money by 6:00 on Friday, which would give me time to get changed and go to the bank. I could meet you there about 7:00 and we could walk to the church together."

"It sounds like you got this all figured out, how can I possibly say no?" I answered. "But I have to check first with my mom to make sure I don't screw up something she has planned. You never know with moms."

"I hope you can make it; I have my fingers crossed." She said.

So I picked up my papers, pulled up my hood, and walked out into the drizzle, waving bye as I walked away outside.

"I'll miss youuuu!" she yelled out as I walked away.

Walking to the route I thought out the rest of the week. "There is no paper on Saturday because it's Christmas. Friday is Christmas Eve, but we have off all day from school, and people will be busy with church and all. I'm hoping for some more of those Christmas tips. Maybe I should collect Thursday and play it safe."

Wednesday brought more rain and the snow from the beginning of the week was nearly a distant memory, except for the large dirty piles that still remained in the corners of parking lots. I asked my mom if it would be ok if I went with a friend to St. Aloysius Church for the 7:30 service and she said that would be fine, but reminded me that I had to be an acolyte at our church at 11:00 for our midnight service.

"If you don't mind me asking," she said. "Is that the girl from your paper route you're going with? The one your father saw last Sunday?"

I answered, "Yes, her parents are deaf and don't usually go to church, and she doesn't want to go alone."

"I understand," my mom said, knowing from experience not to prod too deep into her children's budding romances. "Plus it can't do anybody any harm by going to church an extra time on Christmas Eve. You'll have to bring her around some time when you're ready. I'm sure she's great, and I can't wait to meet her."

Thursday morning the sun finally broke through the clouds and it stopped raining. We had sort of a half day at school, with a vocabulary and science test in the morning and a Christmas assembly in the afternoon to hear the band concert. Zack was one of the drummers and as far as I could tell he was clearly the best. Mr. Tamburino made the band kids dress nice for the performance and Zack looked a bit funny playing the drums while wearing a tie. After the band played, we had cookies and juice in the cafeteria, and then we went to our last period class, which for me was health with Mrs. Henry. After a short review of how to treat snakebites, she passed out a Christmas crossword puzzle that she had copied from *Boy's Life Magazine* to keep us busy.

It felt great once school was over and we set out for our safety corners, knowing Christmas was only a day away and we had off for the next week. I scurried off to serve, knowing I'd also be collecting today. I decided not to collect at Smythville - just the main route home - saving those houses and my gift for Mrs. Mac Mullin for Christmas Eve. Because there was no paper Saturday, theoretically we were told to only charge 65 cents for the week instead of our usual 75 cents, but nearly everybody told me to keep the change from the dollar, and nearly everybody gave me an extra dollar or two as a holiday gift. I collected from all but seven houses, and four of those were from Smythville. I was careful to keep the extra Christmas dollars in a separate pocket. Counting the money from the previous week, I had made 58 dollars, but if I included the extra money from the change for the 65 cents; I had made about 14 dollars more.

I woke up Friday early even though we didn't have school. The day wasn't going to get busy until the afternoon, but there were still things to do in the morning. I hadn't wrapped my presents yet, so I set out looking around the house for some wrapping paper, scissors, and tape. My mom was downstairs drinking a cup of coffee, and she had off from her job at the Borough Hall for the day. She said my dad had to work, but he promised he was only going to be there a half day and would be home early. I asked her where I could find stuff to wrap my presents, and she said she would get it for me, because she didn't want me snooping around upstairs. She went upstairs and came down with some red wrapping paper with Santa and his sleigh being pulled by reindeer, and I took the paper and wrapped my presents in the sunporch. Once I was done, I stacked them under the tree in the living room.

At my mother's urging, I got a shower right before lunch, and then made myself a peanut butter and jelly sandwich. I ate it while I looked at the Schwinn brochure that I had picked up Monday and compared the different ten-speed models. At 2:15 I got ready for my paper route, and by 2:30 I was at the station. I saw Deanna in her kitchen, collecting money from some of the carriers, and I decided I would go serve now and stop back to pay my weekly bill later.

I made my way to Smythville and collected from the houses on the street, arriving at Mrs. MacMullin's house last. I brought the card and gift for her, and I knocked at the door, anxious to see her reaction to her present. Answering the door, she asked me to come in while she got the collection money and a little something else for me for Christmas. She went into the dining room and came back with her purse and a small wrapped box. I told her that because there was no paper delivery on Christmas that the paper charge for the week was only 65 cents. She handed me a dollar and waited for the 35 cents change. She then handed me the present and asked if I would like to open it now. I said sure and tore off the paper and opened the box to reveal a gold money clip with the HBS initials on it. Opening the clip, there were three dollar bills inside. I told her I had never seen a more handsome money clip and I thanked her for her generosity.

I then pulled out the card and present I had for her and gave it to her, saying "Merry Christmas". Her hand began to shake as she opened first the card, and then the present. As she read the card silently to herself, she stopped briefly to wipe her moistened eyes with her handkerchief. Then she opened the present.

"The star - it's so lovely. You know, I think this may be the first present I've received in the past ten years." she exclaimed, clearing her throat as she spoke. "Oh, I'm so old and rickety. Do you think you could put it up on the tree for me?" she asked.

I took the star from the box and reached up to the top of the tree and placed the star on it. Then I put the lid on the empty box and put it under the tree, and stood back to view the star.

"Thanks ever so much." She said. "It reminds me of the one my late husband gave me almost sixty years ago."

I mentioned that I had something else and that it was small, then I took the bulb from my pocket, and I held it up for her to see. "It's for the string of lights on the door," I remarked. "I noticed one was out the other night when I put them up, and I wanted to fix it for you."

I open the door and removed the burnt-out bulb and screwed in the replacement. Then I tucked the burnt-out bulb in my jacket pocket. Once done, I plugged in the string of lights and all the bulbs lit up in their holiday splendor.

"You know," I said, "the other night I was down by the creek after it snowed, and I looked over to your house and I could see your door shining so brightly, it lit up the whole block. It was so beautiful seeing the lights as they reflected in the snow." I really wanted to tell her the story of Deanna and me at the creek, and how the river had seemed to bring us closer together but I didn't. Instead I thanked her for the money clip, and wished her a Merry Christmas.

"The same to you," she said, and then she leaned over and gave me a hug. "You've certainly made Christmas Eve the highlight of my holiday season!"

With that I bade her *adieu*, and left for the rest of the route. I stepped sprightly as I served, happy with myself and my good fortune. As I walked along, I took the money clip from my pocket and examined it and then the bills. The clip was spring loaded, and engraved inside with the words "*with love from Agnes, Christmas 1890,*" and although I wasn't certain, I was pretty sure it was made of real gold. The three dollar bills, were equally old with some of the printing in blue. Near the top were printed the words "Silver Certificate," and on either side of the portrait of George Washington were the words *This certifies that there is on deposit in the Treasury of the United States of America One Dollar in Silver to the bearer on demand.* I tucked the bills back into the money clip and pushed it back deep into my pocket. I then finished serving my route, collecting the last of my houses and amassing an additional eight dollars in Christmas tips, not counting the money from Mrs. MacMullin.

Completing my route, I headed back to the station to pay Deanna my bill. I climbed up her back steps and tapped at the door, and she yelled for me to come in. She was seated at the kitchen table, rolling quarters into paper wrappers when I entered. She was wearing a Snoopy Christmas t-shirt which showed out from under a pair of denim overalls. No matter what the outfit, she looked like a million dollars to me.

"Ah, my Christmas Eve date," she sighed. "I thought for a moment you were going to skip out on me."

I looked around the room, and realized the back room was actually a little dinette with a small four seat kitchen table. The actual kitchen with the stove and other appliances was in the adjacent room, which had the lights off. Looking at the clock on the wall, I said, "It's not even 5:00; our date's not until 7:00. I'm here on business."

"Oh yeah, that's right, business before pleasure," she replied.

"So boss, how is business?" I asked.

"Pretty good," she answered. "Just you, Kevin Leahy, Joey Gilmore, and Dave Parker, and I'm done."

I started to pull out my money, when she said, " there's somebody I want you to meet." Then she went into the other room and came back with her mother.

"Mother," she said. "This is the boy I told you about. His name is Bill. He's been helping me with the papers. Remember, he helped shovel the snow the other day. Isn't he cute?"

I felt my face grow a bit flush from her introduction. Her mother was about the same height as Deanna, but numerous pounds heavier. Her hair was dark and graying and she wore a pair of black rectangular glasses.

It's...nice...to...meet...you," her mother said. "Deanna... has... nothing ... but... good... things... to... say... about... you."

She smiled, and I said, "Thank you, I'm pleased to meet you."

"The...pleasure...is...mine," she replied.

Although she spoke very slowly and enunciated her words a bit hollow, I was surprised at how well she communicated with me despite her lack of hearing. I also noted that when Deanna spoke with her that her enunciation changed a bit, and she assisted her speaking with hand-signing.

"I'll...be...seeing...you...later," she said as she left the room.

"Well that's Irene, my mom" said Deanna. "Ready to dump me yet?"

"For her? Sure, she seems great," I replied.

"Yuck," Deanna replied.

Just then the phone rang in the kitchen and the whole room lit up. I was surprised for some reason that they had a phone, and even more surprised that when it rang that two lights that hung over it lit up with over 100 watts of brilliance. Deanna answered the phone, and by the sound of the conversation I guessed it was Kathy Milano.

"Yeah, I'm doing fine…only three more to go….yeah, he's here paying his paper bill right now…no we aren't meeting officially for church until 7:00 at the bank…yes...yesssss…I still gotta get ready…how about I call you later?"

There was a knock at the back door and it was Kevin Leahy. I opened the door to let him in, and Deanna hung up the phone.

"Here, let me finish paying you," I said, lining out my money to pay Deanna the amount owed on the ledger. "You still have a bit to finish up and I don't need to keep you. I'll see you promptly at 7:00 at the bank," I said.

"With bells on," she replied.

I opened the door and started out. Then I stopped and put my head back in the door. "It is the Bank of New Jersey, on the Pike at the corner of Haddon Avenue, right?" I asked.

"Yeah, yeah," she answered.

"See you," I said.

"Not if I see you first," she joked.

I got home at 5:20 and my mom told me she had made spaghetti with meatballs for dinner, but she had made me spaghetti with eggs which I preferred to tomato sauce. She told me to eat, and then get dressed for my date.

"And you better wear something nice!" she added.

I ate quickly, and then went upstairs to change. I opened my closet and stared for a while, wondering what I was supposed to wear. Finally I decided to go back downstairs and ask my mother.

"Put on a nice pair of church pants and a button shirt and a tie," she said.

"Ah, mom, a tie, you gotta be kidding!" I griped.

My sister came by laughing after hearing the commotion and she told me to come upstairs with her and she would help me. She went through my closet and my bureau drawers and we compromised on a pair of dark khaki pants, my brown shoes and socks, a tan button-down collar shirt, and a dark green crew neck sweater.

"And you better let me help you comb your hair," she said.

Dressed and with my hair combed, I came downstairs at 6:25 and walked into the kitchen, where my mother and father were cleaning up the dinner dishes. My mom acknowledged that I looked passable but she really would have preferred a tie.

"And you better not wear that crummy jacket and sweatshirt your father trash picked!" my mother declared. "Go get your good grey coat out of the dining room closet."

I went in the dining room and struggled a bit with the closet door. We all kept our best coats in the dining room closet, which we seldom wore. From years of being repainted, the closet door had swelled a bit in size, and since the door didn't get opened very much, it explained why it often got stuck shut. Seeing me struggle, my dad came over and pulled hard. The door sprang open, and I looked through the tightly packed jackets to find my good coat. Pulling it off the hanger, I put it on, only to find it was way too small. When I showed it to my mom, she asked why I always waited until the last moment to tell her these things.

"Then wear your brother's coat!" she said.

I pulled his coat out and tried it on. The coat was a little big, but at least it felt a lot better than mine, so I showed it to my mom.

"That looks fine," she said. "What time you leaving?"

"I figured about 6:50." I said. "We're not meeting until 7:00 at the bank."

"Well keep an eye on the time," my mom said. "Don't get sidetracked and keep that girl waiting."

At 6:45, I decided to leave for the bank. I put on my brother's coat, and buttoned it up and started out the door for the bank. The bank was only up at the end of my street, near where we usually crossed the Pike going to and from school, so I knew it well. There was a lot of activity in the bank parking lot, with many cars coming and going, and there was a long line of cars leading up to the drive through window. I went inside the bank and waited for Deanna in the lobby. There were two couches in the lobby positioned at a ninety degree angle to each other just to the right of the entrance, and that seemed as good of a place as any to sit and wait. I sat and watched as the clock hands hit 6:55 on the big Roman numerals, then as it tripped past 7:00, and 7:05.

"This is as painful as waiting for the fire siren for a snow day," I thought.

But at 7:07, the twin doors opened and in bounced Deanna. She had on a knee-length grey dress coat, with a black scarf and black heels. She was carrying a black pocketbook, and a tan sack which I presumed to be holding the paper route money, a considerable amount of which was in change. I got up as soon as I saw her enter, and she instantly saw me and walked over to greet me.

"Sorry to be late," she apologized, "but it took a bit longer than I thought for my nails to dry."

She handed me the sack, and she loosened her scarf and unbuttoned her coat a bit. Her hair was a bit more primped than normal, and she seemed to have on a small amount of makeup which made her look slightly older and a bit more mature. As usual, she looked absolutely lovely to me.

"Well, I never did this before, but how hard can it be?" she remarked.

We walked over to the shortest line, and waited our turn for the bank teller.

"The cashier's check I need is for $568.70," she said. "That's how much is in the bag."

As a station manager, Deanna was the middleman, and paid about a half cent less for the papers than she charged the delivery boys. So for a typical week Deanna made about $1.26 selling me my papers. Multiplying this across all the carriers she could make about $25/week. She was paid for the papers at our rate, and she paid Mrs. Galinskie at her rate and kept the difference.

When we got up to the counter, Deanna asked for a cashier's check for the $568.70, then proceeded to pull the stacks of bills and rolls of coins out of the bag and place them on the counter.

"The cost for the cashier's check will be 35 cents," the teller stated, and Deanna pointed to a separate quarter and a dime, to the left of the money stack.

The teller counted the money and said there was an extra ten cents, and Deanna replied back, "Ok if you say so, but I counted it twice."

The teller handed Deanna the cashier's check, which she folded and put into her pocketbook, followed by the sack, which she had rolled into a ball. She handed me the pocketbook while she rebuttoned her coat and put on her scarf, and we walked out the door, feeling like two adults on the way to a Broadway show.

We crossed the Pike and walked down a block to West Haddon Avenue, where we turned left to head to St. Aloysius Church. The church complex was much larger than ours, and literally took up three-quarters of a block between the church, the school, the parking lot, and the rectory. We walked up the massive steps into the church and through the large front doors. Inside in the church narthex it was dimly lit, and to the left there was a room to hang your coats before you actually entered the nave through another set of double doors that were attended by a group of ushers. Deanna pulled off her coat and scarf, revealing a long burgundy dress with buttons that ran up the entire front length, with a black open collar and black cuffs about the wrists. She again wore a short gold necklace around her neck and a pair of gold hoop earrings that peaked out from her dark curly hair. The dress pulled in at the waist, and accentuated her figure. To me, her appearance was one of pure beauty, and I felt a bit self-conscious that I had not elected to wear the tie. Grasping my hand, she led me into the church, stopping for a moment at what looked like a baptismal font, and dipping her finger in it before making the sign of the cross over her chest. She selected a pew about two-thirds of the way up the aisle for us to sit in. The sanctuary, which contained the altar and pulpit area of the church was currently unoccupied. As she turned to enter the pew, she blessed herself again, and we sat down.

Once seated, I waited in silence for about 5 minutes, taking in the grandeur of the church interior, from its glossy wood-honed pews to the enormous sculpture of Jesus on the cross beyond the altar, posed in his final suffering posture. At the sides of the church were large stained-glass windows, dimly illuminated and revealing various scenes from the Bible, including the Christmas manger scene in a window about four rows up from our pew. At the front of the sanctuary, beyond the altar were wooden chairs appearing even larger than life-size, designated for the priest and his more earthy assistants, including at least four altar boy's for this service. As we sat, I saw a number of people I knew enter and get seated. At one point, I even saw Joey Gilmore walk by with his family and give me the thumbs-up sign as he passed.

At 7:30, the service promptly started and the priestly procession up the aisle included none other than the altar boys Danny and Bobby Dobalo both wearing traditional cassocks, one carrying a Bible and the other a cross. I watched the two of them as well as the other two altar boys very carefully, noticing that their behavior and ceremonial rituals were much better practiced and rehearsed compared to the acolytes at our church. When they passed the altar, they went to one knee to bow, with none of the head nodding on-the-fly pass-bys that we were apt to perform. Heck, once while being an acolyte at our church I saw Dave Parker light the six front candles at the front of the church in the reverse order, going from big to small instead of the customary small to big order. In all I was sincerely impressed by their performance, and I vowed to do a better job myself in my acolyte duties later that night.

Once the church service began I got a bit lost in the proceedings, despite having attended service at my church nearly every week. At one point I asked Deanna what the priest was saying and she said she had no idea, and if I thought this was difficult to follow, I should have been here a couple of years ago when the service was conducted entirely in Latin. Still every once in a while, something sounded familiar, except for a *thine* or a *thou* in place of a *your*. Of course the Christmas readings were the same and the sermon carried the same messages. At one point during the sermon, Deanna grapsed my hand, running her fingers through my hands, finally resting one hand below mine, and the other above, gently rubbing her burgundy nails over the back of my hand in a small circular fashion.

When the sermon was over, the plate was passed, and we prepared for receiving communion. Deanna informed me I was not allowed to receive here, which really was of no major significance to me as I would be breaking bread at my church in less than four hours. Instead, I watched Deanna go up to the altar without me, receiving a round Eucharistic wafer while one of the Dobalo brothers held a metal paten under her chin in case the wafer should suddenly drop through a finger to mouth miss-exchange. She drank from the cup and then blessed herself again, an angelic vision walking back to the pew to me, her unworthy suitor. The service ended shortly thereafter, amid a series of bell rings, a final song, and a procession led by a cross-bearing boy who had likely participated in the theft of my bicycle. Yet overall I was dutifully impressed, and concluded in my mind that the same message had rang clear and true, despite a bit more formality and absence of familiar songs.

As we stood up to leave the church, the push from the crowd allowed me the chance to rub momentarily beside Deanna's body, and catch the fragrance of her hair and suppleness of her body. Unfortunately the night had to end, and we pushed over to pick up our coats and start on the walk home to her house.

We walked from the church hand in hand, and we talked first of the service and then of our family's customs at Christmas. At my house we always waited until Christmas morning to open our gifts, but at Deanna's house, this was performed before going to bed on Christmas Eve. This difference could have been due to the fact that we generally stayed home on Christmas, with a grandparent or two arriving at our house for Christmas dinner. But at Deanna's house, the family left early Christmas morning to spend the day with her relatives in Philadelphia at her grandparents' house.

As we neared her house, I mentioned I had a small gift for her, and I pulled the card and the two wrapped gifts from my coat pocket. She opened the card first, saying, "Now isn't that sweet." Then she opened the first of the gifts.

"Just what I always wanted," she said, "a pair of giant pliers."

I explained that they were wire cutters, to help her to better open the wire straps around the bundles of papers each day at the station.

"Your cutters are so dull, I can barely open the bundles," I remarked.

"Oh, I thought it was just me being a girl," she replied.

She then opened the second present and smiled. "I really need this," she said, "a chocolate version of my favorite sheep, Blacky! Unfortunately he won't last long; I already ate all the Hershey kisses."

She then put a slight frown on her face, and said, "You're so good to me, putting up with all my shenanigans and wisecracking. You got me a card and two presents, and all I did was make you go to church with me."

I looked her in the eye and said, "There's no place I would have rather been tonight than with you."

She then stopped for a second, and kissed me up on the cheek, a few inches from my ear. Then she whispered, "Thanks for being you. I'm really not used to people being so nice to me."

Then she backed away, and in a fake show of emotion, she said, "Oh wait a minute…you know what, I think I do have something for you."

From her purse she pulled out a card and a box wrapped in blue and white snowman paper.

As I had observed with both Mrs. Mac Mullin and Deanna, it was customary to open the card first, so I did. The card pictured a smiling young girl, and above her it read, *Next to you.* Opening the card, it said: *Is where I like to be the best!*

I acknowledged the same sentiments to her, and shook the box before opening it. Its contents moved a bit with the shake and I wondered what the gift could be. I pulled back the paper and opened the box and inside there was a familiar shaped package wrapped loosely in tissue paper. Pulling back the paper, I saw the familiar Hot Wheels logo, and inside was the Volkswagen Beetle. The car was dark green in color, had an open hood with exposed engine, and a sliding clear sunroof. I could hardly contain my excitement.

"This… this is just the greatest thing! I've wanted one of these so badly, and I've looked and looked but nobody ever had one! Where in the world did you find this?" I asked.

"Well let's just say that I have a grandfather with a lot of connections. You really like it?" she asked.

"I love it!" I said.

"Whew!" replied Deanna, "I was afraid that you might already have one, but I checked with your friend Zack and he said you didn't."

"Thank you. This is the greatest gift, and this is the greatest night!" I exclaimed.

I tucked the card and car in my coat pocket, and we walked a few feet further, stopping about two houses up from her home.

"Oh, I got a big favor to ask. I hope you don't think I'm a creep," she said. "But tomorrow we are going to my grandparents' house in Philadelphia to see my relatives for Christmas. We will be there all day tomorrow, Sunday, and Monday. I was wondering if it would be possible for you to unload the papers and put them out on Monday for everybody."

"That shouldn't be a problem," I said.

She took a key from her purse and handed it to me. "This is the key to the garage," she said. "Hang on to it, and use it to unlock the door."

I put the key in my pocket, and it made a clinking sound when it hit the other keys. The front light to her house came on, and she said, "I think they're starting to worry about me."

She leaned over and gave me a short kiss on the mouth. It happened so quickly, I barely had time to react.

"Thank you for a most wonderful night, and card, and presents," she said. "Have fun at your church tonight, and have a wonderful Christmas. I'll miss you!"

"I think I already am starting to miss you," I replied.

The door to her house opened and her mom called out her name. Deanna ran up and in the door. I looked at my watch and it was 9:30. Church was at 11:00, and I was due there at 10:30.

Everybody was excited to see me when I got home. I didn't mention the present or the card, and just told everybody the night was fun and I had a good time. After my interrogation session ended, I went upstairs and removed my sweater and put on a tie. I left for church at 10:25, and went up into the second floor of the parish hall and into the acolyte vestibule and put on my acolyte attire, a long sleeved black floor length robe with a square cut neck and a short white tunic overtop. Zack joined me and after he dressed, I helped him straighten his tunic, which he always seemed to put on crooked. I then did the same for the other two acolytes, Robbie McGirr and Robert McMahon. Zack and I lit the altar candles using the wick end of the candle snuffers, and I was careful to do a true stop and genuflect whenever I passed before the cross. We all headed down to the front of the church, via the lower floors of the parish hall. Pastor Heft was in the church narthex, and we met up with him and he gave us the once-over of the night's activities. Zack was to hold the cross, I was to hold the Bible, and Zack was to handle the offering plates, while I assisted Pastor prepare communion.

Our church was smaller and not as ornate as the Catholic Church, but they still had similarities. There were stain glass windows and a large cross up in front of the altar, but no pictures of saints or confessionals, or fonts of holy water at the church entrance. Tonight the church was adorned with candles on spires at either side of each pew, along with a candle in each window, surrounded by a decorative pine candle ring. The junior acolytes lit each of the side wall candle spires, while Zack and I lit those on either side of the aisle leading up to the altar. When the service began, we all walked up to the center aisle to the singing of *Hark the Herald Angels Sing*, stopping in the center, with Zack in the back with the cross, the two younger acolytes in the front, and Pastor and I in the center. When the song was over, I opened the Bible to Luke 2:1-20, and Pastor read the Christmas story out loud. At its conclusion, everyone sang *Joy to the World*, and we all walked up to the sanctuary, where Zack and I sat on either side of Pastor on engraved wooden chairs, and Robbie and Robert sat on folding chairs directly across from us, on either side of the deacon.

At offering, Zack forgot and only took four collection plates to the ushers, forgetting that two extra ushers were present tonight for the church balcony, so Pastor told me to discreetly join Zack with two additional plates. I was back in time to assist Pastor with the ritual of the Lavabo and his preparation and blessing of the sacraments. I received my communion with the choir, and I sat just beyond the railing while my family received their communion, my brother and father silently acknowledging me with a quick wave while they knelt down to receive.

The last hymn of the service was *Silent Night*, during which Zack and I lit our candlesnuffer wicks, extinguished the altar candles, and carried the flame down to a central candle located in the narthex. With our jobs done for the night, we raced under the church through the Sunday School hallway and into the parish hall and its second floor vestibule, where we changed out of our acolyte robes. In a flash, we went back to the narthex to meet up with our families for the trip back home. Our church had an interesting Christmas tradition, where upon leaving the church on Christmas Eve, all were given a white tapered candle about four inches in length with a paper wax drip-guard. We were to light the candle from the flame in the narthex and carry our lit candle out of the church and into the night as a symbolic sign of carrying the light of Christ into the world. The idea was to see how far you could travel before the flame was blown out from the wind or carelessness. Since we lived within walking distance of the church, the task was not quite as daunting for my family as for others, unless of course it was raining or snowing, or especially windy. This year the weather was calm, and I quickly made my way down the church steps and to our house without my candle being extinguished. Cupping my hand about the flame, I waited on the porch for the rest of my family to appear. About five minutes after my porch arrival, the rest of my family appeared with their candles extinguished. My dad unlocked the door, and I carried my lit candle inside, where my mom instructed me to light a large bayberry candle that sat in the center of our dining room table. After successfully lighting the bayberry candle, I blew out my taper, having succeeded in the quest of carrying home the light.

Chapter 23 - The Bike Shop

I woke up Christmas morning at about 7:00. Like every other Christmas growing up at home, it always seemed that I was the first one up. I went downstairs and looked under the tree, but I knew the ritual that no presents could be opened unless the rest of the family was in attendance. We also had to alternate, with everyone opening one present at a time, until all the gifts had been opened. This not only made it possible for everyone to see what each of us had gotten as gifts, but it also stretched the process so that it covered a good part of Christmas morning. After seeing the wealth of presents under the tree, I went back upstairs and made some general clamor to help wake up the remainder of the household.

Eventually everybody woke up and made their way downstairs. Mom put on the coffee, and made a quick batch of scrambled eggs, Polish kielbasa, and toast, a meal that had somehow evolved into our standard Christmas breakfast fare. We were allowed to open our stockings before this morning meal. The small gifts in the stockings usually amounted to something like candy, maybe a new toothbrush, or some socks – really nothing to get overly excited about. We finished breakfast, and without cleaning up the dishes, proceeded to the living room and the tree. My father was always the chairman of the ceremony, and he made sure the tree was lit and some Christmas music was on before we went any further. He then donned a Santa hat and passed out a single present to each of us. Being the youngest, I was always allowed to open the first.

By the end of our first hour, I had received several pairs of pants and shirts, a new pair of pajamas, some white socks, and a Trenton State College sweatshirt, the latter gift being from my sister, and the only gift of major significance. By hour two, we had worked into the better gifts, which included a box of one dozen baseballs from my brother, a Lego truck builder kit with forward and reverse motor from my grandparents, and a Hot Wheels Supercharger from my mom and dad.

I had particularly wanted the Supercharger. Hot Wheels cars typically were meant to drive on a plastic orange track, about one-quarter inch wider than the car itself. The track was raised off the ground about three feet and could be clamped to things like chairs or end tables. By rolling the cars down the track, gravity supplied the power for the cars to move forward and around curves, or through a loop-the-loop. The battery operated supercharger consisted of a plastic box designed to look like an automotive store, with one entrance and one exit door on either side which could be connected to the orange track. On the top of the supercharger unit was a shift knob which controlled the speed of two spinning foam wheels that resided between the entrance and exit door. When the car sides contacted with the revolving foam, the car was propelled forward. By carefully building a circular track with the Supercharger in line, it was possible to propel your car through the Supercharger, around the track, and back into the Supercharger, in a sort of perpetual motion. At least that's the way it worked on the TV commercials. In real life, you were lucky to get the car to go around once without it flying off the track. Nevertheless, the Supercharger was a step up from the ramp, and provided countless hours of entertainment, as well as a method of shooting your cars out at the cat.

My last gift of the day was one of those that everybody paid attention to, and mom took the camera out for. The box was not extremely large, maybe a little smaller than a shoebox, and it was not particularly heavy. I opened it up slowly to reveal a Schwinn bicycle generator light set, consisting of a front and back light, both of which were powered by a friction generator. As the revolving top of the generator rubbed against the side of your bicycle tire, it turned some internal coils and created electrical power. Pedal the tire faster and the light got brighter, stop the wheel from spinning and the light went out.

Inside the box with the generator, my mother and father had included a handwritten note. It said that this light was to be attached to a new ten-speed bicycle of my choice, which would serve as a combination Christmas and birthday present.

My father, a practical man who knew the value of patience and doing a bit of research before making a decision, explained, "The reason we didn't just buy you a bike and put it under the tree is that you will likely only get one brand new bicycle in your lifetime. That's why you should be allowed to pick out the model and color that you like most. I have off on Monday, and we can go down to Millar's Bike Shop together and you can pick out the bike that you like the best."

I looked at my mom and dad and felt like celebrating. "This is the greatest present ever, because I really wanted and needed a new bicycle."

"Now remember, that this bicycle will cost us a lot of money," my mother reminded me, "so we are giving it to you as combination Christmas and birthday gift. So just remember that on February 2nd, when you get a cake and an empty box."

"Oh I understand," I said. "That sounds like a great deal to me."

My brother, always eager for attention, emphasized that the generator light had been his idea, and that he also wanted to go with us to the bike shop to offer up some pointers.

On Monday morning, I again got up bright and early in preparation for the trip to Jippo's. The store didn't open until 9:00, and since it was only a few blocks away, my dad said that he, my brother, and I should all walk to the store together to mark this momentous occasion. We got to the store about ten minutes after it opened, and old Chip Millar was eating a doughnut and drinking a cup of coffee as we entered through the front door.

"Oh, you brought the whole family this time sir," Mr. Millar said to my father. "And which is the lucky boy that's getting the new bike?"

"That would be the smaller guy here," my father said, tapping me on the head. "I know he has a Schwinn catalog and he's probably got a good idea of the model and color he wants."

"Is that right, son?" Chip asked going into his salesman routine. "Well maybe before you pick you might want me to go over the pros and cons of each model."

"Well, ok, I guess," I replied.

"Now the Paramount model here is our best model, but it's for the true bike enthusiast that's interested in a premium lightweight ten-speed bicycle. This particular model goes for $350. Next in line is the Sports Tourer, which has a three piece aluminum alloy crank set and a ten-speed Gran Tourisimo rear derailer. It has a gear range of 28 to 104, and quick release hubs, and my favorite item – a chrome plated front fork; all this for $196."

"What about the less expensive models?" my father asked.

"Well the Varsity Sport starts at $96.95 and has a 38 to 100 gear ratio, and the Continental has the same gear ratio, but has a lighter diamond style frame for only $8.00 more. That leaves only the Super Sport model left. It has a wider range 33 to 100 gear ratio, and a hand brazed chrome molybdenum alloy steel frame that is lighter and stronger than those on the other low price models. This model is what I personally consider to be our best value at $136.95.

"What about colors?" I asked.

"Well they all come in campus green, sierra brown, lemon, and burgundy."

"Can you show me the burgundy one?" I asked.

"Well we need to talk about frame size," Mr. Millar explained. "You see these bikes come in a 22-inch, 24-inch, and 26-inch frame. We should measure your leg length from the bottom of your shoe to your crotch to pick the best size."

My father suggested that I was still growing and that I should get the biggest frame I could comfortably ride. So I tried both the 24 and 26-inch bikes, feeling they were both acceptable.

"Then I'd get the biggest," my father recommended. "You're still growing."

"Well, we only have the Super Sport in burgundy in a girl's model."

"How about the Continental in burgundy?" my father asked.

"Same thing," said Mr. Millar.

"Well how long is it to order it?"

"I'll have to get my associate and lead mechanic from the back," Mr. Millar said. "Oh Billy, could you come out front."

Billy Proudst came out, cleaning his hands with a towel .

"Wha...Wha...What can I help you wi...with?" he asked.

"Billy, what's the delivery time on a new burgundy Super Sport?"

"Oh th...they're on backorder, s...so are all of the burgundy models. You're probably looking for delivery around March."

"Wow, that's a long time." I commented in a disappointed tone.

"Well the 1972 Super Sport model also comes in an opaque blue color. Any idea when that model would be available?" Chip asked Billy.

"I ac...actually saw a couple that went out last week," Billy stammered. "My guess would be we should be able to get one in and assembled by early February."

I looked at the opaque blue color in the new 1972 catalog and it was definitely sharp.

"I think I actually like the blue more than the burgundy," I said.

I went to ask my brother what he thought, but he had lost interest and was over looking at the car models.

"I want it," I concluded.

Mr. Millar and my dad proceeded to fill out the paperwork, and my dad wrote a check for the full amount. Mr. Millar went into the back room and came back with a color copy of the new 1972 catalog.

"Here you go," he said handing me the new catalog. "It's hot off the presses. Now, I should have a firmer delivery date once I call in the order. The boy can stop in later today or tomorrow if he wants to know the exact date. Then we will call you when it's in and assembled. Of course, if you bring the generator light in a day or so before the pickup date, I'll have Billy here install it on the bike, free of charge of course."

Both my dad and I started for the door, both of us feeling satisfied that we had made an excellent purchase. My brother caught up with us as we were leaving, "So, what was the choice?" he asked.

February really wasn't so long off, and with our weather, I probably wouldn't have been doing much riding in January anyway; I thought. I went home and we relayed the information to my mother and sister, showing them a picture in the new 1972 catalog. Everybody agreed that we had made the right decision on the color.

I went back into the sun porch and played with the Lego truck on the step to the living room. My dad sat back in his chair, listening to a new Johnny Cash album he had received for Christmas.

"What we need now is a newspaper to read," my dad said.

"Well, the truck doesn't get there until at least 2:30," I said. "And today I'm putting the papers out for everybody because Deanna is at her grandparents' house."

"You're getting to be quite the entrepreneur," my father commented.

After lunch I decided to leave for the station at 2:00, just in case the truck pulled in early. It turned out the garage key was for the back door, and I had to walk in and open the overhead door from inside. There was a note on the table in the garage from Deanna, with the new pair of wire cutters placed on top. "Billy," it said, "got these newfangled cutters for Christmas from my boyfriend. I'll let you use them since you're doing me such a big favor. Don't break them, or he'll get mad. See you soon. Luv Deanna."

I took the note and after reading it, shoved it into my pocket. Then I looked around the station, thinking of Deanna and her family and how they managed to lead a normal life without hearing. The paper truck pulled up at 2:15, and the driver Curt opened up the back of the truck.

"You in charge today?" he asked.

"Yes, the Kolakowski's are on vacation," I replied.

"Lucky them," said Curt. "These babies are heavy, only twenty to a bundle with all the after Christmas sales. And there's a Korvette's circular."

We unloaded the truck and I began to put out the papers, pulling the correct number of papers per carrier according to the ledger on the table. The papers were thick and there were a lot of bundles. I was glad I had the new cutters. The circulars were wrapped in stacks of 500 that were less than four inches high. I estimated the number of circulars and put them on each pile. Most of the boys filed in early, and everybody complained about the thickness of the paper. John Shelly even demonstrated that the rubber bands could barely contain the wrapped-up paper size. By 3:15, things looked pretty much in control, and I decided to leave and serve my route. By 4:00, I was done, and I walked back to the station to close things up. All the paper piles were gone except Dave Parker's, and I proceeded to tidy up the garage while I waited for him to arrive. He showed up via car at 4:15 and carried his large stack in three trips to the car.

With everyone now gone, I pulled down the overhead door and locked it, then exited through the back door. I walked home along the Pike, so I turned left onto Greenbriar Avenue and followed it up the street. Walking past Millar's Bike Shop, I decided to stop in to see if he had a delivery date yet for my bike. He said that it should be in on February 3rd, and I should be able to pick it up February 4th, which was a Friday. Exiting Millar's, the wind seemed to have picked up, and the temperature felt like it had dropped at least twenty degrees. I arrived home and told my father and mother the confirmed delivery date.

"That's not too bad," my mom observed. "That's just a few days after your birthday."

"Yep, I can't wait," I said.

"Oh, by the way," my mom added. "Your friend Deanna called while you were out. She said there was an unexpected change of plans and asked me to tell you she would need you to put out the papers tomorrow at the paper station like you did today. I said that I didn't think it would be a problem and you would do it."

Chapter 24 - Meeting in the Parish Hall

Tuesday morning Zack stopped over to see how I had made out for Christmas. He brought with him the Hot Wheels Supercharger he had gotten. We set up a track in my living room with both his and my Supercharger, and we were able to construct a circuit that the cars could circle nearly endlessly without prodding or falling off. I showed Zack all of my gifts, including the baseballs, the Lego truck, the money clip, the generator light, and the picture of my new bike. All the gifts were great, he conceded, but the Hot Wheels Volkswagen was by far the best. He asked me why it was still in its original plastic display package and I said I didn't want to take it out for fear of scratching it or bending its axle.

"Your friend Deanna asked me after the play if you liked Hot Wheels and had the VW bug, but I had no idea that she intended to give you one as a gift," Zack said.

We talked at length about a replacement bike for Zack, and he said he had received almost $40.00 in money as Christmas gifts, and that his mom had managed to get $50.00 back in insurance money from the theft, so it wouldn't be long until he could afford a second Continental model. He was thinking about getting the sierra brown color this time around, so he didn't have to worry about a long delivery time. I mentioned that I had some extra cash that I could easily lend to him if he wanted to speed up the purchase. He said he might take me up on a loan, and maybe borrow enough so that he could also get a generator light.

"After all," he said, "I do plan on painting Mrs. Mac Mullin's living room walls, and that should easily make up the difference."

Zack left right after lunch, and I spent the next hour trying to perfect a track with the single Supercharger. At 2:00 I left for the station, hoping today wouldn't be another twenty to a bundle day. The cold wind whipped around a bit, causing some leaves in the street to swirl, and making my hands feel numb when I didn't keep them inside my coat pockets. When I got to the station I was surprised to see Kathy Milano there. Apparently Kathy also had a key for the garage door. It seemed Deanna was concerned that I may not have received the message from my mother, so she had called Kathy just in case I did not show up on time.

"So, I noticed that you've been seeing a lot of Deanna," she said. "Do you like her?"

"Yes, I do," I answered.

"Do you love her?" she asked.

I didn't answer, not because I didn't know the answer, but because the truck screeched up to the driveway. The papers were lighter today at forty per bundle, and Kathy and I set up the stacks, with me cutting the bundle wires and setting the base pile and Kathy counting the remainder and writing on the carrier names. We finished fairly quickly, and she told me she would watch things and lock up, so that I didn't have to stick around. So I followed her lead, and left to serve.

I was home by 4:00 and bored by 5:00, as I stared at the Volkswagen box and debated whether I should open or not. I finally couldn't take it any longer, and carefully opened the box, and held the pristine car in my hands. It was shorter than the other Hot Wheels cars, but this was the only model I had with a working sunroof.

At 7:15 I was watching the *Glen Campbell Goodtime Hour* on TV, when the phone rang and my mother asked me to go and answer it. I gave her a bit of static, saying it was never for me, and then was very surprised when it turned out to be Deanna. She had just gotten home, and she said she had been thinking about me since Christmas and she had to see me.

"Do you think you could get out for an hour or so? Nothing special, just a walk or something?" she asked.

I said yes, and we agreed to meet each other about halfway between our houses. She suggested we head towards the bank again, and meet up somewhere along the way. I told my mother and father I was going out for about an hour to meet with some friends, and they both nodded ok, with my mom noting, "Pull up your jacket tight and wear your gloves. It's really bitter outside tonight."

I walked up past the bank and saw Deanna coming down the Pike, a little past the bike store. We met up and walked back in the general direction towards my house, for no real reason other than it put the wind behind our backs. Deanna gave me a quick hug along my arm.

"All I could think about the past few days was you," she said. "And my parents bug me so much I just can't take it."

Deanna was dressed warmly with her blue winter jacket with the white fur-lined hood, her mittens, and ski cap. I had on my Harvard jacket and hooded sweatshirt, but the wind seemed to blow right through me and chill me to the bone. We talked about the gifts she had gotten for Christmas, but after a few more blocks, even she said the cold was getting to her.

"I don't know how you can stand it without gloves," she said.

"I left them at church," I replied.

"I don't remember seeing them Christmas Eve."

"No, at my church, the day of the play," I informed her.

Then I remembered that Zack had given me a key. "Well, I do have the key for the parish hall door, and we could stop in for a bit to pick up the gloves," I mentioned. "But the key is really on loan from Zack, and I really don't know if we should be in there."

"Sounds good to me," Deanna said. "It's not like we're going in to steal anything."

We quickly walked up to the church property. There were no cars in the parking lot and the lights were off in the church and the parish hall windows. We continued up the single step to the parish hall door, past the railing where Zack's bike had been stolen. I removed my key ring from my pocket, and held the keys up to the streetlight to determine which one fit the door. Unlocking the door, we walked inside the hall in the red glow of the exit signs and into the multipurpose room where a little more than one week ago Deanna and I had stood following the Christmas pageant. The chairs that had formed an auditorium were now all down and put away. Similarly, the stage was empty of the manger scene and the inn, restored to its original state with the small altar and portable piano on the carpeted floor. Only the aluminum foil star hanging above remained as a remnant of the previous week's performance. The room was still a bit cold, but much warmer than the windy weather outdoors, and it felt good to be inside. I didn't turn on the lights, but instead we walked over to the stage and sat down. Deanna pulled off her hat and started to faintly weep.

"I just don't get it. It seems so unfair. My parents don't understand or care about me," she sighed. "When I tell them I want things, they tell me to get a job. And when I get a job running the paper station, they ignore my responsibility. They didn't tell me we were staying until Tuesday night at my grandpa's until late Monday. And when I told them I needed to get back for today, they just laughed at me. What if I hadn't been able to get you to fill in for me? You know sometimes when I sit at home at night with no one to talk to I feel so alone. It's been like this since my grandmother died, and my brother Joe left. I don't know if I can take it anymore."

I listened to her while she whispered her problems to me, and looked through the darkness into her wet eyes.

"At least I have you," she said. "Can you just hold me for a while?"

I leaned over and hugged her, and she laid her head on my shoulder. I felt her tremble slightly, and then she looked up at me.

"Please don't think I'm crazy. I usually don't act this way. I've just felt so different lately, and all I want is to be with you."

She put her head back on my shoulder. I felt her pain and wanted to hold her and protect her for the rest of my life.

"Things will be ok," I said. "And I don't think you're crazy. You're the best thing that's ever happened to me, and I never want to leave you."

We hugged in the dark room for several minutes. The room was silent except for the sound of our breathing. Then we heard the sound of the heater kick on somewhere within the heart of church, which made a strange creaking sound, a bit more on the scary side then the angelic.

Then unexpectedly, we heard some voices from near the door, and the sound of some jingling keys. Startled, we both ran over and ducked behind the piano. Two men entered the parish hall and turned on the aisle lights, then continued into the multipurpose room. One of the men walked over near the electrical box and fumbled with some switches. Feeling helpless, but wanting to take control, I left Deanna behind the piano, and walked over to the men by the electrical box. Opening it, I switched on a few switches, illuminating the back of the room.

"Can I help you?" I asked.

The larger of the men I instantly recognized as Mr. Shuster, the father of one of the girls in my class at school. Mr. .Shuster's daughter rarely went to church and was not part of our church Youth Group. Her father said he was having a party at his house on New Year's Eve and that he was there to borrow about twenty chairs for the occasion. Mr. Alkins, a deacon at the church, had lent him the key to get the chairs. I showed him where the chairs were in the back of the room, and I helped him and the other man carry them out to their truck. Collectively, it took us about three trips.

When we finished and as he was about to leave, Mr. Shuster leaned over to me and in a low tone said, "I don't know who you are kid, but I do know that you really shouldn't be in here. I'm not going to say anything to anybody about this, because you seem to be alright, but I would suggest that as soon as I leave that you get your ass out of here. And the same goes for your girlfriend back behind the piano."

With that the two men left. We waited a few minutes after the door shut and collected ourselves, then I shut out the lights, and we left the church. I didn't tell Deanna what Mr. Shuster had said. As I walked Deanna home, I realized that I still did not have my gloves. Instead of them, I had left with a small handful of problems that I didn't have at the start of the day.

Chapter 25 - Epiphany

Once New Year's day and Christmas vacation were over and school started again, things got back to a normal routine. It was January 6th which by the Church calendar was Epiphany and supposedly marked the day the three Wisemen finally met up with baby Jesus. This of course disagreed with most of our church plays and manger scenes where the three Magi were present at the blessed birth on Christmas night. From my family's perspective, Epiphany marked the end of the twelve days of Christmas, which according to my father meant that this was the last night we were supposed to turn on our outside Christmas lights. The joke was that Epiphany also was a name for a sudden revelation, which my father said came from the realization that the Christmas bills were coming in fast and furious, and nobody had the money to keep the Christmas lights on.

Apparently Mrs. Mac Mullin and my father subscribed to the same rulebook, as Mrs. Mac Mullin had asked me the day before if I could stop back soon to take down her outside Christmas lights and tree. I mentioned to Zack on the walk to school that I would be stopping by her house after papers, and asked him if he was interested in coming along to meet her and get an idea of the painting job. Zack said yes, and he agreed to meet up with me on my route so we could go together. We decided I would serve the route in reverse, and I would meet him around Haddon and Coldspring.

I met Zack at the Engwalls' house, and we walked the rest of the main route together. We then walked down the steps to the creek and over past the mill to Smythville. It was cold, but there was no wind to speak of, so even though a good portion of the creek was frozen, the chill didn't feel too bad on our bodies. Finishing up the Smythville homes, we went up to Mrs. Mac Mullin's door and knocked. Zack had brought his small tool pouch, although I was not really sure why. He said it made him seem more professional, and besides it had a tape measure and he might need to measure the walls. My question to him was just how professional could you be at age fourteen anyway?

Mrs. Mac Mullin answered, and I noticed she was using a cane to help her walk. She said she had been feeling a bit sore lately, and showed us a bruise on her leg and arm from where she had recently fallen. The cane gave her a bit more stability, and she figured she could put it away come spring when the weather warmed up a bit and her arthritis felt a bit better. I introduced her to Zack, telling her that he was interested in the painting job, and she sat down on the couch after shaking his hand, excusing herself for her impropriety and asking forgiveness due to her age.

Zack took a look at the water stains on the wall, and then took a quick measurement of the room. He and Mrs. Mac Mullin talked a bit about the room color, and she requested an off-white shade, a bit darker than present. Zack did a rough calculation in his head and concluded two coats should not take more than two gallons of paint. He estimated the paint cost to be about $9.00 and his labor to be $20.00, a price Mrs. Mac Mullin reluctantly agreed to, saying she could do without her nighttime snack of tea and shortbread cookies for a month, to help foot the bill.

With the painting details settled, she told me where the key for the basement Bilco door was, and I went in the next room to get it while Zack went outside to take down the lights. Zack and I then both went to the basement to get the dolly and the trunk to put away the decorations. Zack was fascinated by the age of the basement and its hardened dirt floors. Together we brought the trunk inside and opened it. Zack peered inside the trunk, as I had before, and commented on its rusted-out base.

"Say, that trunk looks like it has a false bottom. Look how part of the inside metal is rusted through, but there is no visible deterioration through the base," Zack observed.

He then pulled a screwdriver and pliers from his pouch, and used the screwdriver to pry between the base's side and the wall near the rusted section, and the entire floor could be moved up a bit. The act of dislodging the false base revealed some papers with writing, and he asked Mrs. Mac Mullin if she wanted him to see if he could get them out. She said fine, and he pried a bit more around the trunk inside edges until the whole false bottom was free. He then took his pliers and pulled the rusted bottom piece up, revealing the true base of the trunk and several envelopes of what appeared to be official paperwork. Zack laid the false bottom in the trunk lid, then pulled out the envelopes and handed them to Mrs. Mac Mullin.

"Well, I'll be!" she said as she gazed at the envelopes. "Please fetch my glasses off the dining room table so that we can see what these are."

I got her the glasses. There were six envelopes in all. Three looked to have been sealed with sealing wax and embossed with the HB Smyth stamp Zack had found in the old mill factory desk. The other three looked to be just loosely closed. Seated on the couch with her glasses on, Mrs. Mac Mullin started with the unsealed envelopes. From the first she pulled out the deed to the Smythville property in a document from 1871. Other than some rust damage and a slight tear on the front page, the document was legible and in fairly good shape. The second envelope contained a series of business documents that detailed several equipment purchases but didn't seem of any relevance anymore, since the machines were likely long gone, serving their manufacturing purpose over 75 years ago. The third envelope contained five $100 bills, which is more money than Zack or I had ever seen at one time in our lives. I asked Mrs. Mac Mullin if I could hold one of the bills for a moment to look over its printing details.

That left the three sealed envelopes, and Mrs. Mac Mullin seemed just as excited as us with the prospect of opening them. She asked that I get a letter opener from the dining room buffet drawer, and she slipped the knife into the first envelope and opened it along the top seam. The envelope contained the marriage license of H. B. Smyth and Eveline English Smyth from June of 1869. The document was quickly read by Mrs. Mac Mullin, and placed back inside the envelope. It seemed she did not like to be reminded of Hezekiah's first marriage. The second envelope, once opened, was met with a greater degree of pleasure, as it contained Hezekiah's second marriage license, dated April 1882, to Agnes Gilikson Smyth. This document was notarized in the city of Burlington, NJ, and despite its age and slight yellowing, it remained in good shape. Mrs. Mac Mullin left this certificate out of its envelope, and placed it next to her on the couch.

Only one more envelope was left, and Zack and I wondered out loud what could possibly be in it. I asked if anyone knew the largest denomination of US currency that existed, and when no one could answer, I said I hoped it was another $500. Mrs. Mac Mullin slipped in the knife, and pulled out what appeared to be another legal document.

"Nuts," I said. "There's no money in this one either."

The notarized document was a birth certificate for Enola Maybelle Smyth, dated May 8th, 1882. The certificate listed the place of birth as Camden, New Jersey, and the baby's father and mother as Mr. Hezekiah B. Smyth and Mrs. Agnes Gilikson Smyth. Mrs. Mac Mullin smiled, and momentarily held the certificate over her heart.

"Who's Enola Maybelle Smyth?" Zack asked aloud.

"Why, that's me," answered Mrs. Mac Mullin. "Smyth is my maiden name."

I felt good for Mrs. Mac Mullin since from the stories she'd told me, proving her relationship to Hezekiah Smyth had always been a point of contention.

"Mrs.Mac Mullin! Isn't this the birth record you have been looking for? It's the legal paper trail that proves you are the daughter of Hezekiah Smyth and that you are the heir to his fortune!"

"Dear boy," Mrs. Mac Mullin said. "I always knew I was Hezekiah's daughter and that Agnes Gilikson was my mother. There is no surprise here. And as for his fortune, I believe all that is left is the $500 that we found tonight in that envelope. But looking on the bright side, at least I know I can get this room painted and still afford those shortbread cookies."

I looked at Mrs. Mac Mullin and she smiled the tired smile of an old women. At one point the papers before us had importance, but at this stage in her life, the game was over, like being dealt a winning hand after all the big players had left the room and all that was left to win was the ante.

"Come on boys, it's been a long afternoon, let's pack up the tree and the lights and decorations in the trunk, and put them away in the basement until next year. In the meantime this is for you two, providing the living room paint job meets my expectations."

She handed Zack and me one of the $100 bills.

"Gee, thanks," Zack and I said in unison.

"Now pack that stuff up," she said, as she pulled all the envelopes, documents, and money up off the couch and placed them in a big pile on the end table.

Chapter 26 - Bobby Dobalo

February 4th had arrived at last. After school I was to pick up my new Schwinn Super Sport from the bike shop. A day earlier I had dropped off the generator light and checked to make sure the bike had arrived. Chip Millar pointed to the box and promised it would be assembled and ready to ride by the time I got out of school. In preparation for the big day, I had already collected, so I had time to pick it up and immediately go for a test ride. Zack was going to come with me, but we had promised Mrs. Mac Mullin that her living room would be painted this weekend, so on the walk home Zack peeled off into the hardware store, while I continued down the Pike to Jippo's. When I arrived at the bike shop, Billy Proudst was finishing up the assembly and adjusting the back derailleur. My father had insisted I get a new lock and chain, even giving me an extra $10 for the purchase. So while Billy finished work on the bike, I looked at the bike chains and locks, and selected a set marked *guaranteed deterrent*, which looked to have the heaviest poly-covered chain in the store.

"This is a real fine bicycle," Billy Proudst commented to me as he wheeled it out. "It's the first one I've put together in the opaque blue color and it's really sharp." he said. "It's a shame you're going to add an extra three pounds to its weight with that lock and chain," he added.

Billy wrapped the chain around the frame below the seat, and handed me the lock key, which I put on my key chain. Then Mr. Millar told me to get on the bike, and he had Billy adjust the seat a bit to fit me better. Next he told me to take a ride around the block and come back in and let them know if anything seemed out of kilter or needed an adjustment. The bike rode extremely well, but the front handbrake seemed to rub a bit during normal riding, so Mr. Millar instructed Billy to adjust it.

As it was Friday, Deanna was busy back at the station collecting the weekly paper money. I had promised her I would bring the bike around, as she was also anxious to see it. Zack had picked up his sierra brown Continental ten-speed the week before, and after dropping the paint at home and searching for rollers, he got on his bike and went looking for me. Figuring I would be at the station by now, he stopped at Deanna's house. Seeing my papers in the garage, he went up to the back door to ask Deanna if she'd seen me and the bike yet. She said no, but that I would likely be there soon.

"Well I kinda have to go back to the hardware store to get some rollers for painting," he said. "I thought we had some extras at home, but I couldn't seem to find them. Could you tell Bill to meet me tonight at 7:00 over at Smythville for the job? And tell him to bring the new bike. I can't wait to see it."

"I'll let him know," replied Deanna. "I can't wait to see the bike either. I even got him one of those little license plates for it."

Then she held up a miniature three-by-five inch replica of a New Jersey license plate that had *Billy* written on it.

"Let's see if I have enough influence to get him to hang it from his back seat," she joked.

"You are one tough cookie," Zack retorted.

"Yeah, but I love him," she said.

Thinking a bit more about my paper habits she added, "Hey Zack, sometimes he just picks up his papers on Fridays and I don't see him until later in the afternoon after he comes back to pay his paper bill. You may want to go into the garage and write him a note and leave it on his paper pile. That way he'll be sure to see it before he serves."

Zack agreed that would be a good idea and he went out into the garage, and taking a piece of brown kraft paper from the trash can, he jotted down a quick note and put it on the paper pile labeled "Bill:"

>*Bill,*
>
>*I got the paint from the hardware store, but had to go back to get a couple of rollers. I'll meet you tonight over at Smythville by the mill. Be sure to bring the new bike so that I can see it.*
>
>*Zack*

Most of the papers in the station had already been picked up, with only three stacks remaining. Shortly after Zack left, Bobby Dobalo came in to pick up his brother's load. Entering the station, he saw Zack's note on the top of the stack and came over to read it. Bobby knew through Billy Proudst all about the new opaque blue Super Sport. Thinking back to our last encounter when he was on his mini-bike, Bobby picked up the papers and he forcefully shoved them in his bag. While he packed, his slow-witted brain concocted a plan.

I arrived about ten minutes later. The bike was now perfectly adjusted and safe at home in the garage. There was no need to use the bike for serving my papers, but it sure would make the return trip to the station to pay my bill a lot faster. Reading the note from Zack, I checked the dial and there was still plenty of time to serve, pay my paper bill, and make it back to Smythville by 7:00. What's more, it would be dark by then, and give me a chance to try out the generator light.

I breezed through the papers, stopping at home for a quick dinner of SpaghettiOs, bread and butter, and a dish of Cool and Creamy chocolate pudding for dessert. I showed my mom and brother my new bike and went off to pay my paper bill. My mother told me to be careful and be sure to lock up the bike in a safe place. It was now 5:25 and stars began to appear in the moonless sky.

When I depressed the switch on the top of the generator, its spring mechanism caused the top rubber bearing to tilt into position against the bicycle back tire. Pushing up the kickstand with my foot, I hopped upon the bike and began to peddle. Each revolution of the generator caused a faint whirling sound, and the white headlight on the front of the bike and the red taillight on the back began to glow, dimly at first and then increasing in intensity with each revolution of the tires.

The month of January had been unusually cold, as evidenced by the amount of ice cover on the creek, but tonight the temperature was warm enough to prevent any sting on my face or hands from the air that rushed by as I rode. I peddled to the corner, and then shifted from fifth to tenth gear, and the bike sped even faster with each pedal revolution. I whizzed past Clinton and Collins and on to Greenbriar, to my interim destination. As I braked to turn into the driveway at the station, my lights faded as the bike slowed to a stop.

I got off the bike and walked it across the grass to the back door. Deanna saw me at the door and opened it for me to come in.

"You got the bike?" she squealed.

"Yeah, come out and see it," I replied. And in an instant she was outside with her mother to take a look.

"Wheel it into the garage so we can see it under the light," she instructed.

So I wheeled the bike through the garage back door, and Deanna flipped on the garage light. The fluorescent light in the garage made the bike's blue color even more intense, and both Deanna and her mother agreed the bike was the sharpest they had ever seen.

Deanna pulled the license plate from her pocket and handed it to me.

"It's special, just for you and your new bike," she said as she placed two paper clips through the holes at the top of both sides of the metal plate. For her I would do anything, so I fastened the clips just beneath the seat, and the license plate found its new home.

I left the bike in the garage, Deanna shut off the lights, and we all walked into the house. I pulled out my money and placed it on the table, and she picked it up and put it into her cashbox without counting a cent.

"Just Dave Parker left," she said. "You would think just once that kid wouldn't have to be last."

Deanna got up from the table and swished into the kitchen, her burnished curls tousling with each step.

"You want some beef stew?" she asked. "We're having it for dinner."

"No thanks," I replied. "I already ate, and besides, I only eat beef stew as a leftover, because that's when the gravy is the thickest."

Deanna came back with a bowl full of stew, plopped down on a piece of bread. She also brought over a glass of milk, and proceeded to eat her dinner while I stacked and counted coins for her and put them into wrappers. Dave Parker finally showed up and paid his bill, and Deanna counted out the total check amount, putting the appropriate amount of money into her tan money sack.

"I know you're meeting Zack tonight, but do you have time to walk me to the bank?" she asked. "There might be a kiss in it for you," she said with a wink.

It was only 6:30 and I said yes. Deanna put her coat on, and her mother came into the room.

"We…are…going…to…the…bank," she said and signed simultaneously to her mother. "Don't…worry. He's …standing…me…up… tonight. Going…out…with…the… guys."

Her mother laughed and shook her index finger at me, then Deanna put on her coat and hat and we walked together out the door. I went into the garage and got my bike, and we traveled together to the bank, Deanna on foot and me peddling beside her as slowly as possible. When we got to the bank, she thanked me for the company and gave me a quick peck on the cheek.

"Call me tonight on the phone when you get home," she said as she walked into the bank.

I turned my bike around and started for Smythville, taking a slightly alternate route along the Pike since I was already there. Past the hardware store, the candy shop, the bike shop, the Shop 'N Bag, and the Save-A-Lot Pharmacy I rode. Pedaling faster I passed the Heritage Room Bar, the A&C butcher shop, and Nastasi's furniture store, finally reaching Ormond Avenue. Turning left onto Ormond, I rode up two blocks, passing Jimmy Reeder's house, and approaching the Dobalos' house. Looking at their house up ahead on the left, I noticed the front porch lights were out, which made me glad. I really didn't think anybody was waiting there to intercept me, after all it was February and 6:45 at night. Nevertheless, I pumped fastest while I passed their house, my generator light screaming as I shot like a bolt of lightning past their door. Once safely by the house, I rested my legs and coasted forward. I took a quick glance backward, and wondered if I saw a dark figure on a bike shoot out of the driveway and turn up the street behind me. Looking a second time, I saw nothing, and figured I was imagining things. I continued the length of Ormond Avenue, past the woods and the weeds. As the road became narrower and started to slope downward towards the water, I picked up additional speed, and my headlight beamed an intense ray of white light on the road ahead. I was traveling so fast that I needed to brake before turning left on to Landing Street where Mrs. Mac Mullin resided.

Once on Landing Street I pedaled slowly, in part due to its gravel surface, and in part because I wasn't positive where to meet up with Zack. I knew Zack had brought some supplies like a stepladder, some brushes, and some drop cloths over to the old factory during the week via the shortcut,. I assumed he would be traveling the same route tonight with the paint. I rode on past Mrs. Mac Mullin's house towards the mill, then I stopped my bike to check the time. It wasn't quite 7:00 yet. In addition, the porch light at Mrs. Mac Mullins' was not yet on, so I figured Zack must be coming up through the trail. As I looked up, I thought I saw a figure on a bike turn off of Ormond Avenue onto Landing Street, and I wondered if I was being followed.

Rather than turn toward the figure and head back toward Mrs. Mac Mullin's house, I decided to meet up with Zack at the mill. The starlit sky shone brighter in the darkness by the creek as I got off my bike and walked it towards the gate. With each step, the generator gave a dim glow to the bike's headlight, which intermittently lit the path. When I reached the gate, I looked back to see that the figure was definitely following me, but intentionally keeping a distance between us. In addition, whomever it was had abandoned his bicycle and now appeared to be following on foot.

Holding on to my bike with one hand, I put my other hand in my pants pocket and pulled out the key ring attached to my knife. The ring which once held only one important key, now was rife with extras that made finding the gate key difficult. I felt the keys with my fingers and held them up to the stars but was having no luck finding the one I needed. With a flash of inspiration, I raised my bike's back wheel, and pushed down on the pedal long enough to shine the headlight on the set of keys. The gate key was second from the left, and I took the key between my thumb and forefinger, and slipped it into the gate lock as I had done at least a hundred times before. The lock popped open, and I entered the gate and carried my bicycle inside. Switching off the generator light, I walked over to the abandoned factory. Opening the factory door, I went inside the dark building, only to be startled by Zack, who was inside with a flashlight, having just arrived with the paint, and about to pick up the ladder.

"Jesus Christ, Zack! You scared the hell out of me!" I whispered out to him, my heart beating a mile a minute. "Turn out the flashlight! I think somebody is following me!"

We scampered over to the office window, and sure enough, we could see the figure by the fence.

"Do you know who it is?" Zack asked.

"I'm not positive, but it could be one of the Dobalo brothers," I whispered.

"Did you lock the gate?" he countered in a hushed tone.

"No," I replied. "I was scared, and the keys were hard to see."

"Shhhhhhh," Zack continued. "Whoever it is…is at the gate."

We watched as the figure slowly approached the gate and walked through.

"I got an idea," Zack whispered, "Let's sneak out through the back, and go around the side. If he comes in after us, they'll be no one inside to find."

We both scrambled out of the office door, leaving my bike inside. Then we went to the back of the factory, outside through the fallen wall, and around the side of the building. Now standing at the building's side we watched as the figure went over to the factory door. Zack went to crouch down slowly to get a better look at the stranger, but he knocked into me, and we both fell forward making a muddled sound. The figure looked over at us, and Zack flipped on the flashlight revealing one of the Dobalo brothers.

Instinctively we ran for the gate. I got there first and exited, and Zack followed, falling once and dropping his flashlight. Once through, Zack slammed the gate shut and pushed the lock shut, but our perpetrator did not follow. Instead he went into the factory and came out with my bicycle.

"He's got my bike!" I yelled.

The lone brother then started for the gate with the bicycle in his hands, while we stood and watched.

Zack yelled out, "We got you trapped! Caught you red-handed stealing the bike, just like you stole my bike from the church railing, and Bill's stingray from the tree on Collins Avenue. You can't get out from this gate. You're locked in, and we're going up to those houses and call the cops to arrest you!"

With that, the thief turned around and started walking towards the creek which was covered with ice. In his hands he clutched the bike, and walked with it by his side, stopping briefly to flip on the generator light. Then with its dim light as a guide he continued to the creek, surveying its surface and the distance across the dammed area to the other side. Pick the spot and cross a little more than 25 feet of ice, and he could be on the other side of the creek and free. The figure crept closer to the creek's edge, and dropped the bike, its metallic license plate making a ringing noise as it hit the ground. Leaving the bike on the grass, he gently set one foot on the ice and then the other, as he began his trek across the frozen creek. Under the ice, the creek's silent rushing waters flowed swiftly, spilling out in a gush over the dam a mere thirty feet downstream. Zack and I watched in amazement as the figure moved slowly across the icy surface. One foot, two feet, four feet, six feet. Suddenly there was a large vibrating noise, similar to the sound of someone hitting a metal pole with a hammer. It was followed by a tremendous cracking crescendo, and a soft splash. Through the darkness, we saw the figure slowly sink into the deep. It seemed to occur almost in slow motion, and was followed by the brief sound of someone calling for help.

I grabbed the keys again from my pocket, and fumbled through them to find the proper one. Unlocking the gate, Zack and I ran to the creek, but we were too late. Zack picked up his flashlight and shined it on the ice. A six-foot section of ice was now missing, but there were no signs of movement or splashing, or any traces of clothing. We stood looking over the area for nearly an hour, and finally concluded that our perpetrator had either made a valiant escape, or had been sucked by the rushing water under the ice and had either drowned or frozen to death.

"What do we do now?" I asked Zack.

My question was answered at first only by silence.

"...Nothing..." Zack replied. "...There's really nothing we can do. If he crossed he's probably home by now; if he's dead we can't undo it. I suggest we make a brief appearance at Mrs. Mac Mullin's, tell her it took a while to get the paint, then stop back again tomorrow just like nothing happened. After all, we didn't force him on the ice; he went on it of his own free will. And why should we be guilty of a crime? He was the one taking your bike!"

We vowed that we would not say anything of this night to anyone else, worried that they would blame us for killing him. So we swore on our lives we wouldn't utter a word. I picked up my bike, and Zack got the ladder and painting supplies, and we headed to Mrs. Mac Mullins house. It was nearly 9:00 when I knocked at the door and apologized for the late hour.

"We had a problem getting the paint, but we promised we would stop by," I said. "If it's ok, we'll just drop things off tonight and stop by early tomorrow and get started."

"Oh, that will be fine," she said. "And I'm so glad you stopped by to tell me. I was waiting for you around 7:00 and I thought I heard some commotion outside, and I was worried that something might have happened and one of you might have gotten hurt."

"No, that wasn't us, "Zack said.

"So how about we see you at 9:00 tomorrow morning?" I interrupted.

"That sounds like a good plan to me," she said. "It's almost 9:00 now, and I'll be in bed in another hour, so you wouldn't be able to get much done tonight anyway," she continued.

"Sounds great; have a good night," I replied as we left out through the door.

I grabbed my bike, and we started to walk onto Landing Street. Not more than ten feet from where we were standing we saw an old Stingray style bike lying on the ground.

"He must have been riding that when he started to follow me," I guessed.

"Let's not take any chances." Zack said. And he picked the bike off the ground.

"What do you say we head back along the trail, and ditch the Stingray somewhere far from here?"

There was no argument from either of us, and the quicker we got away from there, the faster we could put the events of the night behind us. The same couldn't be said for a second figure, however, standing in the shadows of the woods just beyond Landing Street.

Chapter 27 – The Body

The night did not bode well for several of us living on different perimeters of the town - at least as far as sleeping was concerned. Over on Greenbriar Avenue, Deanna laid on her bed all night in her clothes, having fallen in and out of sleep waiting by the phone for a goodnight call from her fantastic boyfriend who once vowed he would do anything for her.

Over on Landing Street, Mrs. Mac Mullin laid awake in her bed, unable to move her leg due to the arthritic condition of her knee and the soreness of her side and head from a second fall she had experienced walking upstairs to go to bed. As she lay in her bed she thought of the emptiness of her life, and wondered how things might have changed if she only had the written proof of her relation to Hezekiah Smyth just following his death.

"He was in his mid-seventies when he died," she thought. "At that point in his life, you would think he was beyond the events which happened nearly forty years earlier. Would people really think less of his many successes in life because he had impregnated a sixteen year old girl that he would eventually marry? Why wouldn't he have shared the birth certificate at that late stage in his life, or even have left a note, or a will?"

Over on Haddon Avenue, I lay awake beneath my covers afraid to shut my eyes, because each time I did, all I could see was a vision of a blue and bloated figure, trapped underwater beneath a sheet of ice, banging to get free from his watery grave. Just the thought of the figure made me feel sick to my stomach and caused shivers to run up my spine.

Lastly there was the young man who lay awake in his bed on Ormond Avenue, cursing his cowardice as he had watched his brother die before him. How could he have let this happen? Why didn't he come to the aid of his brother? And how could he best exact revenge on the two who had led his brother to his demise?

There was one in town who slept soundly however. Over on Bettlewood Avenue, Zack slept an exhausted sleep, having rode the perpetrator's Stingray over six miles to a remote area of woods just beyond the seediest part of Camden. There, he left the bike in a heap, just as we had found it earlier that night. He then proceeded to walk the six plus miles back home again.

I awoke, still exhausted from the night's sleep, on Saturday morning at 7:00. I was to meet Zack by the mill at 8:00 and then go on to Mrs. Mac Mullin's for a morning of painting. As I walked towards the creek, the sick feeling in my stomach returned, as I dreaded any chance of seeing a floating corpse on the creek surface. As I went down the steps at Collins Avenue, I saw Zack about fifty feet behind, so I waited for him to meet up with me. We didn't speak as we met, and we both walked silently to the gate, both fearing what could be there, and knowing we were thinking the same ugly thoughts. I reluctantly unlocked the gate, and we both walked inside and wordlessly walked over to the area where the figure had fallen through the ice the night before. But there was no hole in the ice, or trace of a fall, or signs of anything abnormal. Only a solid sheet of unbroken ice was visible to us. Over by the dam, the water continued to pour over its edge, falling down to the stream below in its typical wintry fashion. At the bottom of the fall were some stray sticks and logs, some encrusted in ice, but there was no sign of a body below, nor a jacket or any other article of clothing.

We left the creek and continued through the other gate and up the hill to Landing Street and Mrs. Mac Mullin's home. We arrived at the house at 8:45, and I knocked on the door, turning to look at the view of the creek and the dam from the porch in the early morning sunlight. The view through the barren trees was spectacular as the sun sparkled over the stream and the tumbling water.

Mrs. Mac Mullin answered the door at last, a cane in her hand, and with a heavy sweater wrapped around her thinning bones. She greeted us, and Zack and I instantly went to work, moving the furniture of the room to one side, and laying down the canvas drop cloths to keep any stray paint off of the room's dark hardwood floors. Zack set up the stepladder and took the lid off the can of paint and began to stir it, while I positioned a roller tray and took out a trim brush. When the paint was sufficiently stirred, Zack took the brush and instructed me on the proper method to paint the wood trim. Completing his instruction, he grabbed the roller and put paint into the pan and began to cover the stained wall. The paint went on easy, the color was instantly appealing, and Mrs. Mac Mullin clapped her hands to her face and asked herself why she had not had the painting performed sooner.

Zack stood back to admire the color and Mrs. Mac Mullin teased, "Now don't you stop, or I'll have to ask for my money back."

"Well you'd be out of luck," Zack replied, "because the money has already been spent on a brand new bicycle."

"Oh, is that so?" she questioned. "Well I might have to take it, and you would be left with the old one."

"The old one's gone," Zack said. "It was stolen. Stolen right from the step of the church where it was locked up on the railing. It was the worst day of my life."

"As bad as that was, it couldn't beat last night," I thought.

"Nothing worse?" Mrs. Mac Mullin mused. "But then you're still young."

"It's strange," Zack said as he resumed painting," But even when my father died, it didn't feel quite as bad. I guess it's because he was sick for so long before he died that it actually came as a bit of a relief when he finally passed."

"Come to think of it, I believe you're right." Mrs. Mac Mullin said. "When my father and mother died after long sicknesses, it wasn't such a horrible day, more of a liberation, knowing they had gone to a better place. As crazy as it sounds, even when my late husband died in the war, he had been missing in action for so long before I knew of his fate that I actually felt some closure the day I learned of his death."

"So what was the worst day of your life?" I asked, regretting that I had asked such a miserable question as soon as the words left my lips.

"Well that would have been the day my step-brother had the statue of my mother ripped from the garden of the Mansion and destroyed, with its bits thrown into the creek," she said. "It all happened so suddenly; it was such a shock."

Mrs. Mac Mullin shook her head, and wiped her eye. "Let's talk of happier things," she said. "Like how wonderful the freshly painted room looks."

"Agreed!"

Zack was a quick painter and he finished the first coat of paint in no time. By 11:30, Mrs. Mac Mullin had dozed off asleep on the couch. The wall where Zack had started to paint was now dry, so he began to apply a second coat. I moved around the furniture as best I could to make Zack's job easier, and by 12:30 the job was done. We began to pack up our things when Mrs. Mac Mullin awoke.

"Thanks for such a wonderful job," she declared.

Zack decided to leave the remaining paint in Mrs. Mac Mullin's living room closet and to throw out the brushes and rollers rather than clean them. That left only the ladder and canvas drop cloths to take home. We put on our coats and Zack carried the ladder and I the cloths. Walking back through the trail I noticed some wet paint had rubbed off of one of the drop cloths onto my Harvard jacket, so I left the drop cloth inside the old factory, figuring I could pick it up another day after it had fully dried. We silently checked the site again, and all was in place. Still the inspection left me again with an uneasy feeling, and I wondered if this place which had once seemed so magical to me would ever feel the same.

We left the second gate and headed home, splitting up at the steps at Collins Avenue so that I could get home to get my paper bag and make the return trip. Zack took the remaining drop cloth from my hand and he said he'd see me Monday before school.

At the station that afternoon, I apologized to Deanna for not calling her, saying we ran into some problems with the painting and didn't get home until very late. She said it was fine and made a wisecrack about the streak of paint that had dried on my jacket. I sat on Kevin Leahy's newspaper pile and folded my papers, making a quick perusal of the news to see if there was any report of a missing boy, which there wasn't. John Shelly, Alvin Morrison, and Joey Gilmore all came in and no one had any stories of unusual activities, and Danny Dobalo's pile of papers was already gone from the station when I arrived there.

This all changed by Tuesday, when Deanna reported that an announcement had been made at school that Bobby Dobalo had been missing since Friday evening. If anyone knew of his whereabouts or had seen him since Friday night they were immediately to let one of the Sisters know. In the station, John Shelly said he had heard that they found what appeared to be Bobby's old Stingray somewhere in Camden, and the police had begun their search there. The overall consensus was that no real foul play had been involved and that Bobby had just wandered off somewhere and gotten lost, or had just decided to leave home. Rumors were that Danny Dobalo knew nothing of his poor brother's whereabouts. He continued to regularly attend school, but he had quieted down somewhat. Several people in the station, Deanna included, had begun referring to him as that *Poor Danny Dobalo* because they sympathized with the pain he must be feeling from the loss associated with a missing twin brother.

The days turned to weeks after the death of Bobby Dobalo and he ceased to be a topic of conversation. Yet I still felt pangs of nervousness every time I entered the mill gate, fearing the body would materialize along the water's surface. All remained in this fashion up until the first full week of March. It was also during this week that Danny met up again with Billy Proudst. The week began with some heavy rain that made serving a wet mess, and by mid-week the temperature had warmed unseasonably into the 70's. On Thursday March 9th, as I walked past the factory, I looked over to the dam as I had every day since Bobby's death and I saw a figure floating face down on the surface of the water, his hand lying over the concrete weir of the dam. As I walked closer, I could see he was still fully clothed, with a heavy jacket on, his boots pulling his legs down slightly below his torso and beneath the water. Although the body appeared swollen and waterlogged, I instantly recognized it to be approximately the shape and size of Bobby Dobalo.

It seems that when a body drowns, it starts to sink once the lungs become filled with water. Once submerged, the body will stay underwater until the bacteria in the gut and chest cavity produce enough gas -- methane, hydrogen sulfide, and carbon dioxide -- to float it to the surface. In the case of Bobby, the process took nearly a month, most likely due to the cold temperature of the water which dramatically slowed down the process. I looked to see if anyone was watching me, but as usual the area was devoid of people. I stood there for several minutes, unable to decide what to do, and then I finally decided to leave the body in place and continue with my route.

That night, as I sat and did my schoolwork, the image of the body repeatedly crept into my mind. Finally, after considering the multiple reasons why I should not return, I was inexplicably drawn back to the dam. Going downstairs, I mentioned to my father I was going out for a bit, and then I grabbed a flashlight and headed back to the mill. I walked to the mill in almost a stupor, with no real plan of action. My best bet was just to leave the body for someone else to find. How could that incriminate Zack or me? But maybe questions would be asked. Who was in the area that night? How did the bike get to Camden? In my state, I knew if I were ever questioned I would likely crack like a stone.

Nearing the mill, I began to walk slower, carefully monitoring the surroundings for others. I entered the gate and sat gazing for ten minutes, still seeing no one in the area and contemplating what to do. Finally I summed up the courage to walk back over to the dam, but when I did, the body appeared to be missing. I gazed around and then flipped on the flashlight. With the beam of light, I could now see the hand and arm lying over the concrete ledge; rust-colored cedar water flowing on both sides of the arm, but the body had sunk again, at least partially. The body was positioned fairly close to the edge of the dam where I was standing, the water and its position somehow forcing it in that direction. I bent down on my knees and shined the flashlight into the water, and to my horror I saw what appeared to be a bluish-white face peering back up at me from about two and a half feet below the water's surface. The sight made me pull backward, and I rocked into a branch that was strewn nearby that made me fall over onto the ground. As I tumbled, I braced my fall with my left hand, smashing my ring finger and pinky finger between the branch and the gravel covered earth, cutting my fingers and pulverizing the branch. With my heart beating uncontrollably, I pulled a handkerchief from my back pocket and wrapped it around my two bleeding fingers. Then I picked up the stick and poked the body about the jacket hood, and its head bobbed up, still attached to the body, but still face down in the water. Shining the flashlight over past the body again, the submerged face again was perceivable, and it seemed clear the face on the weir flooring before the dam was that of a second figure.

Feeling a bit confused now, I took the stick and stuck it deep into the water, tapping the face and feeling it to be hard like stone. This was quite unlike the partially floating body which when tapped was soft and bloated. My thoughts turned to the statue of Agnes Smyth, which was supposedly crushed and tossed into the creek, and I wondered if the statue had not been destroyed but simply was thrown into the rushing water.

Gazing back at the body of Bobby Dobalo, now partially afloat, I thought I might pull the body from the water and move it passed the dam so that it could be carried by the water flow downstream from the area. So kneeling back down I grabbed the bloated body by the jacket and pulled it up from the water and onto the shore. The body turned out to be lighter than I had thought, that was until it was about three-quarters removed from the water. Then it became heavy, with water pouring from the soggy clothes, and an acrid smell that reminded me of digging for clams by the bay. Being careful to keep the front of the head from my sight, I grabbed the hood of the jacket even tighter with my right hand, and grabbed the pocket of the jacket with my left, and pulled once again with all my might. Then with one sudden surge, the body toppled completely out of the water onto land, and I fell over backward, narrowly missing the body and ripping the pocket of the waterlogged jacket in half. From out of the pocket flew a shiny metallic object that skipped across the ground. Regaining my balance, I went for the flashlight and shined it towards the shiny item. The light reflected off the silver base and green top of the object and I picked it up, instantly recognizing it once I held it in my hand. Other than a bit of dirt accumulated during the fall, it was unscratched and undamaged. In my hand I held the metallic Hot Heap die-cast car that I had seen as an enlarged model in Millar's Bicycle and Hobby Shop back in December.

Holding the Hot Wheels car in my hand instantly transformed the gruesome swollen sodden corpse back to what it really was, a misguided boy not much older than I who had made a mistake. I couldn't throw this body back into the river, but I couldn't leave it here either. Remembering the canvas drop cloth back in the factory, I left the body and went to retrieve the drop cloth. Laying the cloth on the ground next to the body, I moved the body onto it, and folded the cloth around it, to hide its disfigured state from my sight and to make pulling it easier. I then dragged the tarp out the gate and around past the dam. The darkness of the night helped me to travel undetected. Reaching the woods, I shone the flashlight until I found a flat spot in the sandy soil in which to dig a shallow grave. Using the old shovel from the factory tool closet, I slowly began to dig a hole about three times as big as the body. I had to stop twice during the digging; the first time due to a session of uncontrollable crying, and the second time due to the overwhelming odor. Then pulling the drop cloth with the body over to the hole, I pulled it inside, unfolded it, and removed the tarp, allowing the body to lie on the freshly dug soil. Ripping a section from the drop cloth, I covered Bobby's face, and as a last rite, I took the Hot Heap Car and placed it into his good coat pocket. I then proceeded to cover the body with dirt, smoothing over the site and covering it with leaves and sticks until its appearance blended in with the general surroundings. After wiping down the shovel and returning it to the factory closet, I folded up the remaining tarp and wiped the dirt from my hands. As the rain again began to fall, I stopped over the grave and prayed, first for Bobby, and then for myself, asking for forgiveness for both of us.

Across town, Bobby's brother was meeting with Billy Proudst at his apartment. Billy lived with his father over in the Manor section of town, in a small apartment near the junior high school. Billy had heard of Bobby's disappearance and had assumed the worst. He had intentionally avoided Danny ever since he heard Bobby was missing, not answering his calls or visiting his house. As far as Billy was concerned, his days of bicycle stealing were over. People were getting suspicious, and with Bobby gone and the way Danny did business, Billy had the most to lose.

"H-H-Hey, Danny," Billy said, "An-Any news about your br-brother? I heard he was missing. Do you think he's off h-h-hiding from school?"

"Come on, Billy," Danny replied. "We all know what happened to my brother. He pushed his luck too far this time. Bit off more than he could chew, and now he's gone, and he's not coming back."

"I'm sorry to hear that, h-he really wasn't a b-b-bad kid," Billy said. "You know what h-happened?"

"Yeah, there were two of them," Danny replied. "They set him up, and I'm going to get them. You want to help?"

"N-N-No, I don't Danny. I've been th-thinkin' about this stuff and what we've been doing lately, and I think it's time we la-laid low before we get c-caught," Billy mumbled.

"I'm not talkin' about bikes," Danny said. "I'm talkin' about gettin' even. This is my brother we're talking about here."

Billy had a worried look on his face. This was something he had no intention of getting involved with.

"N-Not this t-time Danny," Billy said. "Like I said, I g-g-gotta hang low. You should do the s-same."

"Ah, you're just a coward you punk!" Danny said, "I'm through with you, but before I leave you still owe me some money. The last job we agreed to 60 bucks, so with Bobby's portion you owe me $40."

"Y-Yeah, I'll get it," Billy said, anxious to get Danny out of his apartment and out of his life once and for all. "It's in the b-b-bedroom."

While Billy went into the bedroom, Danny snuck over to the desk drawer by the phone and pulled out a Smith and Wesson blue steel Target Champion 59, which was a 9-mm handgun which belonged to Billy's father. Danny had seen Billy toy with it on several occasions. He placed the gun in his inside coat pocket and searched for ammunition. He spied a magazine with just three rounds and slipped it into his pocket, shutting the drawer and moving back into the living room just before Billy came back with the money.

"H-H-Here's your m-m-money, man," Billy said.

"You sure you don't want to help?" Danny asked, "There's $100 in it for ya."

"N-Nah, but t-t-thanks for the offer."

Danny took the money and left the apartment. Little did Billy realize he had been duped again, and he was helping more than he imagined.

Chapter 28 – Confession

As I walked away from the mill, with the tarp and flashlight in my hand, I glanced down at my left hand, which was beginning to throb. I adjusted the bloody handkerchief wrapped about my two fingers, pulling it tight to help deaden the pain. I headed up the steps on Collins Avenue, and continued straight up the street until I reached the corner of Johnson. Glancing over one block, I looked at 28 East Greenbriar and saw a light shining down from Deanna's bedroom window, which was partially covered by a pulled shade. Checking the hour, it was nearly 11:30 PM, way beyond the time I was due home on a school night. I needed to talk with someone I trusted, so I started towards Deanna's house, but the room light went dim before I was even halfway up the street. I continued to the house anyway, standing for a moment before the front concrete steps. I wanted to knock, but reconsidering the hour, I turned back towards home, as the falling rain subsided to a mist.

Halfway to Clinton Avenue, I heard a muddled whistle, and I turned to see a figure approaching, with an umbrella in hand. As the figure got closer, I recognized the familiar gait and flowing curly hair of Deanna.

"I was just heading to bed, and I saw your coat from the window, so I snuck out the door to see what you were up to," she said.

"I'm a mess," I heard myself say. "And I needed to talk to you for advice."

I was covered in dirt, and wet from the rain and the cedar water from the river. My sneakers were caked with mud and made a squeaking sound when I walked. And my pants and coat had stench similar to that of the body.

"Your hand looks so sore. Were you in some kind of fight?" she asked.

"Only with my conscience," I replied, as we continued to walk towards my home.

When we reached my house on Haddon Avenue my father was outside, impatiently walking the dog while waiting for me.

"Where were you?" he asked in a stern, but loving voice. "With all the stolen bikes in the neighborhood, and now that missing Dobalo boy, we were worried sick about you. This town is going to hell in a handbasket and we don't need you leading the way. Your mother's a nervous wreck, and I was on the verge."

Before I could answer, Deanna spoke up and said, "It's my fault, sir. Please don't take it out on him!"

My father nodded in an understanding manner. "You kids need to be more careful. Let us know where you are. Call on the phone if there's a problem," he begged. "I won't ask what you've been up to. I trust your judgment and sense of responsibility. Go in the house through the cellar way. If you track that mud on the rug, your mother will send us all packing. And you little girl, I hope your parents aren't sick from wondering where you are too. You know us parents were once children too, and we know all the tricks kids play, but please remember we worry about your safety and well-being. We don't intentionally try to be overbearing. So now that I'm done with my dad speech, I'll leave you alone, but try to keep the hour reasonable. I'll go in and unlock the cellar door, and then I'm going up to bed."

He went into the house with the dog and we walked over to the side door. The side door opened to a landing that either went down to the basement or up to the kitchen. I kicked off my shoes before entering the house, and then we walked down to the basement. Our basement was not much to look at, just concrete walls, a workshop containing my dad's tools, and a small laundry room towards the back. This room contained an automatic dryer, a washing machine, and a large cast concrete sink. My mother was from the old school, and liked to hang many laundry items outside to dry in the summer. Similarly, in the winter she hung certain articles of clothing, sheets, and towels from a clothesline that ran crisscross beneath the basement ceiling.

Once inside the laundry room, I took off my jacket, sweatshirt, pants and socks, and put them on top of the washer, pulling a dry pair of sweatpants and a sweatshirt from the clothes line and putting them on instead. Walking over to the sink, I began to wash the dirt from my hands, struggling around my wounded fingers. Sensing my pain, Deanna helped me by lathering her hands and gently rubbing my hands clean. She then grabbed a towel from the line, and dried my hands and my hair. She then took a washrag and wiped off my face, which was covered with bits of dirt, until I again appeared somewhat presentable.

She then went to the clothesline and pulled off a clean handkerchief and wrapped it about my fingers. The bleeding had stopped but both fingers still appeared quite tender. As she looked at the cuts, I recalled my childhood and Joey Flaherty and the tale of the lockjaw.

I looked at Deanna and asked if she considered herself to be of the Catholic religion.

"Well, actually I'm a Christian. I regularly attend mass at a Catholic church," she replied.

"Ok," I conjectured. "Do you believe that people who don't go to a Catholic church can never go to heaven?"

"That's ridiculous," she answered. "All who believe in the Lord and follow his teachings are eligible to enter."

"What do you think about someone who saw someone die, but didn't tell anyone for fear that he would be implicated in the death?" I asked.

"It depends if he assisted in the killing," she said. "Why are you asking me all this stuff?"

I looked at her and tears welled in my eyes. "Promise you won't tell this to anyone," I asked.

"I swear," she vowed.

"I'm pretty sure that I saw Bobby Dobalo get killed, but I haven't told anyone."

"But why? You didn't kill him did you?" she questioned.

"Of course not, but it's a long complicated story," I answered.

"Do you know where the body is now?" she asked.

"I kinda really would rather not say," I replied.

She stood deep in thought. "I believe in you and your sense of right and wrong. But I really think it's important that the family know what happened, even if they find out the truth anonymously."

It really wasn't quite the answer I wanted to hear, but I could tell she sensed my conflict so she didn't preach on. We left the basement together and went upstairs into the kitchen. Looking at the refrigerator, she asked if I wanted some ice for my fingers. I nodded *yes* in response, and she grabbed some ice from the freezer and put it in a plastic bag, and handed it to me to hold against my bruised fingers. Closing the refrigerator, she asked about a 2x3 inch school photo of me that hung from under a magnet on the refrigerator door and she asked if she could have it. I said that she could and she carefully put it in her coat pocket.

We then entered into our back family room, which was a large addition that my father had added to the back of the house. When we entered, the lights in the room were off, except for those of a large fish aquarium that sat in the corner of the room next to the couch. We both sat down on the couch in the light from the tank, saying little and watching the fish swim by. I was tired and leaned my head against her shoulder. I gradually reclined on the couch, with my head on her lap, and gazed into the fish tank as she gently rubbed her fingers over my forehead and through my hair. The fish tank was covered with a glass top, over which perched the light. The water level in the tank was high so that the bubbles from the filter traveled upward and hit the underside of the glass top, and rolled outward towards an opening at the back of the lid. The fish darted about the tank, occasionally swimming up to the bubbles along the glass surface. A day ago, I would have shuttered to look at this site, a reminder of Bobby's body gasping for air beneath the ice surface. But Bobby was free from the ice and the water now, and somehow I felt more at peace with his death.

I shut my eyes with the hypnotizing, soothing feel of her caressing fingers on my forehead, feeling somewhat comforted by the night's events, the warmth of her body, and the presence of someone I trusted and respected at my side. In a short time, my body relaxed and fell into a peaceful sleep.

While I slept, she continued to stroke my hair, and look down on the boy she had fallen in love with. As she stared down she prayed that our love would grow stronger and that we could share our whole lives together. Eventually she too began to nod off, and fall into a peaceful sleep.

About 2:30, my father walked from upstairs into the family room and saw us on the couch together. Silently he walked beside the couch and gently tapped Deanna on the shoulder. When she opened her eyes, he put his finger over his lips and motioned for Deanna not to wake me. Placing a couch pillow under my head, Deanna got up and my father covered me with the afghan. Then he thanked Deanna for her support and walked her to the car and drove her home. Once home, she stole up the front stairs and unlocked the front door, waving goodbye to my father as she entered the house and crept stealthily to her bed.

Chapter 29 – Shadows [2]

The next morning I woke up on the couch alone. It was 9:00 and it took me a minute to realize what had happened, and that I had overslept and would be late for school. I could hear my mother in the kitchen, and she walked down into the family room, and saw that I was awake and asked if I wanted any breakfast.

"Your father said you had a rough time last night and he suggested I let you sleep late today," she said.

I told her I wasn't hungry, and she mentioned, "When you feel ready, why don't you get up and take a shower? You can skip school today. I don't know what you did last night, but you had me worried sick. I kept thinking of that missing Dobalo boy, and I was scared something might have happened to you. I'm off from work today, and I was thinking later this morning we should go to Grants and get you a new pair of sneakers and a new coat. This morning in the basement I saw that coat and the pants you wore yesterday on the washer and threw them out. The pants were ripped and caked with mud, and that coat, let's just say that it has seen much better days. The same goes for your sneakers; they were coated with mud both inside and out and smelled like rotten fish. They're also in the trash, we can get you a new pair at Grants as well."

She left and went back to her chores in the kitchen, and I got up to get a shower. While showering I noticed the swelling on my fingers had gone down, and the cuts looked a bit better. After my shower, I covered the cuts with three Band-Aids around each finger, and I got dressed and combed my hair for the trip to the store.

Three blocks away, Deanna was also at home. It seems she hadn't gone to school either, telling her mother she wasn't feeling well in order to get a bit more sleep from her late night out. As she lay in bed, she made up her mind to help, whether I wanted it or not. So she jotted down a few thoughts on a piece of paper. Then thinking about it a bit more, she found her mother's typewriter, and carefully pecked out a letter to Mrs. Dobalo. The letter was short but to the point.

Dear Mrs. Dobalo,

I have known both of your boys for quite a long time, and I was saddened when I first heard that Bobby was missing. Recently when speaking with a reliable friend, I was told confidentially that this friend knew for certain that Bobby had died. Unfortunately, although the friend had nothing to do with the death, he is concerned that by going to the authorities with this information, that he might be wrongly associated in Bobby's death. I am not writing you this note to sadden you, but I hope it might help bring closure to Bobby's life and this difficult part of your family's bereavement.

Respectfully yours,

A Concerned Friend.

Around 11:00 my mother and I went to Grants. I got a pair of black Chuck Taylor Converse sneakers, a new pair of jeans, and a blue hooded jacket. The blue jacket was for school and bumming around. My mom said she would also have liked to get me a new dress coat for special occasions and church, but Grants just didn't seem to carry anything all that nice. By the time we got done at the store and some of the other shopping that my mom had planned, it was already 2:00. So my mom stopped home with the car, I picked up my paper bag, and she dropped me off at the paper station. Since it was Friday, Deanna was inside collecting money from the carriers.

I quickly gathered my papers without talking to anyone and set out on my route. For the first time in weeks I felt no ominous feeling when I unlocked the gate by the paper trail, and felt no need to peer into the water in search of a floating body. When I got to Mrs. Mac Mullin's house I was surprised that she had left a note on the door for me to come in. When I did, I saw her sitting on her couch, still in her nightgown, with a blanket on her lap and another around her shoulders.

"Your money is on the table," she said. "Please go get it. And if you could, please hand me the paper. I'm afraid that I am a bit under the weather, and my legs don't really seem to be getting much better, despite the warmer weather."

I handed her the paper, and told her I hoped that she'd get better soon. Then I asked her if there was anything I could do for her.

"Well maybe if you could bring the paper in to me each day for the next week or so, I would appreciate it," she said, "That'll save me an extra trip to the door while I'm not feeling well. Bending over to pick up the paper can take me quite a while some days."

I served the remainder of my route and collected from all but seven of the houses, and then I stopped home to eat dinner before I returned to the station to pay Deanna and accompany her to the bank. I arrived at her kitchen door about 5:30 which was typical, and Deanna opened the door to let me in. Her appearance seemed even a bit more polished than usual. She had on a dress and a bit of makeup, her nails were freshly primped, and her hair glistened and smelled of Herbal Essences.

"Wow, you look beautiful. You're so dressed up. Are you going out tonight or something?" I asked.

"Nah, I did this because of you," she proclaimed with a smile.

"What, are we going out on a date or something?" I inquired.

"No, silly, because of you I slept late this morning and didn't go to school today, and since I had so much extra time, I figured I'd clean myself up a bit," she explained.

"That's funny. I woke-up this morning alone on the couch. It seems my best girl must have walked out on me last night," I said. "And I slept so late that I missed school today too."

"That explains it," she declared. "Looks like you cleaned up a bit too since last night, and even got new sneakers and a new jacket."

We continued to talk and wrap up coins until Dave Parker finally arrived about 5:50, and when he left, Deanna packed up the money and we walked together to the bank. Once we were through, I asked her if she wanted to come over to my house for a bit.

"I got into a little trouble from my parents about the late hours I've been keeping lately, and I promised I wouldn't be out late tonight," I explained. "Besides, my mother and sister are dying to meet you."

Deanna said ok, but she also needed to get in early tonight, by 9:30 per her mother's orders, so we headed to my house and visited with my mother and sister. My father also talked with us a while, never mentioning the night before or his drive with Deanna back to her house while I slept. We even played what I thought would a tedious game of Yahtzee with my parents, which turned out to be a whole lot more fun than I ever imagined, especially when Deanna pulled out a roll of five 6's on the last throw of the dice to win the game.

At 8:30 my mom pulled out an apple pie and some vanilla ice cream and served us all some dessert, then she and my father retired to the living room, leaving Deanna and I alone in the back family room. We watched TV a bit and cuddled until about 9:15, then Deanna said she'd better start for home, so we got our coats and I walked her home.

When we got to her house, she thanked me for a great night and she gave me a slow kiss on the mouth. She then pulled away and said she had something to tell me.

"I hope you don't get mad at me," she said, looking at me with her big brown eyes. "But remember our conversation last night about Bobby Dobalo and bringing closure to his family over his disappearance?"

"Yes, I remember," I recalled.

"So I sent a letter this morning to Mrs. Dobalo, telling her that a friend knew for sure that Bobby…was…dead…and that I was writing her in hopes that this might help bring a proper…closure to… his life," she explained.

"You did what?" I questioned.

"Please don't be angry with me," she protested. "I did it for you."

"I don't know about this," I argued. "And you promised me you wouldn't tell anyone."

"I didn't tell her. I wrote it in a letter. And besides, I kept it anonymous," she went on. "No names or times were mentioned."

"I have a bad feeling about this," I objected.

"Just be that way," she sighed. "But I was just trying to do the right thing."

And with that she ran up her front steps and into the house.

By Monday of the following week the letter reached Mrs. Dobalo, and by Tuesday the letter was with the local police. It didn't take long thereafter until the news spread to the entire media.

The following Thursday, the majority of us carriers were waiting at the station for the paper truck to arrive. Deanna was seated at the table, but we were not talking. At 4:00 the truck drove up and backed into the driveway. As Curt the driver got out of the truck he commented, "Don't blame me; they held the presses for the breaking story!"

As the truck pulled away, Deanna began dividing up the papers. Alvin Morrison was the first to read the headlines.

"Hey look, Oaklynne made the front page!!"

There on the front page was the headline, "ANONYMOUS LETTER ASSERTS MISSING BOY DEAD." And there below the headline was a story about the letter sent to Mrs. Dobalo and an actual transcript of the letter. The story quoted Detective Sergeant Hebner saying they were stepping up the investigation. Then the story went on to recount the approximate time and day that Bobby Dobalo had disappeared and then recounted how his bicycle had been found in Camden several days after his disappearance.

Just reading the story brought back the tragic memories of that night and made me feel sick. I immediately packed up my papers and started off from the station, passing a silent Deanna as I left, looking her straight in the eye and shaking my head. By Friday there were stories about the letter and Bobby's disappearance on the local TV news, and by Saturday the story had actually gone national. Because of the attention to the story, I had decided to stay clear of the paper trail, delivering to the Smythville homes by bike, figuring the odds of an attack by Danny during the media frenzy over his brother's story was fairly remote. In fact when I rode by the Dobalo house on Saturday afternoon, there were several TV news trucks camped out in front of the house obviously in anticipation of a comment or two from Mrs. Dobalo.

By Monday, Danny Dobalo had stopped going to school because of all the attention. He had also stopped picking up his papers, electing Paul Slason to serve in his place. On Tuesday, Detective Hebner reported in the paper that they were making great strides in the case and they had now positively identified the make and model of the typewriter that had been used to prepare the letter, and that they had also narrowed down the time that the letter reached the Oaklynne post office to within a four hour period.

Now we all began to sweat out the details of every breaking story or news flash. Of course we all feared different events, and although none of us talked about the proceedings together, we all sensed each other's trepidation. Deanna and I were now not talking to each other at all. I feared the buried body could be somehow uncovered. Deanna feared the letter would be traced to her. Zack feared the body would be found floating in the creek. Billy Proudst feared that the bicycle stealing coup would be uncovered. And Danny Dobalo feared the story would be discovered of what a coward he was as he watched his brother drown and did nothing to help him.

On Friday I collected my route, and when done I rode back to the station. Tapping the door, I silently opened it and handed Deanna an envelope containing one twenty dollar bill, three one dollar bills, three quarters, a dime, a nickel, and four pennies totaling exactly my bill of $23.94 as payment. Then without saying a word I walked out. I rode my bike home feeling miserable and wondered exactly how I had let this small crack between Deanna and I grow into a huge chasm.

Once at home, I moped, feeling worse than ever, knowing I had no one with which I could share my feelings. Plopping on the couch before the fish tank, I turned on the TV and sat in a funk until about 10:15, when the show I was watching was interrupted by a breaking news story. In an interview, Detective Hebner stated that the partial remains of the missing Dobalo boy had been found in an abandoned lot in Camden, not far from where his bicycle had previously been found weeks before. While the cause of the death was still undetermined, it was believed to be drug related.

I couldn't believe the news I was hearing. It was obviously all in error, but it could clear up the mess in my life and let things settle back to normal. Although I am ashamed to admit it, the news made me feel like celebrating, but it didn't matter because I had no one to celebrate with. With a less heavy chest, I decided to go out for a walk, covering up any secret agenda by bringing the dog with me. Being late March, the temperature had become a bit more pleasant, and we walked down Haddon Avenue to Coldspring, and over to Collins. I stopped by the steps leading to the creek and while the dog busied himself smelling the steps, I looked up at the sky. The moon which had hours before shown full had turned a sour shade of blue as a cloud passed over it, and even as the cloud appeared to dissipate, its penumbra remained, some of it a reddish brown, and some of it blue. The moon light flickered on the creek's surface, appearing almost bloodlike, and I pulled the dog away from the steps and away from the scene.

We continued up Collins to the corner of Johnson, where I stood once again and peered over at the Kolakowski home. The upstairs lights were off, and we walked over the block and I stood before the house front steps as I had done before, trying to find the courage to apologize and make things right again. I stood like a fixture on the corner, the dog straining his chain to smell the hydrant, while my shadow from the streetlight cast down on her steps and up on her door, as if it was about to knock to say, "I'm sorry."

But my resolution weakened, and as the dog grew tired of the hydrant, he pulled me away, back across Greenbriar Avenue and again toward home. As we slunk silently away, my shadow resisted, falling behind me as if saying it wanted to retreat and go back to her house. But the shadow was overruled, and before I knew it, I had recrossed Collins Avenue and was halfway over to Clinton Avenue, now out of sight of her house.

> *Won't you reach out love and touch me, let me hold you for a while?*
> *I've been all around the world, oh how I long to see you smile.*
> *There's a shadow on the moon, and the waters here below,*
> *Do not shine the way they should. And I love you just in case you didn't know.*
> *Let it go.*
> *Let it happen like it happened once before.*
> *It's a wicked wind and it chills me to the bone,*
> *and if you do not believe me,*
> *come and gaze upon my shadow at your door.* [2]

Deanna had seen the same interview with Detective Hebner on the 11:00 news and felt the same sense of relief as I had once he gave his report. She headed up the stairs to bed, stopping momentarily by the phone in her bedroom and debated whether she should call me to ask if I had heard the news. But either because of the hour or her pride she resisted. Taking off her clothes, she slipped on her pajamas, and then looking at her dresser, she picked up the picture she had taken from the refrigerator weeks before and held it in her hand. She then turned out the light and walked over to the window, and pulling up the blind she looked out first at the moon, and then to the street where I had passed not more than five minutes earlier. The streetlight dimly lit her window, and her shadow cast down on the bed, with its outstretched arm still cast down beside the phone.

With a final sigh, she pulled the blind half down, and lay on her bed, holding the picture in her hands. Contemplating, she took the picture and placed it beside her on the other pillow, and closed her eyes and began to dream.

Won't you lie down by me baby, run your fingers through my hands?
I've been all around the town and still I do not understand.
Is it me or is it you, or the shadow of a dream?
Is it wrong to be in love?
Could it be the finest love I've ever seen?
Set it free.
Let it happen like it happened once before.
It's a wicked wind and it chills me to the bone,
and if you do not believe me,
come and gaze upon the shadow at your door. [2]

Chapter 30 – The Statue

The news that Detective Hebner had found Bobby's partial remains in a field in Camden came as a huge shock to Danny. After all Danny had seen his brother's body fall through the ice at Smythville, but this wasn't something he was ready to admit to the police or his mother. The body found in Camden had gone through substantial deterioration, and a good part of the skeletal remains were missing. It seems that the strongest tie to his brother was that the bones of the lower torso were of the approximate size and age of Bobby, and that a sneaker on the site matched the type that Bobby was wearing. Danny was especially furious with the comments that the death was drug related. Bobby had never done drugs, and although he had performed some bad deeds and stolen quite a few bicycles, being categorized with the drug crowd was something Danny felt was insulting. Always thinking of himself, Danny also figured that he could be labeled as a druggie as well. After all, if others thought that Bobby was taking drugs, they would probably think that Danny was taking them too.

Despite all the media fanfare over the letter, the funeral passed by almost unnoticed. The remains were cremated, and the burial was a small ceremony attended only by the family. Because of general embarrassment, the feeling was to move on quickly, and soon everyone with the exception of Danny had pretty much removed Bobby's death from their minds. Danny had formed his own opinion of who was accountable and he planned retaliation when the time was right.

By the middle of April, the weather had warmed and spring was in the air. On the morning of Saturday April 22nd, I headed over to Zack's house on my ten-speed bicycle. I had my tire-shaped car collector case in tow, which now even held the Volkswagen, although its cubicle was specially lined with a Kleenex to keep its paint from scratching. We had decided to play with our cars on Zack's porch like we had done in the past, assembling a town with some blocks, and building houses and garages, and roads for the cars to drive on. We played for about thirty minutes, but the activity didn't seem to hold our interest as much as it had in the past. Instead we decided to go for a long ride on our bicycles. In preparation, Zack got his canteen and filled it with water and we set out. The morning was especially beautiful, with what baseball players called a high sky. Not a single cloud was visible and the sky was a tremendously clear shade of blue.

We rode down Bettlewood Avenue and across the bridge over the creek into Collingswood. In Collingswood, there was a road called Lees Lane that rode along the creek and eventually meandered through the woods and followed it as it grew into the lake. Eventually the road fronted lakeside residences, some of which were extremely large with wealthy owners. Along the route, the lake often became blocked from sight by the homes and the woods, only to come into view again up the road by an occasional clearing or a park. We had traveled about five miles, nearing the midway point around the lake, when we came upon one such clearing with a small playground consisting of a swing set, a few see-saws, and a large sliding board. There was also a large circular shaped stone building with a fireplace, built during the Depression for picnicking, before a path that led down to a small concrete fishing dock on the lake.

Zack and I rode our bikes down the path and stopped and sat down on the grass. The air was cool, but the sun was warm, and we sat and gazed out over the lake. Looking at the tremendous volume of water, it was hard to believe that it really was the result of the dam, blocking the creek and creating a reservoir of water about twelve feet higher than the creek's eventual course downstream.

Zack took a drink from the canteen, and then handed it to me and we began to talk.

"So how are things with you and Deanna now?" he asked. "You don't talk as much about her anymore."

I had never told Zack about my burial of Bobby's body or about Deanna and the letter, but somehow I figured he may have suspected that she was the one who wrote it.

"I guess things are pretty bad, but at least when we see each other now, we can muster up a hello," I replied.

"You should try to patch things up," Zack continued. "I like her a lot, and I know that you do too."

I picked up a small stone from the ground and threw it into the water.

"Yeah, well that's easier said than done."

The stone made a splash and scared off a group of ducks that changed the direction of their paddling away from the edge of the lake and into deeper water. As my eyes shifted from the ducks and back across the lake I changed the subject.

"You know, if you look carefully, you can actually see the old factory building on the other side," I said. "But I can barely make out those Smythville houses."

Zack squinted his eyes. "I can't see the houses or the dam," Zack said.

"You know that Mrs. Mac Mullin has taken a turn for the worse. Mrs. Welsh who lives up the street said she is having a really difficult time getting around. She has to go over more and more frequently to see that she's ok, and bring her food. She said that some days she can barely get out of bed. I know she's really old. I wonder if she'll ever get any better."

"Yeah, it's a shame she doesn't have anybody she could go live with; you would think everybody has got some kind of family somewhere," Zack said.

"Well you heard her. He mother and father died and she didn't have any brothers or sisters, at least any ones she was talking to," I answered. "You know she's lived in that house so long, I don't even think if she had any relatives she would leave. Heck, she barely even went outside except for the porch when she was well. Once I was talking to her and I realized that she hadn't walked down to the creek for so long that she didn't even know that the fence around the area was locked. I guess that's why she never questioned how I could come up through the trail each day when I delivered the papers."

"I wonder what ever happened to the creep step-brother of hers who had the statue of her mother destroyed," Zack asked.

Just then I remembered the statue.

"You know Zack, I don't think I ever mentioned this to you, but one day I was looking over by the corner of the dam when the water was running slow, and I thought I saw a face in the water. At first I was scared that maybe it was Bobby's dead body, but when I poked it with a stick it seemed to be made of stone. I'm not sure if the statue really ever was destroyed. I think that maybe they just threw it in the water and it eventually was carried by the current to the edge of the dam."

Did you try to pull it out?" Zack asked.

"No, it's way too heavy. It's a shame. I remember Mrs. Mac Mullin saying the day they threw it in was the worst day of her life. It probably would brighten up her spirits if we could pull it out," I theorized.

"You want to go take a look?" Zack asked, never afraid to tackle a challenge.

"Sure," I replied.

So we got back on our bikes, and continued our ride around the lake. Rather then turn back, we continued forward on Lees Lane around the lake until it intersected with Park Avenue, which led to Heather Avenue, which eventually intersected back with Johnson Avenue in a huge loop. Altogether the trip to Johnson was a bit further than we had traveled earlier, about seven more miles, so that by the time we had traveled from Zack's house, around the lake, and back to Johnson Avenue we had pedaled about twelve miles. Once on Johnson Avenue, we rode over three streets where it intersected with Ormond, then we took that road to Landing and over past Mrs. Mac Mullin's house to the mill.

Once at the gate, I unlocked it, and we parked our bikes inside the old factory, and headed over to the dam. With the spring season, the water flow over the dam was greatly increased, making it more difficult to walk out onto the dam ledge. The extreme water flow and the glare of the sun off the water's surface made it difficult to see what lay below.

"I can't see a thing," Zack said. "I wonder if I can feel anything."

We looked around and Zack found a relatively straight stick about five feet long. I continued a bit further and found a clear soda bottle, and I picked it up and carried it with me saying this might help.

Outside the fence and up the hill, Mrs. Mac Mullin strayed from her bedside, struggling with each step due to her chronic knees, and peered briefly from her bedroom window. From there she had a perfect view of the dam. Although she could barely walk, her eyesight with glasses was still good, and she instantly recognized me and Zack down by the water.

"I wonder what those boys are up to?" she thought, and she grabbed a chair from the other side of the bed and she sat it in front of the window.

Zack took the stick, placed it in the water, and felt around the area where I remembered seeing the statue.

"I can feel something hard," he agreed. "And it seems like it runs about four or five feet in length and a little less than a foot and a half in width."

I took the soda bottle and positioned it so that the bottom was pressed against the water, and using it almost like a sight glass I looked through it and could barely make out what appeared to be a face in the water, about two and a half feet below the water surface.

"If only we could figure a way to pull it out," I commented. "We can't very well construct a lift out on the dam ledge."

Zack looked around and noted a tree growing about twenty feet away, fairly close to the fence.

"We might be able to fasten a pulley up on that tree over there," Zack said, "and tie a rope around the statue and pull it out, or better yet, put something heavy on the other end of the rope like a log and lower it down over the dam to help pull up the statue. But we would have to find a heavy log and drag it over here."

In a moment of inspiration, I mentioned that rather than using a heavy log, we could be like Hezekiah Smyth and let the river do the work.

"Maybe we could get an empty 55-gallon drum and fasten it to the rope that went through the pulley to the statue. Then lower the drum over the side of the dam and let it fill with water. As it filled with water it would get heavier and travel the full twelve feet down and pull the statue out of the water. If I'm not mistaken, there's an empty blue plastic open-top drum over by the old factory we could use."

"That's a great idea," Zack said.

"I think a gallon of milk weighs a little more than 8 pounds. 55 gallons times 8 pounds would weigh almost 450 pounds. I doubt if that statue could weigh much more than that," I said.

"We probably would need to make sure the drum stayed close to the water flowing over the dam. We could wrap the rope attached to the drum about that steel support about four feet over by the dam ledge, which would ensure the drum stayed next to the dam so that it would be sure to fill with water," Zack said. "I could easily drill two holes into both sides of the top of the drum so we could tie the rope to it. It all sounds pretty easy."

"But how do we get the rope around the statue?" I asked.

Zack thought out loud. "We have a big fishnet back in my garage. It's more than two feet in diameter. We could loosely attach the rope around the circumference of the net hoop. Then we could position the hoop under and around the statue head, and pull the rope taunt and tie it. Then do the same thing on the statue's foot end, and tie them both together, and to the rope to the pulley on the tree."

"It all actually sounds pretty easy," I said. "Let's go into the old factory and see what we can salvage."

We walked over into the factory. The blue plastic 55-gallon drum was there, in good shape and relatively empty except for a few items of trash inside. And in the tool closet, there were several pulleys and chains which all looked plenty sturdy for the job and large enough to handle a very thick rope if need be.

"So what else do we need to get to do this? We should make a list," I commented.

"We need a good heavy rope about one-hundred feet long, and we need the drill for the drum," Zack said.

"We need the net, and maybe some thin wire to hold the rope around the net," I added.

"And maybe a sandwich," Zack said. "I'm kinda getting a bit hungry."

I looked at my watch. It was 1:15. "We could go get something to eat, stop at your house and get the net and drill, and then get a rope and some wire from the hardware store. We could easily get back here today and do this, except I gotta stop around 2:00 or 3:00 to do my papers, I said.

"Sounds like a plan," said Zack.

We got our bikes and locked the gate, and rode up Landing Street towards Ormond Avenue. Mrs. Mac Mullin watched us leave from the bedroom window. Her room was warm and a bit stuffy, so she forced open her bedroom window about three inches until a slight breeze of fresh air entered the room, then feeling a bit weak from the exercise, she laid back on the bed to rest her eyes for a few minutes.

As Zack and I headed up Ormond Avenue I mentioned that I had a few dollars and that maybe we could stop at the A&C Deli just up on the Pike and get us a hoagie and a couple of Cokes to drink. It seemed like the kind of thing that would make our day's adventure a bit more memorable, so we continued up Ormond and I bought the sandwich and a bag of chips and the sodas. There were some tables out front of the deli and we ate there. The spring temperature was perfect, the air was crystal clear with a slight breeze, and the lunch really hit the spot.

It was now about 2:00 and we weren't far from the paper station, and I suggested we swing by Greenbriar Avenue on the way to Zack's house to see if the papers were at the station yet. We approached the station on our bikes, riding up Johnson Avenue towards the south side of the garage. The paper truck had arrived early and Deanna had just finished putting the papers out in the station, and had stepped out the back door of the garage and into the house to get a drink. She was coming out of the house on the north side of the garage when we pulled up. She heard me talking to Zack, and she hesitated out of sight from us, debating whether to confront me or go back into the house. We were clearly one of the first to arrive, and the papers looked extremely light, maybe sixty or even seventy to a bundle.

"Wow, we're in luck. The papers are already here, and they are really light," I said to Zack as I looked at my eight-inch pile. "I really don't feel like riding all the way home to get my bag. If you don't mind, maybe we could each carry half the pile, and serve the route together. It really won't take us long. Maybe together we could serve Collins, and Coldspring, and Haddon up to Johnson Avenue. Then you could break away and go home to get the drill and the net, and I could finish up Haddon to the Pike and stop at the hardware store to get the rope. We could easily get everything done by 3:00 and meet back by the mill by 4:00. I could serve the houses at Smythville, and then we could get to work on the statue. Heck, at that rate we could set things up and easily have it out of the water by 6:00."

Deanna listened to our muddled voices from the outside of the garage. From what she could hear we were working on some kind of a project near the mill and we would be there working around 5:00 to 6:00.

"That sounds pretty good to me." Zack said. "It would be great if we could do this today. I think tomorrow it's supposed to rain."

"Only one problem," I suddenly realized. "We don't have any rubber bands."

We looked around the floor and there were several rubber bands strewn about.

"What about those?" Zack said.

So we both started picking up stray rubber bands.

"That's five, six, seven, eight, nine, ooh ten, eleven... twelve ..."

Deanna could hear us counting rubber bands as we picked them from the floor. Her emotions had tossed inside her for weeks like a shaken bottle of soda ready to explode, and she couldn't take it any longer. She suddenly burst in the garage from the back door, walked briskly to the cabinet over the table, and grabbed a handful of rubber bands.

"Here!" she said grabbing my hand and forcing the red bands into it. "Take these! Maybe at least I can do one thing right for you!" she sobbed.

Then she ran out of the station and out the back door and up the steps of the house. I ran after her as quickly as I could, catching her on the steps and grabbing her by the arm. She turned back and looked at me with tears pouring down from her eyes.

As I held her outstretched arm and looked into her streaming eyes, I said, "I'm sorry, please believe me, I'm sorry!"

She was in no mood for apologies, and pulled away and ran in the door. I stood for a moment on the bottom step in silence. After taking a moment to compose myself, I wiped my eyes, and returned to the garage. Joey Gilmore and Jon Shelly were now in the station, along with Zack, and they had watched the whole event. All were silent as I entered the garage and handed Zack half the stack of rubber bands. Quickly I bent down and split up my pile of papers and we left. As Zack and I rode off on our bikes, Jon and Joey started to giggle. They were facing each other, each sitting on a pile of papers while they folded.

"Ah, the essence of true love," laughed Joey, his back facing the front door of the garage.

"Ohhhh, help me," laughed Shelly, as he fell to the ground and acted like he was dead. "My heart is broken!"

They both squealed and giggled with delight. Then as they were snickering, Danny Dobalo walked into the garage. He was clearly a foot taller than either of them, and at least forty pounds heavier. He was totally pissed off since he had just seen Zack and I ride off from the station. And seeing Jon on the floor acting dead and Joey giggling made him feel they were somehow poking fun at him and his brother.

"What's with you two punks!" he yelled. "I oughta kick each of your arses outta here!"

Jon Shelly got up quickly off the floor, and looked solemnly down, quickly picking up his papers and putting them in his bag.

"You make me sick!" he said to Jon, then he spit onto one of Jon's papers in his paper bag.

He then looked around the station for his papers, and realized Joey was sitting on his pile.

"Pardon me, but didn't I tell you to get your fucking ass off of my papers!" he yelled at Joey. Then he kicked the pile of papers with his boot, sending Joey and the paper pile flying.

Joey jumped up, grabbed his papers and quickly left the station, with Shelly close behind. Then Danny walked over to Dave Parker's pile of papers, counted out his 53 papers from Dave's pile, and then he threw the remainder of Dave's papers on the stack which had been knocked over, dropping the newspaper with the word Parker written on the top corner on top of the pile that was strewn about the floor. He then sat down on Donald Elfrith's stack and lit up a Marlboro. As Danny took the last drag from his cigarette, Deanna walked into the station. She had calmed herself down and wiped away the tears and had hoped that Zack and I were still there. At first she noticed the strewn pile of papers, and then she noticed Danny Dobalo.

"Well good afternoon, my dear lady," Danny began. "Can you believe the nerve of some of the kids in this place? I was just about to pick those up."

"Oh, I'll get them," Deanna said, as she bent over to pick them up and straighten the pile.

"I haven't seen you in a while, Daniel," Deanna said. "I see you had Paul Slason filling in for you. I'm really sorry to hear about your brother."

"Paul did an ok job, but he's not quite as conscientious as me. And as far as my brother Bobby, it was really a rough time. I still find it hard to believe that he's gone for good."

"Well, at least they finally found the body and you and your family could get some closure. It would probably be really tough if you still hadn't found out where he was, and you weren't sure if he was gone or just missing," Deanna speculated.

Danny wasn't paying much attention until he heard Deanna use that word *closure*. It was the same word that was in the letter, and Danny became a bit more certain that it was Deanna who had written it. Even when the letter first was received, Deanna had been on the short list of people he guessed to have been the author.

Danny nodded. He hadn't really even listened to her comment, as he had his own agenda.

"Hey let's not talk anymore about Bobby and the past; it's too depressing. How about you and that boyfriend of yours? Seems like you two might be getting a bit serious?" Danny asked.

"Well, we were kind of serious for a while, but things have cooled off. We really aren't seeing each other anymore," she answered.

"That's a shame. A pretty babe like you should have someone nice to pamper you and keep you happy, not some creepy kid with a dirty jacket and a loser friend from that key shop. What's that kid's name again?"

"You mean Zack Mausser?" Deanna asked.

"Yeah, that's the one," Danny replied. "Say, where do those two hang out anyway? I got something for that Zack and I'm not sure where he lives. I think your boyfriend lives over by the bank."

"Yeah, Bill lives over on East Haddon Avenue. Zack lives over on Bettlewood." Deanna replied.

"Haddon and Bettlewood, you say?"

"Yes," Deanna went on. "But I believe I heard them both say that they planned to be over on Landing Street tonight around 6:00. You know, over by the dam. It's really not far from your house on Ormond. I think they are doing some kind of a job for Mrs. Mac Mullin, one of the old women on Bill's paper route."

"Is that right?" Danny said. "Maybe I'll look them up."

Danny picked up his papers and tucked them into his bag.

"Hey, it was real nice talking with you. Keep up the smiling, babe. If you ever start feeling lonely, give me a call. A cute girl like you needs a guy that can give her some sweet lovin', if you know what I mean," he said with a wink. Then he walked out the door and lit up another Marlboro, and started walking south on Johnson Avenue.

Zack and I pedaled down Johnson and onto Collins Avenue, each riding one-handed with a stack of papers tucked under our right arms. When we got to the corner of Coldspring, I stopped and folded two papers and tossed them to my two customers on the right-hand side of the street while Zack did the same to the houses on the left. We quickly served the homes on Coldspring, and then traveled down to Haddon. With each of us picking a side, we stopped and rolled and served several houses at a time, Zack on the left and me on the right. Zack didn't know the houses on his side, but somehow through a silent communication of head nodding, we communicated without error until we made it up again to Johnson Avenue. Once at Johnson, Zack handed me what remained of his half of the pile of papers and headed home to get a drill and the fishing net. As per our prediscussed plan, I continued up Haddon and served out the papers to both sides.

With only the papers left for Landing Street in Smythville, I decided to stop quickly at home. I had been trying to keep my parents more aware of where I was, and besides I needed to get some money for the rope. As I pulled up the driveway my father was on the front porch. Earlier in the day he had taken down the enclosure, and now he was putting up the outdoor screens on all the house windows. Our house had the old type of sash windows, and the way they worked was that a wooden framed screen hooked at the top of each window, then fit inside of a recess in the sash frame. In the winter, the screen was replaced by a secondary wooden frame window which we referred to as the storm windows. So in the spring my father had to remove all the storm windows and install the screens.

Inside my mother was cleaning the sun porch's aluminum venetian blinds, taking them down one by one and washing them in the bath tub, then hanging them outside on the close line to dry. My mom asked me if all was alright, then mentioned that she and my father were going over to Gloucester that night to eat at O'Donnell's Restaurant, and asked me if I wanted to go with them or do something else for dinner.

"No thanks, Zack and I sort of have something planned for tonight," I said.

"Ok, then you can take two dollars out of my wallet, and both you and Zack can go over to the Burger Chef tonight and you can both buy dinner on me," she replied.

I went upstairs and got some of my money from my bedroom, then came down and took two dollars from my mom's pocketbook, which sat on the dining room chair by the phone. I also decided to grab my paper bag and a flashlight from the basement, just in case we went longer tonight than expected, or we needed to get something from in the old factory building that was always relatively dark, even in the daylight.

Putting the flashlight and the four papers in my bag, I headed to the hardware store on my bike. Inside the store there was an entire section devoted to rope and wire. There was a large sign instructing how to select the right rope for your application, and I decided on a $^3/_8$ inch diameter, 700 pound static weight rated Dacron rope in a 200-foot length. I also picked up ten feet of bell wire, just in case we needed it for the net. The cost of everything was $3.49. I paid, went outside, and put everything into my paper bag so I didn't have to hold anything while I rode my bike.

I elected to stay on the Pike until Greenbriar Avenue, which I turned down, riding past the station in which sat Alvin Morrison and at least three still-unclaimed stacks of papers. I continued on to Ormond, past the Dobalo house, and on to Landing Street, where I served the last four papers, stopping last at Mrs. Mac Mullin's house. As instructed, I first knocked, then opened the door to drop off the paper inside on the couch. When I entered, I heard Mrs. Mac Mullin call down from upstairs.

"Who's that?" she hollered. "Is that the paper?"

I yelled back, "yes," and she asked me to come upstairs with it.

When I got upstairs, Mrs. Mac Mullin was in her bedroom. She had on a robe over her nightgown, and she was sitting with her legs up on the bed. I went over to the bed and handed her the paper.

"Oh, thank you," she sighed. "I was wondering if you could be a dear and go down in the kitchen and get me an orange and a muffin, and a glass of water. I just don't have the energy today.

So I got her what she asked, and I peeled the orange when I saw she was having a problem with it.

"Is there anything else you would like?" I asked.

"No, this is just fine," she said. Then she added, "I saw you earlier today down by the dam. You and the other boy seemed very busy. What are you fishing or something down there? Take my advice, if you are, you won't catch much of anything right before the dam."

"Oh no, we're not fishing. But I'll let you in on a secret. We think we located the statue of your mother, and we devised a way we think we can pull it up. I don't want you to get your heart all worked up over it, because we might be wrong, but if we are right, we are going to bring it up and put it on your porch."

"Well, I'll let you in on another secret," she laughed. "I think you would stand a better chance of catching a fish in front of the dam, than pulling up that statue. But I wish you luck. Please just be careful. I don't want either of you to fall and get hurt. You could trip and kill yourself if you fell over that dam."

I looked at the window and I could see Zack over by the dam. I also noted the window was open about three inches to the outside air.

"Hey, you be careful. That window has a broken rope to the sash weight inside. There's nothing really there inside to hold the window open. It could fall at any moment and smash those old fingers of yours."

I took the eight-inch by two-inch stick that usually propped the window open in the summer and I laid it down on its side under the open window. "Keep this stick here so if it falls you won't smash your fingers," I cautioned.

"Oh you worry too much," she cajoled.

"You sound like the pot calling the kettle black," I commented back. Then I left the room to meet up with Zack, while Mrs. Mac Mullin eased herself over to the chair in front of the window with her dinner, to watch Zack and I as we tried to raise the statue.

I reached the dam a few minutes later, and I saw Zack had left the gate unlocked, with his bike locked to a post on the inside of the fence. I locked my bike to the same post, leaving my paper bag with my bike, but taking the rope and the wire with me. When I reached Zack, I saw that he had already set up the pulley on the tree and had taken a second pulley and attached it to a circular chain which he intended to slip over the short post on the dam ledge to hold the drum close to the cascading water. He had already drilled one hole in the top of one side of the drum, and he was working on the second.

"Hey Zack," I said, "Looks like you've made a lot of progress!"

Zack said that so far everything had gone real well, and that drilling the hole in the drum was even easier than he had originally thought it would be. His drill was a hand drill that looked a little like my mom's egg beater, except for the half-inch drill bit on its underside.

"You get the rope?" he asked.

"Oh yeah, here it is," I replied. And Zack nodded his head in a positive fashion.

"It looks plenty strong enough," he figured, "and it's good you brought the longer length just in case something breaks or we find out we need more."

He finished drilling the hole, and we carried it down by the dam and began setting things up. Leaving about five feet of slack, Zack attached the rope to the drum through the two holes he had drilled and then slipped the rope through the pulley attached to the circular chain. Next he went over near the fence and threaded the rope through the pulley attached to the tree. He pulled the rope taut through the pulley and walked back over to the dam. Zack then took the pulley mounted on the circular chain and used the outstretched net pole to position the circular chain over the steel post on the dam ledge.

"I get the idea of the second pulley now," I said. "All we have to do now is push the drum off the side here and it will swing over next to the dam and start to fill and descend, pulling up the statue. It's a good thing I got here when I did, or you would have kept adding pulleys, and I would have had to go back to the hardware store to get more rope."

Now came the hard part, attaching the rope to the statue.

"If this goes as easy as the other stuff, that statue will be up by 5:00," I predicted.

Of course my prediction must have jinxed us, as pushing the net under the statue with the rope attached to its circumference proved particularly difficult. Making little progress except for snagging the device, Zack decided to cut the netting from the hoop which he reasoned should make the job a lot easier. By 5:30 we had got one rope loop around the head section of the statue, but the loop around the feet was much more difficult. We suspected it was due to the lower end of the statue being attached to a somewhat larger base, which made pulling the net hoop over it a lot more difficult. We continued to persevere with the statue base, or I should say that Zack did, as I watched him struggle time after time with near misses. Like me, Mrs. Mac Mullin watched the action, except from a much higher perch through her bedroom window.

Back on Greenbriar Avenue, Deanna had evaluated her plans for the evening several times. As irritated as she was, she wanted nothing more than to be back together, but her pride kept making her reconsider. As the clock ticked later and later, she finally made a decision.

"I'll go down to Landing Street to see what those guys are up to. After all, he did kind of apologize to me," she thought. "I can sort of keep in the background, and depending what's happening I'll decide to either meet up with the guys or leave."

With that she looked at herself in the mirror and forced on a smile. Then she headed over to Landing Street with the hope that things would turn out for the best, and she wouldn't make herself look as forlorn as she did earlier in the day. She arrived on Landing Street about 5:30 and looked around. Over by the dam she could see Zack and I with the net hoop, standing next to the dam by a drum. Zack was repeatedly placing the hoop in and out of the water, but for the life of her she had no idea why. As much as she wanted to join us, she resisted, but slowly crept closer to the gate to try to get a better view. Eventually she had made her way to the gate and noticed it was unlocked. She could clearly see both Zack's and my bicycles were chained to the fence, but she still was uncertain as to what we were doing. She decided to enter in through the gate, so she quietly opened it and pushed it softly until it closed. From there she tiptoed over to the old factory and stood in the shadows where she could get a closer look at what was going on.

Danny Dobalo shared none of the reservations of Deanna. As soon as she told him that Zack and I were to be over on Landing Street about 6:00 he had made up his mind exactly what he was going to do. He went home to his nightstand and pulled out the Smith & Weston blue steel handgun from the drawer and unwrapped it from the undershirt he had hidden it in. Similarly he pulled out the revolver magazine, wishing that he had more than just three rounds of ammunition. Danny had already acquired some experience with rifles and handguns before, having shot at targets in camp over a series of summers. This gun was a bit different than what he had used before, but the cartridge was easy to load, the safety was easy to locate, and the size and shape were a relatively good fit for his hand.

"How ironic," he thought, that these two would pay their dues at the same location from which they had sent Bobby to his grave. He had no intention of giving himself up or getting caught as he worked his plan of revenge.

"Don't fire until I'm at close range. One shot, and then throw them into the creek, just like Bobby," he thought.

And just to help create an explanation for the deaths, he had brought along two plastic bags, each containing some pep pills of his mother's that he planned to plant on the bodies before they were thrown in the creek.

"If the dead bodies are found by that Detective Hebner, that lazy clown will just think they were shot as some part of drug deal," he speculated.

Danny put on a baggy pair of dark pants and a dark shirt and tucked the loaded gun deep into his pocket. He routed through Bobby's things until he found his pocketknife, a six-inch switch blade that he had picked up mostly for show in case he ran into trouble on a botched-up bike heist.

"It's a shame Bobby wasn't carrying this knife on the night of his murder," Danny lamented.

With his weapons concealed, he started for Landing Street. It was almost six o'clock, and dusk had set in as the sun began its descent from the blue evening sky.

Chapter 31 – Danny Dobalo [2]

As the water began to reflect the intense orange glow from the descending sun, Zack finally looped the base of the statue.

"Success at last!" he yelled in a voice so loud that both Deanna and Mrs. Mac Mullin could hear it from their vantage points.

He pulled the rope tight around the base with a slipknot, and then carefully tied both the front and back statue lift ropes to a metal ring he had found in the factory tool closet. He then cut the rope leading to the pulley on the tree to the correct length, and also tied it to the lift ring. The job was done. All that was left was to push in the barrel.

While Zack was doing the rope tying, Danny Dobalo had arrived on Landing Street and made his way over to the gate. He had seen the two boys over by the dam as soon as he arrived, and he blessed his good fortune that this was going even a bit smoother than he had anticipated. He noticed the gate was unlocked, and that its open lock had been hooked but not closed on the fence just to the right. He was tempted to lock the gate and scream out that he had them penned up like fish in a barrel, but this barrel was a bit too large to ensure a good shot. Looking inside the fence, he saw the two bikes both locked to the post, and he thought it a shame that his band of thieves would not be able to take advantage of two last bicycle heists.

Zack looked over first at the drum, and then the pulleys, and then the lift ring, checking them all one last time to make sure things were tied properly. As a last check he gave the rope a quick short tug in both directions and confirmed all was secure.

"It looks like this baby is ready to fly," Zack said.

Then he looked at the side of the dam and its lip and he stroked his chin for a minute.

"You know, I'm a bit worried about that lip, "Zack observed. "If the statue pulls up on an angle, it could catch on the lip and get stuck. I'm pretty sure I saw a long metal crowbar in the factory tool closet that might come in handy. If the statue gets stuck, we could use the crowbar to pry the statue from the lip and keep it moving. The only problem is that it's starting to get dark and hard to see in that closet. I hate to take the chance that it could get stuck. You know I'd leave it for tomorrow if it wasn't supposed to rain and I wasn't afraid of leaving all this stuff up so that someone might see it."

"I'm one step ahead of you Zack," I said. "I figured things would go late so I brought a flashlight. It's over by my bike in my paper bag by the gate."

"I knew there was a reason I let you stay to see this," Zack laughed. "I'm going to get the flashlight, and then go get the crowbar."

I watched as Zack walked towards the bikes. Then, I turned my head in the other direction, looking over the dam to the west, and watched as the sun made its final descent into the dark stillness of the lake. As it sank from view, the evening sky was suddenly transformed from its jet-blue appearance to a vivid swirl of pink, orange, and yellow. Its appearance was a sight of beauty, and I thought back to the night I had stood in this same spot with Deanna, transfixed by the natural beauty of that wondrous winter night.

Seated by her window, Mrs. Mac Mullin had also shifted her eyes to the sunset, and she marveled at its glowing splendor. She also reminisced about the past, and thought that she hadn't seen such a sunset by the creek since the night before her late husband had left for the war.

Zack headed over to the gate towards the bikes to get the flashlight. Danny who was standing in the shadows couldn't believe his eyes when he saw Zack walking over alone towards him. At first he thought maybe Zack had seen him, but as Zack veered towards the bikes, he realized he had not been seen. As Zack reached down into the paper bag to pick up the flashlight, Danny grabbed him from behind and pushed the barrel of the blue steel revolver right under his chin.

In a cool, quiet tone Danny whispered, "Now it looks like I have you trapped, you murdering son of a bitch! Don't do anything fast or I'll pull this trigger and you'll be with my brother pushing up daisies or carp, or whatever he was pushing the night you forced him through that ice."

"Hey we didn't force him to do anything, he walked out on that ice all by himself," Zack blubbered.

"Shut your mouth, you lying sack of shit!" Danny blurted out. Then he took his left hand without the gun and pulled it back as hard as he could into Zack's stomach.

"Now here's what I want you to do and you better do it slowly, and you better keep it quiet or you're a dead man. Unlock your bike from the fence and take the chain, then wrap it around your neck. Then lock yourself up to the fence," Danny said.

Zack took the keys from his pocket. There was his large key ring, held to his pant belt loop with a chain. But as hard as he tried, he couldn't help but fumble the keys in his hand.

"Hurry it up," Danny said urgently, looking over at my silhouette by the mill. "What's taking so long?"

"I can't see the keys, and I can't look down with that gun pointed into my neck!" Zack retorted.

Danny gradually lowered the gun to Zack's back.

"I'm giving you to ten, and if you don't get it done, I'm killing you. I got nothing to gain keeping you alive, and you have everything to lose," Danny went on. "One, two..."

Zack popped the keys from the chain and using his fingers he located the bike key in a second. He swiftly unlocked the chain, and wrapped it about his neck. Danny took the lock with his left hand, while holding the gun in his right. Zack turned slightly and ran the chain through the fence, and Danny pulled it tight and placed on the lock, pressing in the shackle and effectively rendering Zack nearly motionless.

"Now keep it down or I'm coming back for you!"

Danny started to walk away, and Zack stood motionless. His would be killer had forgotten that he still held the key ring, and he slowly slipped the keys back into his pocket, so they wouldn't be seen. As the ring of keys descended they clinked together on the chain. Danny, realizing his stupidity, walked back to Zack.

"Give up the keys!" he scolded. "Or give up your life."

Zack remained motionless. Danny groped him for the keys and with each push and pull, the chain strained tighter around Zack's neck. As Danny leaned in, the chain pulled fast around his neck. As he began to choke, Zack kicked him hard in the groin. Danny took the back of the gun and whipped Zack on the back of the head, making the chain constrict even tighter around his neck. In severe pain Zack choked back and admitted the keys were in his pocket. In pain himself, Danny ripped the keys from Zack's pants. Then with an enormous scream he took the ring of keys and threw them with all his might towards the dam and into the creek.

Deanna had noticed Danny shortly after Zack had walked over to the bikes. She recognized his long blonde hair and muscular build and remembered that he had said he had something to give Zack. At first she thought they were talking and Danny was giving Zack something, then she saw them fighting and Zack go to his knees. She wasn't sure what to do, and then she heard Danny's loud scream.

Danny's dark figure started running towards the dam, waving his hand which held the gun. As I saw him coming, I momentarily froze, thinking first it was Zack, and then realizing it was Danny. Suddenly he stopped and took aim. A shot rang out in the evening air, and I swear I heard the bullet buzz just past my ear. The shot had missed, but I was an open target and I instinctively dove for cover behind the blue plastic barrel.

Mrs. Mac Mullin looked down from her window, clearly hearing the shot, and seeing Danny running with the gun. She screamed in horror as I fell to the ground behind the barrel.

"My God, not the boy, don't let him kill the boy. He's so young and has so much to live for. Sweet Jesus, please take me in place of him," she prayed out loud.

Deanna heard the gun shot too and she also fell to the ground. Crawling on the earth she tried to stay down and out of sight from the gunman. Finally reaching a tree, she stood up, and looked to see if I was hit, and where he was going next.

Danny looked around the dam, then looked back at Zack and cursed, "One bullet gone, so these next two have to count."

He started walking slowly with the gun raised towards the drum. As he walked closer, I peered from behind the drum, wondering how to escape from my predator. I was literally stuck between a rock and a hard place. I couldn't run towards Danny or I would get shot, and I couldn't run backwards or I would fall into the river.

Sensing my predicament Mrs. Mac Mullin stood up on her creaky legs, and with all her might, she pushed open her bedroom window. As it opened, the propping stick fell forward, falling onto the porch roof. Mrs. Mac Mullin screamed that she was calling the police, and they would soon be there to get the marauder with the gun. Unfortunately her yelling fell on deaf ears; we were too far away from her, and the roar of the water over the dam made it difficult to hear any specific speech from her bedroom. We only heard the muffled words of her elderly voice nearly seventy feet away.

Deanna dropped to her knees and grabbed some large stones, and standing behind a tree by the factory wall, she began throwing the rocks at Danny, narrowly missing him once and distracting him momentarily so that I could run out from behind the drum. As I ran, Danny lifted the gun for a second shot, and both Mrs. Mac Mullin and Deanna simultaneously yelled for me to duck. Diving to the ground, a second report rang out, whizzing past the drum and glancing off the concrete of the dam.

Mrs. Mac Mullin pumped her clenched fist and rose up her head and hit the bottom of the window. Abruptly the window crashed down on her neck, effectively pinning her head between the window and the sill.

The sun which had put on a marvelous display earlier disappeared into the lake, and the evening transformed to a greyish twilight, making it more difficult to see Danny's silhouette from my perspective on the ground against the backdrop of the dark trees. Danny raised the gun again and took aim to shoot for the third time.

"Run, Bill, run," Deanna cried out, and I scrambled out onto the concrete weir of the dam, where the cold rushing water pushed steadily across my feet.

"Keep running to the catwalk," Deanna screamed at the top of her lungs. "He's going to fire again."

I tried to run for the catwalk but the force of the water made me slip. I instinctively grabbed for the steel pole which held the chain with the pulley. As I fell, I hit the side of my head on the concrete, and the heavy stream of cold water enveloped my body. For a moment, I felt as though I had been pushed into a water tunnel with a white light at the end. I could see water rushing around me as I looked forward, and the glowing white light got closer. In a mystical way the light appeared to motion me to go back, and suddenly my eyes again opened and I was back holding the metal pole, with one leg hanging over the dam, while my neck struggled to keep my head above water. Through the rushing water I could clearly see the darkened shadow of Danny moving toward me as he stepped out onto the dam ledge. At first he walked cautiously, then sped up a bit in order to position himself for his final shot.

As he lifted the gun, I pulled the rope which ran through the pulley and to the drum with all my might. The drum lurched towards me and the dam, falling about a foot below my leg, and instantly filling with water. As the drum filled, the rope became taut as the statue raised. Unaware of the rope and not being able to see it in the darkness, Danny took a last step and his foot became entangled with the rope. With a loud scream, his body fell from the dam, crashing twelve feet below on the rocks and branches that lay in the creek bed below. His head bounced off a rock, then into the side of the dam, and he was pulled for a good five minutes under the plume of cascading water.

I looked down at the rocks, wondering how long I could hold on before I joined Danny at the base of the creek. Then from out of the corner of my eye I saw Deanna, with Zack's netless fishing hoop. Reaching out with the stick end, she looped the net over the metal pole I was holding. Seeing the hoop, I readjusted my hands so it draped over the side of the dam. Then using the bottom of the loop as a step, I climbed back up onto the ledge. Then, unlike earlier in the day when she pulled back her arm on the steps, she now offered her hand and grabbed onto mine, tugging with all her might as we tumbled onto the dry land.

Deanna embraced my waterlogged body and hugged me with all her might.

"Thank God you're safe," she rejoiced. "I could never have forgiven myself if you had been killed."

We both stood up, a bit bruised, wet, and woozy, but all in one piece. I looked over at the statue and it was caught on the edge of the dam, just as Zack had predicted, pulsating up and down as the drum which hung below the dam bobbled in the downward rush of water.

"What happened to Zack?" I asked, fearing he may have been shot.

"He's over by the gate," Deanna recalled, and we rushed over to see his upright body still chained by the neck to the fence.

"What happened over there?" he questioned. "I thought maybe you were shot. I couldn't tell who let out the scream. Is he gone?"

"He fell off of the dam. I got chased on the ledge, and he followed. When I fell and grabbed the drum rope, the statue popped up and he tripped over the rope," I explained. "I don't think he could have survived the fall."

We looked at how Zack was chained about the neck.

"How can we get you unlocked?" Deanna asked.

"I don't have my keys," Zack exclaimed. "He took them and threw them into the water."

"I'll be back in a flash," Deanna said.

Then she hopped on Zack's bike and rode back to her house as quickly as she could. Zack and I figured she went to call the police, but were surprised when she returned ten minutes later with the wire cutters from the station. Taking the cutters, I clipped the fence links which the heavy chain ran through. After three cuts, the chain became free, and Zack was released from the fence.

Grabbing the flashlight, we walked over to the dam to survey the situation. The statue still bobbled, stuck on the lip of the ledge. One side of the statues face was intact; the other side was smashed undoubtedly from the repeated blows of a sledge hammer over fifty years ago. I pulled the pocketknife from my pocket, and looked over at Zack. He silently nodded his head yes, and I cut the rope holding the statue at the ledge. The rope whipped through the pulley freeing the drum which fell into the creek below. The statue still caught on the edge of the dam fell slower, eventually freeing itself from the lip and disappearing back into the water which flowed before the dam.

Looking down near the ledge lip on which the statue had gotten caught, we saw a shiny object just below the water surface, stuck in a clump of branches which had accumulated by the side of the dam. I pointed the flashlight towards the object in the water and it reflected back the light, appearing to sway in the current, as if it were some type of fish lure being pulled from a fishing reel. Zack bent over and grabbed the object at its center, and lifting it up, he held his key chain, his thumb and forefinger grasping the center gold key his father had left him.

I pointed upward and spoke to Zack and Deanna.

"Somebody up there was really looking out for us tonight," I whispered.

Seventy feet away in her room, Mrs. Mac Mullin silently struggled to free herself from the window. From the side of her head she felt an unbearable pain and a warm liquid flowing down the side of her neck. Taking her strong right hand, she smashed the window, lacerating her wrist. She forced up her head one last time and the weakened sash broke apart as the rotted wood from the base of the window fell to pieces. A large piece of glass fell forward as the window broke free, and her body propelled downward, toppling the chair and smashing to the floor below. As the chair fell over, it hit the nightstand and the pictures on it fell onto the floor. Her ancient eyes opened and she grabbed the picture of her uniformed husband and pulled it to her chest. Then closing her eyes she felt herself enter a tunnel and she focused on a bright light which appeared before her. The light took the form of her late husband, and he beckoned her to follow. Still clutching the picture, Enola silently rolled over on her side and moved away to a place where her loneliness would finally disappear.

> *Please kiss me gently darling where that river runs away,*
> *from the mountains in the springtime on a blue and windy day.*
> *Where there's beauty all around as the shades of night grow deep.*
> *When the morning stars grow dim,*
> *they will find us in our shadows fast asleep.* [2]

Chapter 32 – The Station

Zack, Deanna, and I stood next to the dam and surveyed the situation. I shined the flashlight down below the dam and there was no trace of Danny. Taking the key to Zack's bike lock, I unlocked the chain from around his neck, and we stood together in the starlight, each wondering which step to take next.

"What do we do now?" I asked, directing the question to Deanna this time. She thought for a while and then responded.

"Well, Danny is most likely dead," she supposed. "And he pretty much brought about his own demise. We could call the police, but there's really nothing they could do now. The only good such a call would do is explain what happened to his body. In the end, all that would be remembered of Danny's life would be how tragically it ended, and the evil he perpetuated along the way. On the other hand, we could do nothing. Collect up these ropes and chains, and leave the area not saying a word to anyone. Eventually Danny's body will be found downstream, but it won't be linked with us. They'll probably report that he fell, or that maybe he jumped, distraught from the recent loss of his twin brother. But in any case, his end will be viewed more positively than that of a gun-toting hoodlum. I think in the long run that ending is better for him and his family and his legacy."

We stood and listened as she finished her decision.

"My vote is we pick up our things from the area and we leave. Let's promise not to say anything to anyone about the night, and simply go on with our lives."

Zack and I agreed wholeheartedly with her assessment. So we picked up our things and left.

The following Monday, I returned to the paper station. The papers were out just as normal, and Deanna had written: *For my Blacky from Shep* on the top paper. Below the heading were the words ...*oh my little sheep, I thought you were lost and confused, but I was wrong. I should have followed you*...

Danny's body showed up three days later, washed ashore a half mile downstream of the mill. The paper ran a front page story on his life. It spoke of his athletic prowess, his days as an altar boy at the church, and his loyalty to his somewhat slower twin brother. The evidence pointed to his despondence over Bobby's passing, and how it pushed him to leap to his death. There was a massive service held at St. Aloysius Church scheduled for Saturday, which would be attended by Deanna, Zack, and I, and all of the newspaper carriers from our station.

In that same paper, on the back of the obituary page was a four-line paragraph describing the life and times of one Enola Mac Mullin, who had died at home earlier in the week. Her death was ascribed to a tragic fall. The story mentioned how she had once been married to a World War I pilot, and that she had lived in Smythville for the majority of her life. There was no mention of her family heritage, her subsequent empty life, or the site of her funeral. I later heard she was buried in the Saint Andrews section of the Pine Street Cemetery next to her parents, through a special clause in Hezekiah's burial plot arrangement with the cemetery. But when I rode to visit the grave one afternoon in May, I saw no marking to this effect on the tombstone.

I gave up delivery to the Smythville homes shortly after Mrs. Mac Mullin's death, but continued to serve the remainder of the route all through high school, even after Deanna tired of being manager, and the station moved to at least three alternate locations.

Over the years I gradually lost touch with all the friends of my youth, as I moved away to college and eventually moved on with the adult portion of my life. Now over forty years later, in the age of instant communication, most people get their news from the television, or the Internet, or even their phones. I consider myself a bit of an old-timer, and I still prefer nothing more than sitting down with the newspaper after a hard day at work. Gazing at the paper, I often reflect back on those days of my youth and wonder how much more of each story is hidden behind the lines of print. It now also seems odd that I've lost track of exactly who delivers the paper to my doorstep. I guess it's probably much more efficient these days that the newspaper is paid for by the year and is delivered in a waterproof bag by an unseen car-driving adult. In our town at least, the day of the paperboy is gone, but the job and the people will continue to live in the hearts of us childhood carriers forever.